W9-CTB-328

"WALDEN, GET BACK!"

"Behind you. They're behind you!" Higgins cried.

Walden swung around. His laserifle was batted from his hands by another of the mobile steel tentacles. The wall had come alive with them. They wrapped themselves around his wrists and waist and pulled him toward the bulkhead.

He screamed when he saw the heat drill emerging from the wall level with his chest.

His hazard suit turned a cherry red from the heat drill and he felt the pain lancing into his torso. The world became black, as death came to claim him . . .

Books by Robert E. Vardeman

The Weapons of Chaos Series

ECHOES OF CHAOS
EQUATIONS OF CHAOS
COLORS OF CHAOS

The Cenotaph Road Series

CENOTAPH ROAD
THE SORCERER'S SKULL
WORLD OF MAZES
PILLAR OF NIGHT
FIRE AND FOG
IRON TONGUE

The War of Power Series (with Victor Milán)

THE SUNDERED REALM
THE CITY IN THE GLACIER
THE DESTINY STONE
THE FALLEN ONES
IN THE SHADOW OF OMIZANTRIM
DEMON OF THE DARK ONES

The Swords of Raemllyn Series (with Geo. W. Proctor)

TO DEMONS BOUND
A YOKE OF MAGIC
BLOOD FOUNTAIN
DEATH'S ACOLYTE
THE BEASTS OF THE MIST
FOR CROWN AND KINGDOM

The Biowarriors Series

THE INFINITY PLAGUE
CRISIS AT STARLIGHT

BIOWARRIORS
Book Two

CRISIS AT STARLIGHT

Robert E. Vardeman

ACE BOOKS, NEW YORK

This book is an Ace original edition,
and has never been previously published.

CRISIS AT STARLIGHT

An Ace book/published by arrangement with
the author

PRINTING HISTORY
Ace edition/February 1990

All rights reserved.
Copyright © 1990 by Robert E. Vardeman.
Cover art by Richard Hescox.
This book may not be reproduced in whole or in part,
by mimeograph or any other means, without permission.
For information address: The Berkley Publishing Group,
200 Madison Avenue, New York, New York 10016.

ISBN: 0-441-06267-9

Ace Books are published by The Berkley Publishing Group,
200 Madison Avenue, New York, New York 10016.
The name ''ACE'' and ''A'' logo are trademarks
belonging to Charter Communications, Inc.

PRINTED IN THE UNITED STATES OF AMERICA

10 9 8 7 6 5 4 3 2 1

I have dipped into the future,
far as the human eye can see,
Saw a marvelous vision of the world
And all the wonder that is being with you,
Patty

-rev-

CHAPTER
1

Radiation blasted Jerome Walden's body. He trembled and tried not to panic. He failed.

"Calm down," Anita Tarleton said. Her words soothed him a little. He knew they were safe within the *Hippocrates*. Radiation baffles kept out the worst of the solar radiation they were likely to receive. But what he feared transcended mere solar flares and occasional proton event storms.

The entire planet of Delta Cygnus 4 had been destroyed in a single cataclysmic explosion. Tiny pellets of rock, some smaller than ten grams, had been accelerated at near light speed and shot into the planet. Each had produced an explosion rivaling a ten-megaton bomb. Then the alien Frinn had sent in the heavy bullets. Two of the sublight speed missiles Walden had tracked massed more than a kilogram. Thousands had been fired from mass drivers built in the asteroid belt and shot into the planet, cracking it into pieces and completely destroying it.

The released radiation worried him.

"It's all right. Tell him, Egad," Anita said, dropping down and patting a dog turned into a genetic mess. Egad had German shepherd coloration, with his right eye brown and left eye noticeably smaller and blue. A greyhound body supported

1

a Saint Bernard head. Most disquieting were his black ratlike tail and short legs.

For all the hodgepodge of physical attributes, the dog was nearly the equal of many humans intellectually. Egad—Enhanced intelligence, Genetically Altered Dog—was an unexpected and secret product of Walden's genetic research.

"You worry too much," Egad assured the biologist. "No radiation here. Not much," the animal conceded. "I know. I watch all meters. Nakamura not worried. Sorbatchin not worried. Not even Zacharias is worried."

"There," Anita said, pushing back a strand of her flame-red hair with an irritated gesture. "If the good major isn't worried, why should you be."

"I don't credit Edouard Zacharias with enough brains to worry," Walden grumbled. He stood and stretched. He was stiff from lying on the acceleration couch too long. He needed to exercise—and there wasn't time.

"He won the Starburst Medal on Persephone," Anita said. "They don't pass those out for fun." Her irritation with him was obvious for her to actually defend the meddlesome officer this way.

"I've heard the stories of how he rescued an entire battle group," Walden said. "That doesn't keep him from being a pompous ass."

"Smells bad," Egad confirmed. "Let me rip out his throat?" The dog sounded anxious. Walden emphatically refused. The ship was in too much trouble to lose even one more in the chain of command.

The Frinn had destroyed the research planet Schwann—Delta Cygnus 4—and a fully armed destroyer accompanying the hospital ship *Hippocrates*. Walden snorted in disgust.

The *Hippocrates* had been built as a hospital ship. It wasn't used that way. It carried his research team to Schwann to conduct bioweapons research. The planet had been perfect, having a rudimentary oxygen atmosphere with little in the way of higher lifeforms to contaminate. If a project got out of hand, it wasn't the disaster it would be on Earth. Even better, the North American Alliance and the Japanese Hegemony could better control security on Schwann.

Though the Soviet-Latino Pact had similar research stations on the world, security was supposed to be more than adequate.

The memory of the planet turned Jerome Walden cold with fear. Something had gone seriously wrong in the Sov-Lat facility. To eradicate their mistake they had fired a cleansing bomb, an eight-hundred-megaton fusion crust-buster. It hadn't been enough to stop the Infinity Plague.

"What are we getting on the plague?" he asked suddenly. Anita had worked on the data analysis from autopsies of the aliens they had found aboard a disabled alien vessel. The crew had died from the Infinity Plague's effects. The best Walden could tell, the aliens had three more pairs of chromosomes than did humans. The plague worked on the extra pairs and unraveled them, causing eventual autonomic nervous system failure.

The aliens' bodies simply forgot how to function. Over a span of months, they slowly suffocated.

"Maybe it's the Infinity Plague that got to me," Walden said, remembering his long hours working at the dissection of the aliens. Even using nano-miniaturized equipment and robot hands, he had exposed himself to the bodies for needed observation and "feel" that couldn't be obtained in any other way. He had checked his hazard suit; Anita had checked it. Walden still experienced qualms about not being infected, even though the plague affected only the aliens.

As far as they knew.

"You're all right. Look, Jerome," the flame-haired woman said, her exasperation growing. "I had Leo Burch check you out. He said you were fine. Everything is fine. You heard him. You sat there petting that damned cat of his while he did the workups. We avoided the radiation from Schwann's blow-apart. You weren't infected by the plague. You're fine."

"Sorry," Walden said. He didn't feel fine. He rubbed his eyes and tried stretching again. Pain wracked his joints. Only willpower kept him from sinking back to the couch and returning to his fitful, nightmare-filled dreams.

"You're stressed to the breaking point. We all are."

He didn't need this as a rationale. He had accepted the duties of director of research knowing how difficult it would be. He had his own work to do—and he had to monitor constantly what the other scientists in the project did, too. Some worked well with their colleagues. Others were secretive. Still others were paranoid to the point of assuming the others wanted to steal their results.

Walden worked well with them all, keeping his temper when lesser men would have lashed out. Only when one of his scientists—Doris Yerrow—turned out to be a Sov-Lat spy did he begin to truly feel the internal stress. Finding and fighting the Frinn had been difficult. Learning how the Sov-Lats had released the Infinity Plague might be impossible without their help—and he doubted that would be forthcoming, no matter how open Colonel Sorbatchin and the Sov-Lat research director Pedro O'Higgins seemed.

"What about Captain Belford?" he asked. "He's got to run the *Hippocrates* if we're going to chase down the alien ship." A Frinn ship had left after Schwann was destroyed. Only by tracking it through liftspace could they hope to erase the danger to Earth—and stop the spread of the Infinity Plague in the alien population.

Only Walden seemed interested in the latter prospect. Major Zacharias, Colonel Sorbatchin, even Anita and the others considered the plague retribution for what the Frinn had done to a planet populated with fellow researchers. Walden's skepticism about the aliens' culpability kept him at an intellectual distance from the rest.

"No good. Captain man smells of fear," cut in Egad. "When his first officer tried mutiny, it did something to him."

"He lost confidence in himself," suggested Anita. "It definitely left Zacharias and Nakamura in charge. They're running the *Hippocrates* now, if anyone is."

Walden said nothing to this. Zacharias was a pompous, officious fool with more power than he deserved. Miko Nakamura was officially only a civilian advisor. In fact, she wielded the power aboard the ship. She had prevented Captain Belford from returning to Earth immediately upon discovery of the alien Frinn vessels in the Delta Cygnus system because of the complex residue effects left from the starlift engines as they bent space into new fractal shapes.

"We've got to talk with her," Walden decided. "We can't go chasing the Frinn unprepared, without notifying Earth."

"There's no choice." Anita said. She paced back and forth in their tiny compartment. "I've talked with the sensor officer and others. They've located no fewer than ten remote recording devices left by the Frinn. If the *Hippocrates* returns to Earth, the aliens will be able to study the mathematical residue and pinpoint our home world.''

Walden shuddered. The Frinn had blasted Schwann into atoms. Earth wouldn't stand any better chance against them.

''They're infected with the plague,'' he said. ''We ought to track them down and see what we can do to stop its spread on their planet.''

Anita Tarleton's bright emerald eyes widened in shock. ''Let the bastards die! Look at what they did to Schwann. We lost thousands of men and women when they destroyed it.''

''The Frinn aboard the ship did the destroying. There's no reason to wipe out billions—more!—unless we're at war.''

''We are,'' she said hotly. ''What do you call their unprovoked attack on us, on Schwann?''

''We don't know if it was unprovoked,'' Walden said. ''The Sov-Lats aren't saying what went on before we arrived. The Frinn had contact with them for months before the Infinity Plague was released. We don't know if Sorbatchin created the incident or the Frinn shot first.''

''I have no liking for Sorbatchin, but I'll believe him over *them*,'' Anita said.

''Sov-Lat colonel smells sneaky,'' Egad said. ''Don't trust him. Don't trust other one, too.''

''O'Higgins?'' Walden shook his head. He had never heard any good said about Pedro O'Higgins. Vivisectionist was one of the kinder epithets applied to the Chilean biologist. Human vivisectionist was even more commonly mentioned in scientific circles. He might have grabbed an alien and sliced him open to satisfy a deviant curiosity. As private as the Frinn seemed, this might have been enough for them to react with a show of force that ended in a planet's complete annihilation.

From this point, any escalation was plausible. Even the star-spanning war Miko Nakamura feared.

''Egad, where's Nakamura now?''

''In her quarters,'' the gengineered dog said. He twisted his massive head around, getting the transducer squarely under his throat. Only in this way did the computer in his collar pick up the vibrations and translate them into human speech. "She's no good. She doesn't smell right."

"We know," Anita said, patting the dog's shaggy head. They had surmised that the military advisor used pheromone damping chemicals to prevent easy surveillance of her on-board spy activities. They had never discovered who repeatedly bugged their quarters, but Nakamura had the expertise.

"Let's talk to her," Walden said.

"Good," Anita seconded. "She can convince you there's nothing wrong with you physically."

"It's not all in my head," Walden said, knowing how defensive he sounded. He just *felt* wrong. If it wasn't radiation from the devastated planet or the Infinity Plague, it had to be something. Even walking tired him quickly.

The trio went to the military advisor's cramped quarters. Walden hesitated. He never liked talking with Nakamura. The woman made him feel guilty, even when he hadn't done anything. This infuriated him. He was a senior scientist, an administrator in charge of millions of dollars' worth of personnel and equipment. He shouldn't be reduced to a stammering graduate student worrying about his oral examinations when he confronted her.

The door slid open silently. Walden entered, Egad rushing between his legs. The dog settled down in a corner, his rat tail wagging briskly and a large red tongue lolling between vicious teeth. The dog eyed Nakamura with suspicion and a little of the fear Walden shared.

"Close the door," the small woman said softly. Her voice rang out in Walden's ears. "It is good that you seek me. We must talk in private." Black eyes like motionless pools of oil fixed on Anita.

"She stays," Walden said, already on the defensive.

"Very well. The situation is desperate aboard our ship," Nakamura said without further vacillation.

"We know. Captain Belford isn't in command," Anita said.

"He has never truly been in command. I do not refer to that situation. It is well in hand. Between Major Zacharias and myself, we can command the *Hippocrates*."

"Not bad for a mere civilian advisor," grumbled Walden.

"I am not referring to our reluctant guests aboard ship,

either,'' Nakamura said. Her fingers worked on the keypad of her computer. Walden shuddered as he saw the edges of the woman's hands. She had been gengineered into a killing machine. The most obvious parts of her were the sharpened bony ridges along the sides of her hands. She could assassinate with a simple hand motion. Walden wondered what other surprises Nakamura held for anyone trying to attack her.

The vidscreen bloomed into three-dimensional life, showing the Sov-Lat colonel and Pedro O'Higgins huddled together, whispering behind their hands to keep from being overheard. Nakamura touched a button and the sound blared. Walden didn't know how the woman did it, but she was able to spy on anyone anywhere in the *Hippocrates*.

"They pose no problem after their abortive attempt to hijack the ship,'' Nakamura went on. "There is another problem.''

"The Frinn.''

"They are a considerable problem, but possibly not as severe. We rot from within. That Doris Yerrow was not the only spy aboard.''

"You've found someone else?'' asked Anita, appalled.

"That is my problem, I have not found this person—or persons. The spy continues to operate unchecked. Sorbatchin learns too much of our plans, and I am unable to interdict the flow of illicit information.''

"This doesn't change the need to chase after the Frinn, does it?'' asked Walden. A dizziness assailed him that made him wobble. Anita and Egad both came to his aid. He tried to wave them off. His hand twitched uncontrollably.

"This might be a symptom of our unknown spy's activity,'' Nakamura said, studying Walden. "Have you checked for psychoactive drugs in your system?''

"No. Dr. Burch checked only for the Infinity Plague virus.''

"Conduct your own blood analysis. Look for systematic poisoning—or trace poisons. You are vital to the *Hippocrates*' mission, Dr. Walden. Without you, there would be little hope of defeating the Frinn.''

"Why?'' Walden's head cleared and his vision became preternaturally sharp. Even the dim light level in Nakamura's quarters made him squint.

"You are too modest. We need coordinated effort among all scientists to defeat the Frinn. Zacharias and his EPCT troops cannot destroy an entire world—or civilization. Their number is too small. Your work is such that you can."

"The Infinity Plague might do it for us."

"We cannot take the risk. We must know that the Frinn are not able to find Earth." Nakamura sighed in resignation, the first hint of emotion Walden had seen from her. "I have removed all location data from the computers. It will not be enough if we are captured."

"Any race capable of starlifting is able to use our star charts to calculate where Earth must be," said Walden.

"Precisely. We will not be captured intact," the military advisor said. She stiffened and tapped her fingers over the keypad. The vidscreen display altered in a swirl of color. Leo Burch walked along a corridor, Doris Yerrow's obese cat cradled in his arms. He idly stroked the animal's head. Egad growled. Walden motioned the dog to silence.

"I don't know why Leo puts up with that creature," said Anita. "I'm glad, though, Doris' cat isn't off somewhere starving itself to death."

"It's so fat," Walden said, "it could go for a month on stored energy. You wouldn't believe the rolls of adipose tissue I felt when I was petting it." The cat dangled bonelessly over the medical doctor's arm, head bouncing as Burch walked slowly. If it hadn't been for the eyes moving and the tail giving an occasional twitch, Walden would have thought the animal had died.

Nakamura said nothing. Her impassive ebony eyes studied Burch for several more seconds, then she hastily scanned each member of Walden's research team.

"Which of them will give us the key to survival?" Nakamura spoke more to herself than to Walden and Anita.

Nakamura changed the display, once more with dizzying speed. The asteroid belt showed clearly. Magnification on a single rock revealed a long, thin metal tube.

"The Frinn mass driver," said Nakamura. "They accelerated their tiny particles along that track until they reached relativistic speed. I have studied the technology. I do not believe they are any more advanced than we—and perhaps they lack certain touches we take for granted."

"They might not be as dedicated to eradicating their own species as we are," said Anita. "This is a jury-rigged contraption. It wouldn't surprise me if the *Winston* couldn't find parts to put together a more deadly, professional mass driver."

"They have such equipment aboard," admitted Nakamura. "We had no reason to use it against a planet, however. Both the Sov-Lats and our side occupy the same world. We use the equipment to return message packets to avoid interception."

"Did the Frinn ship leave from this asteroid?" asked Walden.

"That is the reason for showing you this particular rock." The vidscreen picture changed. Stars shifted abruptly and then steadied. "It is in this direction the aliens departed. We follow within the hour."

Walden shuddered. The last encounter with the Frinn had been bloody. Both sides had lost, as far as he was concerned. Human life had been lost, along with the Schwann research station. Frinn had been killed, too, and the chance of infecting their home world unwittingly with the Infinity Plague didn't please him. The Frinn seemed to have struck mercilessly and without warning; he wanted more information. He was not a religious man, but the autopsies he had performed on the aliens convinced him they were not a warlike race. They had a *soul* about them, even in death, that bespoke peace.

"The mathematical residue from their starlift drive remains. It is being analyzed now for the precise galactic geodesic that will take us to their world."

"We go, we conquer," said Walden. "Isn't there any way we can let them know we've found their home world without following?"

"You are not a coward, Doctor," said Nakamura. "Consider this a great adventure. Your team might be called upon— *will* be called upon—to insure a victory for humanity. Only by the Frinn's utter defeat can we ever return home."

"We aren't even allowed the honor of being carried home on our shields," Anita said sarcastically.

Nakamura missed the sarcasm or chose to ignore it. "Just so, Dr. Tarleton. We conquer or we die. There is no other option." She stared at the star pattern for several seconds. "We will not die. We will defeat them totally."

Walden grew increasingly uneasy. He hadn't learned what he needed. If anything, he felt nauseous.

Nakamura did not look at him. "I recommend immediate blood chemistry workups, Doctor. If necessary, I can advise you on antidotes if you find a poison in your system."

Walden didn't speak. He silently beseeched Anita to help him from the room. Waves of weakness washed over him. He wasn't sure if it was from some real or supposed poison working at his body or from the knowledge that he was going to be a party to genocide when they found the Frinn's home planet.

Two hours later, as he rested after beginning arterial blood gas tests, the *Hippocrates* shuddered, seemed to stumble, then launched into liftspace. They pursued the Frinn. To the death.

CHAPTER
2

Jerome Walden held his head and wanted to cry. His emotions flared uncontrollably. He looked up at the omni-med analyzer he used to evaluate his blood sample. The first run had been a hunt for the Infinity Plague virus. He hadn't found it. The second run had proven negative, too.

He had changed to a more standard broad spectrum search program. It ran slowly, too slowly. He wanted to cry, to scream, to run around his lab and smash things. But he couldn't. His legs had turned to putty and his mouth felt drier than the Atacama Desert burning under the noonday summer sun.

"You look like cat shit," Egad said from his vantage point on a low table covered with a soft blanket.

"You're supposed to be man's best friend. All I get from you are insults."

"You smell like cat shit, too," the dog added. "Why?"

Walden looked up and frowned. "Explain that!"

"Smell like cat shit. No need to explain."

Walden used a small keyboard to alter the analyzer as it worked on a fresh sample of his blood. If he had been on Earth, this would have taken less than an hour to get a full readout. Even though the *Hippocrates* was a hospital ship, it lacked many of the most recent medical advances, notably in nano-technology equipment.

The display flashed once. Walden smiled crookedly. "Thanks, Egad. You *are* man's best friend. You might have saved my life."

"Cat poisoned you?" the gengineered dog asked, his blue eye peering at Walden.

"Something like that," Walden said. "When Burch examined me, the cat slept on a table beside us. I picked it up and stroked its head. The animal must be laden with poison. The analyzer says I've been contaminated with a slow-acting chemical that works on my prefrontal lobe." Walden started to laugh but broke into tears. He no longer controlled his emotions.

"Cat shit," Egad said firmly, "is bad for you. Cat is bad. Kill cat."

"No!" Walden didn't want the dog near the animal until he had a chance to examine it. "And don't tell Leo Burch about this, either." Walden had been around Nakamura too long. Suspicion flared when he considered how long Burch had carried the cat around the ship and had not become poisoned himself. The particular ferrocyanate compound had numerous antidotes but none that Burch would take—unless he knew the menace presented by the feline.

Walden let the analyzer finish its work. He double-checked the result with a fresh blood sample. Weakness flowed through him like a solar wind. He thought how much blood he had taken from his arm and wondered if his body could ever generate enough replacement for it. Synthetic perfluorocarbon blood might restore him to health faster. He discarded the notion. He had never liked the blood analog because of its side effects.

He rummaged around his lab, programmed his computer process device, and concocted the antidote to the poison working so insidiously at his brain. Walden injected himself with it, waited ten minutes, and ran a new blood sample to verify he had nulled out the poison. He had.

He heaved a deep sigh and leaned back in a chair. His fingers tapped the controls mounted in the arm. Almost of their own accord, they summoned a picture of the gray lift-space bubble surrounding the *Hippocrates*.

"You can go crazy watching that," came a voice from behind. Walden jumped, as if he had been caught in a guilty act. Edouard Zacharias stood in the doorway.

"How did you get in? I had a safe-lock on the door."

"I'm in command of the *Hippocrates* now," the EPCT major said. "There's nowhere aboard that can be denied to me."

"There damned well is," snapped Walden. "This is a research lab. It has dangerous chemicals and even more dangerous biohazards in it. A careless moment and—"

"Spare me your lecture, Doctor." Zacharias reached past Walden and put a new combination into the vidscreen controller. The Sov-Lat colonel and his chief biologist popped into view. "They present the real problem to our mission."

"Sorbatchin and O'Higgins can be put into the brig," Walden said. "Do it. Don't let them run loose, if you're worried about them." He paused and considered the two men. Which was the more dangerous? Sorbatchin was thoughtful and a dedicated soldier through and through. Pedro O'Higgins lacked any guiding moral value. Walden wouldn't be surprised to learn that O'Higgins had developed the Infinity Plague—and had released it knowing what it would do to the Frinn.

"I've considered this," Zacharias said. "Nakamura believes we can learn more keeping them under constant surveillance."

"They tried to take over the ship once."

"They are guarded constantly now," Zacharias said stiffly. "They are a rot inside the ship, but they are not why I've come here, Doctor."

"I'm so happy you've finally seen my sterling qualities and sought me out for my own special self."

"Sarcasm gets us nowhere," Zacharias said briskly. Walden saw the man slip into a rigid attention stance. "We will be in liftspace at least two months. We must make plans for the moment of exit."

"The Frinn might be waiting for us," Walden said. "What then?"

"The *Winston* will exit a few seconds before us. If the pig-faces are waiting, the destroyer will engage them. We are

currently generating battle scenarios to cover this. We will
not be in immediate danger, I assure you.''

"That's more of a relief to you than to me, unless I miss
my guess," Walden said. He couldn't shake the feeling that
Zacharias had lucked into the chest filled with medals he
sported. Being with the EPCT landing force on Schwann had
strengthened this opinion. The combat marines had shown
little confidence in Zacharias as a leader.

Walden had his own battles to fight aboard the *Hippocrates*. He turned off the omni-med analyzer when it flashed
a confirmation that the cyanate compound destroying him by
millimeters was neutralized completely.

"I don't know what you mean, Doctor." Zacharias cleared
his throat and checked a small device he held in his left hand.
Walden recognized it as a military-issue sensor. If any spy
device focused on them, the sensor would report it to Zacharias. Whatever it told him, the major smiled in satisfaction.

"We need backup bioweapons to attack the Frinn," he
said. "Specificity is required. We cannot rely on the Sov-
Lats' Infinity Plague to work quickly enough. Your detailed
report indicates such infection might require months to work
adequately."

"You want to separate factions of the Frinn populace and
eradicate them?"

"Just as we can do on Earth," the major said. "Give us
a variety of options. Slow release, aerosol, contact, anything
else you can think of."

"Two months," mused Walden. "That's not much time
to build an arsenal. Can we get the Sov-Lats to help us? I'm
sure they can be of great help."

"No!"

"They've had direct contact with the Frinn." Walden
couldn't get rid of the notion that O'Higgins had tailored the
Infinity Plague for the aliens. That was a ludicrous notion,
he knew. Such a complicated and slow-working virus required years of careful study and genetic engineering skill.
Even the fastest computers on Schwann wouldn't have been
adequate to model such a plague with any accuracy.

The computers aboard the *Hippocrates* were even less
likely to give decent results. The few pitiful ones he had
brought along couldn't handle more than five hundred simul-

taneous nonlinear equations. Getting time on the ship's navigational computer was out of the question. The smallest
mistake in course meant immense distances to be traveled at
sublight speeds when they shifted back from liftspace.

Tracing the Frinn using the residue from their starlift required computing power. Simply finding the poles of higher
order and performing the summation on the resulting Laurent
series took hours. He had no hope of disturbing the ship's
navigator during those long hours of work.

"I understand the limitations of your equipment," Zacharias said. "Do what you can, Doctor. Consider this an order."

Walden ignored the EPCT major and his superior attitude.
He was responsible for the research team, not Zacharias.
"What of Captain Belford?" he asked.

"The captain is temporarily incapacitated. We are doing
what we can for him, but he has been removed from command because of medical reasons."

"Has Leo Burch signed off on the removal?"

"We . . . are not asking Dr. Burch for help at this time,"
Zacharias said.

"You mean Nakamura isn't. She suspects him of something. What?"

"I have always maintained that he, not your Dr. Yerrow,
was the Sov-Lat spy. He is very clever, however, and I have
yet to catch him doing anything to aid Sorbatchin."

"He wouldn't necessarily know Sorbatchin, even if he were
a spy," Walden pointed out.

"They all know each other," Zacharias said confidently.

Such belief in a monolithic enemy irritated Walden. "We
need to work on the alien corpses if we're to develop the
bioweapons you requested. There isn't any hope we can build
the delivery systems in only two months."

"The EPCT will take care of that," said Zacharias.

"Hand delivery is suicidal. The Frinn are similar to us in
many physiological ways. We both breathe a similar air mix-
ture, gravity seems equal for us, some of the photochemical
responses in the skin are remarkably like ours."

"They are the enemy. We will kill them for what they did
to Schwann."

"Good soldier," Walden said, not even tempering his sarcasm with a faint smile. "Kill first, ask questions later. Did it ever occur to you we're going in shooting because of the Sov-Lats and their diabolical bioweapons? We're locked in a genocidal war because *they* released the Infinity Plague."

"They're humans like us," Zacharias said, his stiffness returning.

"You can't have it both ways. Either they're treacherous scum not to be trusted or they're allies. Do we work with them or put them in the brig?"

"You may work with O'Higgins and the others, if you are careful not to reveal classified material."

"The whole damned lab is filled with classified material," raged Walden. He tried to calm himself when Egad cocked his head to one side and stared at him, brown and blue eyes worried. Walden needed to check his chemical and enzyme balances. This outburst wasn't like him. Some small trace of poison must remain in his system to affect him. He shouldn't let Zacharias bother him more than any of his prima donna scientific staff.

"You're a competent researcher, Doctor. You know what to do." Zacharias spun and marched from the room.

Walden checked his own telltales to be sure they weren't being observed. The spy devices that had plagued him on the trip to Schwann had vanished with Doris Yerrow.

"What do you think of it, Egad?" he asked.

"Let me rip out his throat. Bad smells. Ugly cat shit soldier."

"You tempt me," Walden said. When he saw the dog rise and bare his fangs, he shouted, "No, Egad, that's not even a hint of a suggestion to do it."

"Rhetorical command?" asked the dog. "Don't understand how to say something and not say it either."

"Human speech is complex," Walden said, not wanting to go into the details behind it. The dog had trouble with the more complex human emotions and thought patterns. The notion of a life-guiding philosophy lay beyond the dog's ability.

"We do as cat shit soldier says? We work on pig weapons?"

"Don't call the Frinn pigs. They're the enemy, or so it seems, but I don't want you falling into the habit of thinking of them as animals. They're intelligent."

"I'm an animal," Egad said. "So are you."

"You're more intelligent than any pig."

"Are Frinn smarter than Egad—or you?"

"Possibly," Walden said. "Probably some of them are. They've had their share of geniuses, just as humans have."

"Egad a genius among dogs."

Walden patted the creature's shaggy head and scratched his ears. He was rewarded with a very canine wet tongue on his hand. How little he knew of Egad and his abilities. They had talked at length, and he still had only a dim idea how the gengineered dog viewed the universe. Loyalty entered into Egad's world, but more basic needs could sway him temporarily.

"Find Anita and bring her here as soon as you can. We need to map out a research plan if we're going to accomplish much in the next couple months."

"Anita fine bitch. You're lucky."

"Get going," he said, sending the dog to fetch Anita, more to get Egad out of the lab than through real need. He could easily summon her over the ship's com system if he didn't mind Nakamura, Zacharias, and everyone else knowing about it. The dog trotted on his mission, giving Walden the chance to be alone for a short time.

He sat in his chair and stared into the shifting, formless gray liftspace picture being relayed from the *Hippocrates'* hull. Zacharias had said a man could go crazy watching it. Walden doubted that. Soldiers—and starmen—conjured their own legends. This had to be one of them. He found the formless, shifting gray nimbus soothing.

Dissect the Frinn. Work on their body chemistry to find specific bioweapons. Do to the aliens what he had spent a lifetime of research doing to his fellow man.

The change in direction from human to alien victim didn't strike Jerome Walden as any improvement.

He turned to his small auxiliary lab computer and began setting up the preliminary research assignments. His entire team would be involved—and that included the Sov-Lat scientists who had survived the disaster on Schwann.

CHAPTER
3

Egad rubbed against Walden's leg. The scientist reached down, distracted, and scratched the dog's ears. He didn't want to take his eyes off Zacharias and Vladimir Sorbatchin working on battle scenarios. The vidscreen in the wardroom glowed with possible attacks, counters, and approaches to the type of planet they believed represented the Frinn home world. The process fascinated Walden in a morbid way. The military men had no idea how the Frinn defended their planet—or if they did at all.

Zacharias insisted that the lightning strike favored by Sorbatchin and his Sov-Lat advisors was unrealistic. Only a surreptitious approach and guerrilla warfare would work.

Walden shook his head. The entry of the *Hippocrates* into normal space from liftspace would be anything but unannounced to a starfaring race worried about invasion. The Frinn had shown technical acumen and cleverness in the way they slated the Delta Cygnus system with sensors passively waiting for a lift away. The residue from the lift would be recorded and retrieved later to pinpoint Earth's location.

They were cautious and suspicious, the Frinn. Walden wondered at their contact with the researchers on Schwann. If they were so paranoid a race, why did they bother making what seemed to be open and friendly initial contact? Walden

18

wished he knew what had really happened before the *Hippocrates* arrived at Delta Cygnus 4.

"They dispute trivial points," Pedro O'Higgins said at Walden's elbow. Walden's hand tightened on Egad's neck as he held the dog back. Of the dozen Sov-Lats who had been rescued from Schwann, Egad liked their chief scientist least.

Walden couldn't argue with the gengineered dog's feeling. He shared it. O'Higgins was abrasive and had a subtle cruelty underlying his words and actions.

"They know nothing," O'Higgins went on, oblivious to Egad's start toward him and Walden's grip on his collar. "We blunder about aimlessly when we should make plans. Missiles with appropriate bioweapons. We enter normal space, locate their planet, and fire immediately. We can fabricate anthrax in sufficient quantity for eradication of the pig-faces."

"What happened on Schwann?" asked Walden.

"They attacked. That is all we know."

"Why did they attack? You'd had preliminary contact with them and they didn't seem hostile then." Walden guessed at this from what had been said. Zacharias kept him in the dark about the little the EPCT had gleaned from interrogating the Sov-Lats.

"We retaliated when they began using their MCG weapons against our facilities. The microwaves fried everyone at ground level. Even those two levels below the surface were severely burned."

The microwave-compressor generators struck Walden as an inefficient weapon of war. The main body of the generator was compressed by the rapid application of a magnetic field. The resulting wavefront fed out the end of the projector as intense microwaves. The entire machine had to be rebuilt after every use. The Frinn's compact toroid energy field weapon seemed little better, although it was devastating. The required equipment for creating the billion-g-acceleration plasma doughnut took hours to recharge. Detailed analysis of the Frinn attacks on the NAA destroyers and the *Hippocrates* showed their primary weaponry was no better than that available to humans.

If anything, the Frinn were considerably behind Earth in important ways. Walden sighed. Humanity had spent centuries vying for weapons superiority. The Frinn's only real advantage had been the unexpectedness of their attack.

"Tell me about your work," Walden said. He watched as Sorbatchin and Zacharias continued their computerized war planning. They had reduced a dozen possible attack approaches to three probable ones. He had to agree with O'Higgins on one point. What the tactical computer told them and the reality they found would be vastly different—it was always that way in war.

"You know what we did."

"Anthrax," Walden said, distracted. Miko Nakamura entered the room, nodded to him, and sat quietly beside Sorbatchin. Walden found that interesting and disquieting. Their civilian advisor always sided with power. By this simple act Edouard Zacharias had sunk to number three in command aboard the *Hippocrates*. Walden wasn't sure he liked having Nakamura and the Sov-Lat colonel in charge.

"Nothing else."

"The Infinity Plague," Walden replied. "You worked on it. Why did you choose a DNA unwrapping virus? That's incredibly difficult to control once released."

"You are responsible. The Soviet-Latino Pact would never engage in such reprehensible research."

Egad's reaction to what Walden knew was a lie startled him. The dog tugged in such a way that communicated well. The gengineered dog thought O'Higgins spoke the truth.

"Where did the plague originate?"

"The North American Alliance developed it," came O'Higgins' angry response. "You know that. You and your team of researchers were to perfect it."

Walden started to hotly deny it, then stopped. He was director of research but had not been given full information about the mission. His immediate superior on Earth, William Greene, had given Anita Tarleton an assignment she refused to discuss with him. Because of their personal closeness, Walden had learned that the classified assignment existed. How many others in his team had been given similar assignments classified beyond even the director's need to know?

"You're still developing race-specific weapons, aren't you?" asked Walden, countering. The muscles around

O'Higgins' eyes twitched. From this small clue Walden got his answer.

"We see no reason to destroy entire continents when only small segments need to be dealt with. It is *you* who seek weapons of mass destruction."

Walden didn't bother answering the jibe. He remembered how Zacharias had approached him asking for Frinn-specific bioweapons. The major had spoken enough with Sorbatchin that some of the Sov-Lat philosophy of killing had rubbed off. Walden caught Nakamura's eye and tipped his head toward the hatch leading into the corridor. She followed quietly.

"Can we talk here?" he asked.

"Briefly. There are no probes focused on us. They center on the wardroom," she said needlessly.

"Where did the Infinity Plague originate? Did the NAA or the Sov-Lats develop it?"

"What difference does it make?" she asked.

Walden went cold inside. "We released it," he said, reading her reaction accurately. "The Sov-Lats knew we had and tried to analyze it. That's why we encountered it first in their research facility. They tried to figure out what it was but they died."

"They released their mutated anthrax in defense against the Frinn. Is that not enough for you, Doctor?"

"The NAA is responsible for the plague," he said dully. His world turned around in dizzying circles. What worried him the most was the chance that his lover had been sent to Schwann to work on the Infinity Plague and he hadn't known.

"Chromosome stripping using viral agents is not new."

"It can destroy the Frinn."

"Perhaps that is for the best," Nakamura said. "I have seen how Zacharias prepares for the coming battle. I do not like his choice of tactics."

"You're siding with Sorbatchin?"

"A direct thrust at the heart is more likely to succeed. Sneaking about and giving the enemy the chance to detect us is a poor choice. Excuse me, Doctor. I must do my duty and advise." Miko Nakamura spun and returned to the wardroom where she again sat beside Colonel Sorbatchin, lending weight to the Sov-Lat's arguments for a blitzkrieg attack from space.

"Come on, Egad," Walden said, tugging on the dog's collar. Egad growled deep in his throat. Walden let the canine go his own way. They had been in liftspace less than a week. He had work to do on the bioweapons for use against the Frinn.

And he needed to find Anita Tarleton and find out exactly what research orders she had received from Dr. Greene. Jerome Walden didn't think he would like what she told him.

CHAPTER
4

Walden nodded off over his computer terminal. The outraged beeping his arms caused as they hit unprotected keys brought him awake with a start. He looked around guiltily. Egad slept in his basket in the corner of the laboratory. Other than the gengineered dog, the room was empty.

Walden stretched and then yawned. He didn't remember getting sleep the night before. A quick check of the computer date told him he hadn't been asleep for a few minutes. It had been hours and he hadn't awakened refreshed. If anything, he felt worse now than he had before.

Fingers working slowly on the keyboard, he called up ship's status. He groaned when he saw the report. The *Hippocrates* reentered normal space in less than a week. For almost two months he had been killing himself to work out weapons capable of defeating the Frinn. The past five days had been even more hectic since Zacharias and Sorbatchin— or Nakamura—had decided on the type and delivery system required for the invasion of the Frinn home world.

He could supply it. If only he had a few more days to work on it, a few more hours. Even minutes might help.

"Where's Anita?" he asked Egad. The huge head shook and the greyhound body pushed upward on the stubby legs.

23

The dog yawned immensely and then circled twice before settling back down. Walden repeated his question.

Egad fixed his brown and blue eyes on his master. The expression was one of sorrow.

"Well?" demanded Walden. "Do you know?"

"Know," the dog confirmed. "You won't like it."

Walden wasn't going to argue with the dog if he didn't want to speak. He requested the information from the computer. Everyone with access to the machine would know what he asked but he decided security was secondary to speed. A single beep and a flashing light located Anita as being in . . . Zacharias' quarters.

He frowned. The two of them had spent a great deal of time together since the *Hippocrates* had entered liftspace. Walden discounted it as chance. Anita had argued bitterly with him when he asked for her mission orders on Schwann. The argument had turned more acrimonious than he liked, but he needed to know if she had been sent by Dr. Greene to perfect the Infinity Plague. She had stormed off and hadn't spoken to him for three days. And when she did they quarreled once more over the same topic.

He hadn't learned what he needed to know, and she spoke to him only in passing. He had waited for her several times in their quarters, but the increasingly long hours he spent working on the Frinn physiology and biochemistry kept him away. He assumed she kept similarly long hours on her own analyses. That she had long conferences with Zacharias and not with him struck Walden as odd, but not exceedingly so.

Now he wasn't sure. He tried to push his ugly suspicions from his mind. He tried to convince himself that his fatigue caused needless worry. A second look at Egad told him he had finally guessed what the gengineered dog had known for weeks, perhaps longer.

"She's with Zacharias, isn't she?"

The dog's immense head nodded the barest amount.

"How long?"

"Long enough. Don't like him. Cat shit soldier smells bad. Anita nice bitch."

Walden rubbed his temples and wondered if he had totally eradicated the poison gnawing at his brain. That had been many weeks ago, and he hadn't suffered any recurrent symptoms—that he knew about. His problems ran deeper than the mere attempt to kill him.

"We've got to look over the Frinn ship," he said, more to himself than to Egad. The captured vessel that had held the dead aliens had been magnetically connected to the *Hippocrates* before the ship went into liftspace. "I need to be sure of all the details about their living conditions before proceeding with the weapons."

"Dangerous," Egad cautioned. "We can't go outside."

Egad meant that in a way different from Walden's understanding. Egad had never reconciled himself to being unable to run and play under the sun. Walden had told him it was dangerous outside, therefore he couldn't leave the ship. Egad's limited understanding of space travel and celestial dynamics accepted this.

Walden knew that transferring from one ship to another while in liftspace was extremely hazardous. The destroyer escort *Winston* traveled less than a kilometer away—and it might as well be a million parsecs. However, the Frinn ship was connected to the *Hippocrates* by grapples. The danger here lay in the tiny blister of liftdrive encasing the captured alien vessel. The smallest disturbance might pop the blister and cast off the Frinn ship forever.

The way he felt now, about his work and personal life, Walden didn't care if he was marooned in the ship and died.

"Can I go?" The dog bounded up and dropped his huge Saint Bernard head in Walden's lap. The scientist scratched the dog's ears and lifted his head to stare directly into the mismatched blue and brown eyes.

"No. I'll get Willie Klugel or Paul Preston to come with me. They've been doing work similar to mine. They can use the break from their labs, too." He smiled wryly. Willie Klugel would never acknowledge any danger in the pursuit of project completion. Preston, with his work on angiogenesis factor and blood clotting, took a more cautious view of the world. He stepped close to bioweapons capable of wiping out the world every day and respected that.

Walden wanted to ask Anita to join them, but pride kept him from doing so. If she preferred Zacharias' company to his, that was her business.

"Anita fine bitch," Egad said, still staring up at him.

Walden left without comment. Egad whimpered and returned to his basket, curling up on the blanket but not sleeping.

"I don't want O'Higgins along," Walden protested. Miko Nakamura stood impassively, her dark eyes betraying nothing of what went on inside her head.

"There is nothing to hide on the Frinn ship," she said. "Our Sov-Lat friends requested that he join you and Klugel."

"I want Preston, too."

"We have been over this. It is too dangerous for more than a trio to enter the Frinn ship. Your initial request is most irregular, Doctor." The woman stared at him as if trying to decipher some hidden emotion in him. There wasn't any. He was sucked dry inside from his work.

"Simply looking at the pictures from the foptic camera isn't good enough." He didn't know how he could explain to her. He was a scientist and dealt with enigmatic symbols and concepts as part of his work. But nothing replaced a hands-on feel for a finished product. All the tri-d pictures taken since the ship's capture wouldn't replace five minutes poking around in the Frinn ship.

He needed to know his bioweapons would work. A sense of what the Frinn held dearest would help. He cursed himself for his compulsion to accomplish in weeks what he took years to do otherwise. Walden had long since come to grips with the moral issue of designing killer microbes. He tried to bring some humanity and purpose to the process rather than let researchers like Pedro O'Higgins have free rein.

"You have said this before," Nakamura reminded him. "I accede to your request, though reluctantly. You, Klugel, and O'Higgins will be the first to enter the Frinn vessel since removal of the corpses. Do not disturb anything that might prove useful to us later."

"I'm on your side, Nakamura," he said tiredly. "Just be sure to keep O'Higgins from stealing anything."

"He will be observed closely."

"Did we intentionally release the Infinity Plague?" he asked suddenly.

Nakamura smiled crookedly. "You never rest, do you, Doctor? That is a quality that has much to recommend it."

"It irritates you," he said.

"Senseless refusal to accept the obvious irritates me," Nakamura said. "Now please go and examine carefully your hazard suits. I have carefully inspected them. You should be certain nothing goes wrong."

"It's my life." He started to go, then hesitated. "Where can I reach Anita? I want to say good-bye."

Nakamura shrugged. That simple gesture held more than denial for Walden. The Japanese Hegemony advisor might not know where Anita Tarleton was. That bothered him. He had come to believe Nakamura knew everything happening aboard the *Hippocrates*.

"She is occupied, I think," Nakamura said.

Walden didn't press the issue. He hurried to the airlocks and found his hazard suit in its storage locker. Evidence that Nakamura had scrutinized it for damage was everywhere. Walden did a thorough job of his own. Since his poisoning he had done everything more carefully. That newfound paranoia had helped drive Anita away, too.

"Ready?" demanded Willie Klugel. The short, balding scientist had already donned his suit. The helmet's inner surface fogged with his moist breath. Walden tapped the glasteel.

"Adjust your humidity level, Willie. You'll fog over completely if you don't."

"Damned suit. Never could get this right." He fumbled for a few minutes while Walden finished climbing into his suit. Pedro O'Higgins stood impatiently at the airlock.

"What are you looking for?" Walden asked the Chilean scientist.

"The same as you. Justification for the assumptions made during research."

"What does Sorbatchin want you to find?"

"Let us go. I have had enough of this playing at spy aboard your ship." He cast his brown eyes back toward the corridor leading into the *Hippocrates*. Walden wondered if O'Higgins looked for Sorbatchin or Nakamura. Neither had come to see off the small exploration party.

Even worse, Anita Tarleton hadn't come, either.

Walden pushed into the airlock and sealed it when the other two joined him. They passed through a second lock and waited for what stretched to eternity for Walden. His heart raced. He needed to look at the Frinn controls and check critical gas levels in their biosphere. He really did. He wished he could convince himself as easily as he had Nakamura.

The lock cycling open startled him. For a second he stood and stared. Simply stepping into the Frinn ship would require caution. The vessel existed in liftspace only through certain fudge factors. He didn't understand them—and he didn't think the *Hippocrates'* navigator did, either. That did nothing to inspire him since the man had assured him entry would be safe.

Walden stepped out and screamed as a million knives cut at his brain. His feet disconnected from his ankles and his guts tumbled endlessly. He turned and tried to retreat to the *Hippocrates.* A burning band circled his neck and tightened. Walden stumbled and reached out, only to have his fingers turn icy.

Then the excruciating sensations passed and he stood inside the Frinn ship, sweating but whole. The phase interface between the ships required more to pass than he had anticipated.

Doubt assailed him about the need for entering the Frinn ship. He knew he had made the right decision after only a few steps into the craft. The *feel* told him much about them, and he hadn't gotten any of it from Nakamura's carefully gathered photos of the ship's interior. Klugel and O'Higgins, recovered from the transition effects, then went their separate ways. Klugel wanted to examine their food preparation system. His work centered on destroying the flora responsible for digestion in the Frinn gut. He was an expert in T-odd bacteriophages in humans. Walden didn't doubt that Klugel could starve an entire world in a few weeks with his research.

What O'Higgins sought Walden couldn't say. He had to ask Nakamura later. It might give a clue to the line of Sov-Lat research.

He entered the control room and settled into the commander's chair. The contours poked and bent him in odd ways but nothing he couldn't tolerate for a few minutes. The Frinn were humanoid and, from what he had seen, had thought patterns similar to a human's.

Walden reached out and saw that the Frinn arms were a

few centimeters shorter than his. Opening a case he had brought along, he began analysis of their air composition. The automated equipment worked silently and gave him an excuse to do what he considered real exploration.

To his surprise most of the ship's major systems were automated and ran independently of any Frinn operator. This dependence—over-dependence from his viewpoint—pointed to fewer crew and more comprehensive mechanisms. He made a note about possible low population levels on the Frinn home world.

If he was right, they might defeat the Frinn quickly. Their population might be extremely small compared with Earth's twelve billion hungry mouths. The more Walden thought, the less likely the success for Sorbatchin's quick strike against the Frinn home world seemed. Low population meant fewer to disable and kill. It also meant a scattered population.

The Frinn came from a world similar to Earth in gravity and atmospheric composition. Fewer Frinn meant a lower population density. Their dependence on robotic helpers added to his growing idea that depending on an epidemic style bioweapon wouldn't work fast enough to help those aboard the *Winston* and *Hippocrates.*

But the Infinity Plague would work eventually. It would spread insidiously and tracelessly.

All his work these past months might have been wasted. They might arrive to find a world on its last legs. In a perverse way, Walden hoped this was so. Being responsible for destroying an entire species didn't thrill him any more than the notion that his bioweapons might be used against other humans.

It was bad enough that the NAA had released the Infinity Plague.

"Jerome, you ready to go back? I've got what I need." Willie Klugel tapped the case of his recorder. "They don't eat much, if I interpret their portions correctly. I'll have to increase dosage to be effective."

"They don't eat much individually or as a crew?" asked Walden.

"Both. Small crew, from what I made out. But then this is only an exploratory vessel."

"Not a warship?"

"I meant that," Klugel said, frowning. Sweat ran down his forehead. Too much else occupying his attention, he still hadn't adjusted his hazard suit levels properly.

Walden sat down in the command chair and finished the gas sample analysis. He didn't think Klugel had made an error. The truth had slipped out, as much as they wanted to deny it. Calling this a warship made what they'd done to the Frinn easier to stomach.

Killing peaceable explorers didn't seem as noble.

"This *is* a scout ship," Walden declared. "They didn't invade the Delta Cygnus system. They stumbled on it as explorers."

"But the robot fighting machines! Those aren't something you carry during friendly exploration." Klugel snorted in contempt at such an idea of peace and scientific curiosity.

"They were efficient," admitted Walden. "They were also robotic. Only a few living Frinn commanded them. What if their fabrication was recent?"

"After the Infinity Plague had been released and infected them?"

"Yes," said Walden, warming to his supposition. "They built the war machines in response to what they saw as an unprovoked—and sneak—attack on them."

"The microwave weapon. The compact toroid weapon. Explain those."

"I can't. Not exactly," said Walden. "Zacharias said something about them being inefficient weapons, though, makeshift and not ideal for use in prolonged combat situations. They might have bollixed them together to defend themselves."

"Why defend? Why not run?"

"The liftspace residue," Walden said triumphantly. "If someone shoots at you, you duck and start to run. What good does it do if you're leading the man with the gun home to kill not only you but your family and friends?"

"A beguiling argument, Jerome. It is also impossible to verify."

"It's a good hypothesis," Walden said. "We might be starting an interstellar war over an accident. I can't believe the Infinity Plague was released on purpose."

"I studied your reports carefully," Willie Klugel said. "It

is an odd weapon for use against humans. It strips the wrong chromosomes, then stops."

Walden wished Anita would talk to him about her intended research on Schwann. He *knew* she was supposed to work on the Infinity Plague project. Her silence didn't make sense, otherwise. If he knew what it was intended to do, he might be able to piece together a better scenario of events on Schwann between humans and Frinn.

"Let's find O'Higgins and get back to the *Hippocrates*. I've got work to do."

"We reenter normal space in only three days," agreed Klugel. "I, too, have much to do. So little time, so little time to kill billions." The small biologist shuffled off, stroking his recorder and mumbling to himself.

Jerome Walden followed, no longer caring if they left Pedro O'Higgins aboard or not. He had too much on his mind to worry about the Sov-Lat scientist.

CHAPTER
5

Jerome Walden stepped back into the *Hippocrates'* airlock. The violent wrenching coursing through his body signaled a change in the quality of liftspace bubble. The return marked a doubling of the agony he had endured on entering the Frinn ship.

"What's wrong?" he shouted into his com unit. The reverberation in his hazard suit helmet almost deafened him.

"There is trouble, Doctor," came Nakamura's calm voice. She stood just inside the lock with her arms folded across her chest. "The liftspace blister protecting the Frinn ship is deteriorating because O'Higgins activated some device aboard the ship. The energy imbalance is disturbing the dynamic balance between our vessels."

"He was told not to!" Walden couldn't believe the Sov-Lat scientist had been so reckless—or careless.

"Wait," cautioned Nakamura. "You cannot go back to retrieve him. It is too dangerous."

"I just came from there. I know it's dangerous." Walden didn't think. He jerked free of the woman's strong grip and avoided her long enough to start the airlock cycling shut again. He saw a flash of anger on her face. Then Nakamura vanished from sight. Walden impatiently waited for the airlock to cycle open on the other side.

He experienced unbearable vertigo and senses shifting this time. The break between the Frinn ship and the *Hippocrates* had become even more extreme.

Recovering, he darted back down the narrow connecting tube, felt a different and frightening tingle as he passed through the pseudo-bubble that bulged out to encompass the Frinn ship, and then plunged into the vessel itself.

"O'Higgins!" he called into his microphone. The com unit worked passably inside the Frinn ship. Communicating back to the *Hippocrates* could be done only through the fiber optic circuitry Nakamura had installed.

Walden knew that was a one-way communication. Those on the ship could see his and O'Higgins' fate overtaking them and never be able to give warning.

"Where the hell are you? You've got to return to the *Hippocrates* immediately. The bubble is popping!"

Strangled gasps came to him over the headphones. He turned, trying to decide where the signal was the strongest. He gave up and moved toward what they had decided was the Frinn weapons control room. O'Higgins was a biologist, but his mission had been dictated by Sorbatchin. The GRU colonel didn't care about inventing new weapons if he could plunder existing ones and turn them to his own use. One attempted takeover on the *Hippocrates* had failed. A second might succeed with some mysterious Frinn super-weapon.

For the first time, Walden considered what he was doing. He had rushed back heedlessly to help O'Higgins—and he didn't even like the man. As a researcher, O'Higgins was competent but needlessly cruel. Yet Walden had returned to the Frinn vessel, risking his own life for no reason.

Walden slowed as he neared the Frinn weapons center. He knew the reason. So little had gone right lately, he had nothing to lose. Or so he thought. It was self-despair, self-*pity*, that drove him to such recklessness.

"Pedro, are you inside?" Walden studied the entryway to the weapons control room and didn't like what he found. Small red lights circling the doorway winked slowly. What had the Chilean triggered by entering the room?

"Help me." The signal crackled with static and was so weak Walden barely heard it, even though he stood only a few meters away from the source. "I'm trapped."

Walden wished he could get help from Nakamura, but the advisor could only watch, not aid. He didn't even know where the foptic lines had been laid or where the rice-grain camera lenses had been installed.

He touched the wall and recoiled. It felt hot, even through his hazard suit gloves. The insulation in those gloves could withstand three hundred degrees Celsius before starting to smolder. For him to sense heat through them meant a temperature far above what was to be expected.

Walden frowned and backed off for a better look at the area. The wall didn't appear hot. Such temperatures as he felt should have vaporized a metal wall. And if the Frinn used another material such as a fiber composite, it would sublimate and leave tiny holes. He felt heat but saw no telltale cherry-red glow.

"This is where the bubble into liftspace is breaking," he said, knowing Nakamura would hear. "O'Higgins might be trapped on the very edge of it. I'm not sure how to get to him."

The winking lights hypnotized him. He didn't want to go through the doorway, yet saw no alternative. Finding a laser torch and cutting through the wall would take too long. Walden grabbed the gas analyzer from his belt and shoved it forward. Actinic beams slashed down and microsectioned the device. It sputtered as its battery short-circuited and then fused.

"Whew," he said, rocking back. The Frinn protective device would cut anything—anyone—trying to pass through the doorway. He had to get inside some other way.

He tried to remember the layout of the ship and couldn't. Panic mounted. He knew there were only seconds before the Frinn ship dislodged from the *Hippocrates* and drifted off into liftspace. When the bubble burst, it would be over for anyone still aboard. The Frinn engines didn't function properly after the battle that had brought the humans aboard the ship. He and O'Higgins would drift forever between dimensions, caught in the fractal universe opened by the liftdrive and traveled only by starships.

Walden rushed down a deck and frantically sought an entry from below. He saw no reason for the Frinn to provide such an emergency exit when they had gone to great lengths to booby-trap the main doorway. Although Walden found nothing, he discovered the edge of the bubble pushing its way inside the Frinn ship's hull.

Amorphous gray billowed and sent tendrils like fog into the ship. It lapped and licked at the deck plates. Wherever it touched, it left nothingness.

"O'Higgins, the deck. The floor is giving way under you. Drop down. You'll never make it out the way you came in." Walden hopped up and down, trying to grab the sharp edges of the vanished deck plate. He didn't want to cut his suit gloves, but he did want to see inside the room. Pedro O'Higgins might not be alive. The Frinn protective device might have ended his life.

Or worse. He might have fallen into the gray timelessness of liftspace.

"Help me," came the faint cry. "I'm so far away. I can't see anymore. So far."

Walden caught the sundered edge of decking and kicked himself into the room. He lay flat, not wanting to replace O'Higgins as a target if any robotic sighting devices were activated. Only the deadly laser-rimmed doorway showed any sign of life. The rest of the room was empty—and more.

The gray of liftspace oozed and billowed like a living being. Walden blinked when he thought he saw a hand reaching toward him. The second time it appeared he knew whose hand it was. He grabbed, caught it, and yanked as hard as he could.

His feet slipped on the slick decking. He tried to let go of O'Higgins' hand. The Sov-Lat scientist clung to him with a tenacity Walden couldn't break. Flailing about, Walden grabbed a chair and hung on for his life. O'Higgins slowly reappeared from the shadowy depths of liftspace. His arms and shoulders came into view and then his torso followed. He clung to a small metallic device fastened to his belt.

Walden shrieked as lances of white-hot pain drove into his ears. A burst of static louder than any sound he'd ever heard crashed and echoed inside his helmet as O'Higgins tumbled completely into the Frinn ship.

Walden lay stunned for a moment, then shouted at O'Higgins to get up, to get into the compartment below. To his horror, the gray mist seeped inward and began covering the escape hole.

He shoved the motionless Sov-Lat into the hole and tumbled after him. Walden crashed on top of O'Higgins and chanced a look up. The encroaching grayness filled the hole and started oozing downward. With strength he didn't know he possessed, Walden picked up O'Higgins and ran to the airlock. All the way he shouted for Nakamura to cycle open the hatches.

The transition back to his ship jarred Walden so badly he almost lost consciousness—almost. Grimly, he held on and forged ahead, leaning against the inside of the airlock. Slowly, ever so slowly, it cycled open.

He collapsed inside the *Hippocrates*, unable to move.

"You are very brave, Doctor," came Colonel Sorbatchin's solemn voice. "And very foolish." The blond, powerful officer snapped his fingers. Leo Burch and his medbot Albert hastened to O'Higgins' side. They skinned him and Walden from their hazard suits. Tiny probes snaked from the medical analysis robot and entered the Sov-Lat's arms and legs. Monitors began flashing vital signs. When he was satisfied with what he saw, Burch turned to Walden.

"You don't look any better for the trip, old son. Want a snort of Doc Burch's Magical Elixir to fix what ails you?" He held out a hip flask that Walden knew contained whiskey.

He started to reach for it, then remembered how he had been poisoned. "No," Walden said, scooting away from the doctor. "I'll be fine. I just don't remember much of what happened back there."

"We saw it all," spoke up Major Zacharias. Anita stood beside him. Even in his shocked condition, Walden saw how closely she stood. Her side brushed against the EPCT major's.

"The gray. That's liftspace. I saw it. I rescued O'Higgins from it."

"You should have let him die," Zacharias said. "He disobeyed orders and endangered us all."

"Why did you save a Sov-Lat?" demanded Anita, outraged. "You've become one of them. Why, Jerome? I don't know you anymore."

"Become one of them?" he repeated dully. Pain began

lancing up and down his back and legs from the muscle strain of carrying the heavy Pedro O'Higgins. He had been tired before entering the Frinn ship. The physical and emotional toll on him over the last few minutes robbed him of his senses.

"You've sold out. I'd never have believed it!" Anita Tarleton swung and stalked off. Zacharias watched her go, a smug expression on his face.

"You've lost her with this vacuum-brained stunt, Walden. Taking sides with the Sov-Lats is treason. I'll strip you of your security clearance. You won't work for *us* again."

"Us?" Walden took several seconds to realize what Zacharias meant. Then he exploded in anger. "You pompous fool! O'Higgins is a human being. I couldn't let him die back there!"

"Why not? You've worked on weapons designed to kill him."

This rocked Walden. What Zacharias said was true. Every bioweapon he had designed had been intended for use against the Soviet-Latino Pact nations. Any number of his creations would have ended O'Higgins' life—and he would have felt a sense of accomplishment at so successfully defending the NAA.

But not now. Now the Sov-Lats and the NAA had to work together to defeat the Frinn.

Jerome Walden wasn't even sure *they* were the enemy. He wasn't sure of anything.

"I'll be watching you, turncoat." With that threat, Edouard Zacharias stalked off.

Walden sat on the floor of the airlock and simply stared. He was alone. Burch had taken O'Higgins to the infirmary. Anita and Zacharias had stormed off after calling him a traitor. Of Nakamura he saw no trace. He was more than alone. He was abandoned.

Struggling to his feet, he regained his strength quickly. The muscle strain along his legs and back faded as he stretched and turned. He would live, he thought. That might not be any improvement if Zacharias convinced the others in the research team that their director had betrayed them.

The *Hippocrates* was large, but it was too small for an outcast scorned by his own side and mistrusted by the former enemy.

"Egad cares," came the rasping, computer-generated voice he knew so well. "Master brave. Heard cat shit bitch who doesn't smell say so."

"Nakamura said that?"

Egad bobbed his head up and down. Walden patted the animal and then started toward his quarters. When he stumbled inside, it didn't surprise him to find Anita's belongings gone.

"Bitch moved," Egad confirmed. "Just after you left me in lab, she came and took things."

Walden collapsed onto the bed he had shared with Anita. A migraine headache rose behind his eyes and attacked with savage fury. He tried auto-hypnotic techniques to relax and failed utterly. He rose and fumbled out medication he had concocted in his own lab. The artificial beta endorphins thwarted the pain in seconds.

Walden also sank into a chair, all pretense at strength gone.

When the door chimed, he motioned to Egad to open it. He didn't want to see anyone except Anita—and he doubted she had returned.

Miko Nakamura pushed in when Egad nosed the door button. She turned her black eyes on the gengineered dog and nodded curtly. She had figured out that Egad was far more than he seemed. By acknowledging him, she turned him into an equal—and a reluctant ally.

The dog sniffed loudly and jumped onto Walden's unoccupied bed. He stared at Nakamura, waiting for his master's command to kill.

Walden almost gave it for the sheer pleasure of seeing someone die. He held the command in check. Nakamura was an expert at killing. The gengineered bony ridges along her hands showed that. She might be able to kill both Egad and him and never break a sweat.

Walden didn't care about himself. He had lost everything. Sending Egad to a pointless death bothered him.

"What do you want?" he asked.

"I need to debrief you. When you did not appear in the wardroom, I sought you out. What happened aboard the Frinn vessel?"

"You saw it all on your foptic cameras, didn't you?"

"The bubble discontinuity cut through the fiber optic cable. I lost you within minutes of your reentry. What you saw is of utmost importance scientifically. No one has come this close to a higher order liftspace pole before.''

''You don't want to know what O'Higgins found?''

Nakamura stared at him, then said in measured tones, ''He found nothing of significance. He triggered a Frinn security device. At that point I lost the foptic connection.''

Walden wanted to lie to her, to tell tall tales of the invincible weapons O'Higgins had discovered. He wanted to shake her calm façade and make her reveal what lay beneath. Walden had been stripped of everything he held dear. He wanted others to share the same fate.

''He didn't find anything. He didn't have time before the gray fog drifted through the wall. Hell, it must have eaten the wall. It took out a section of deck plate.''

Nakamura nodded sagely, keeping him talking without verbal prompting. Walden told her all he had seen. He finished by asking, ''What's the prognosis for O'Higgins?''

''I spoke with Dr. Burch before coming here. O'Higgins is in a light coma caused by the trip into liftspace. From what you tell me, he was completely immersed.''

''Only his hand poked out. If I hadn't grabbed it . . .'' Walden shivered at the thought of dooming anyone to such a chasm beyond human reach.

''He will be all right. Burch says that the condition is temporary. No harm has been done to his body. Only his mind has endured trauma from the experience.''

Walden shrugged it off. What did he care about O'Higgins? He was a Sov-Lat, one of the enemy who wasn't an enemy now.

''Was *your* mission successful, Doctor?''

''What?'' Walden had been drifting. Nakamura's sharp question brought him out of his reverie. ''I think so. It ties in well with my research. I got a good feel for how the Frinn live.''

''You worry about Sorbatchin's tactic of a lightning strike at the centers of their power.''

''Their home world will be decentralized. We won't be able to spread any disease vector quickly enough to defeat them.''

"The Infinity Plague will spread," Nakamura said with confidence.

"Slowly, it'll spread slowly," answered Walden. "They use robots for everything. That ship was an exploratory scout ship, and it was almost completely automated. They don't share our distrust of total robotization."

"The Sov-Lats have shown their ability to change programming parameters," said Nakamura. "And we have developed computer viruses which can render their most highly protected programs worthless, should we send the proper signal."

"The Frinn aren't like that. They depend on their machines."

"A decentralized culture supports Zacharias' plan of waging guerrilla war against them. The longer we can draw out the battle, the more likely we are to succeed."

"That's the way it seems. I have an aerosol delivery system you can use for a nerve gas Klugel and I worked up in the lab, but it doesn't look as if it'll be effective enough."

"I must consider what you've said." Nakamura looked lost in thought. "It is too bad none of the Frinn lived long enough to tell us more of their culture."

"Yes, it's too bad," Walden said sarcastically. Nakamura stared at him, then bowed slightly and left.

He didn't have the heart to move Egad from his bed. He slumped over a table and fell into a fitful sleep troubled with dreams of Anita, Zacharias, and planets filled with dying aliens.

CHAPTER
6

"We need to test before we can guarantee such results," protested Willie Klugel. The others gathered around the large table shared his skepticism over Walden's plan.

"Zacharias has to have the bioweapons ready immediately. We shift back into normal space anytime now." Walden glanced at the computer terminal beside the table and saw that the *Hippocrates* had less than three hours before reentry. He had to get his team into action.

"Don't be absurd. These weapons can backfire on us if we're not careful," said Burnowski. "We dare not rush into battle without testing more thoroughly."

"Don't be more absurd than you have to be," cut in Chin with his clipped, precise words. The man lounged back in his chair and hooked his fingers behind his head. He stared unblinkingly at Burnowski. "How can we test what we've devised? The Frinn ship is gone. It drifted away to who knows where in liftspace. All we've got are corpses in a high-vac freezer. Test the microbes how?"

"We can do something more than computer analog studies," insisted Burnowski. Walden appreciated the older scientist's caution. Chin had a tendency to act impulsively. If Burnowski had a fault as a scientist, it was just the opposite. Nothing would leave his lab without hundreds of hours of intense testing on the computer and even longer months of meticulous experimentation on test animals.

"We don't know what conditions will be," said Walden. "I've done some first order approximations on what we're likely to find." He started the projector. The vidscreen filled with his guesses and supporting facts.

He had put together the report and knew its contents by heart. His mind drifted as the others tried to absorb everything he had to pass along. Walden looked around the darkened room. Anita Tarleton was nowhere to be seen. Walden felt a hollowness that refused to go away. By the time the presentation came to an end, he was ready to agree to any suggestion. It was difficult caring about this—or anything—without Anita beside him.

Instead, he kept control. He cleared his throat, got attention back from the vidscreen, and said, "Do your own projections on my numbers. Meet here again in one hour with recommendations and cautions. Any questions?"

"Yeah," muttered someone at the rear of the room. Walden thought it might be Marni Donelli. "Do we get to take a break for lunch?"

He ignored her and pocketed his tri-vid data cube. He left quickly, not wanting to talk to his team. It still bothered him that Anita hadn't come to the briefing.

Then again, why should she? She was able to get her information directly from Major Zacharias.

"Walden," came a harsh voice. "I would speak with you."

He turned to see Pedro O'Higgins striding up. The man had recovered well from his brief trip to the other side of the *Hippocrates'* liftspace bubble.

"What is it? I'm very busy, Doctor. We reenter in less than two hours."

"I have not had the chance to thank you for saving me. Why did you do it? We are not friends."

"We're not even allies," Walden said, bone-tired. "But we *are* humans. We'll be facing an alien military soon. We may not like each other, but we've got to work together."

"You say this because you think the NAA will triumph over the Sov-Lat Pact." O'Higgins almost sneered.

"I say it because I probably mean it." Walden was startled

to find that he did mean what he said. The differences between the Earth superpowers had to be laid aside until the Frinn had been dealt with. The snippets he had discovered about events on Schwann pointed to serious mistakes made on both sides. He wished they could parlay with the aliens before using the bioweapons his team had developed, but that was a small hope.

If nothing else, he hoped for some show of unity among the humans until afterward.

After the genocide. This thought made him shiver. Perhaps the Sov-Lats were right in pursuing race-specific bioweapons. He had heard rumors that they could bring down an Armenian dissident in the center of a Polish city.

He longed for such specificity and control. To pluck out the Frinn and leave everything else would be a miracle. Even with the Infinity Plague working so insidiously at them, they still posed a major menace to Earth.

Walden's mind turned into other paths when the phrase "major menace" stuck and repeated endlessly. Major, major, major. Zacharias. Zacharias and Anita Tarleton.

"You look distracted, Walden."

"I am," he said, forcing the ugly thoughts away for the moment. "I am also very busy. If there's nothing else, O'Higgins . . ."

"Sorbatchin wants to speak with you. It will take only a moment of your time."

Walden heaved a sigh of resignation. He had no time left to do anything. Everyone wanted only a minute here, a few seconds there. He had spent a century chasing others' ideas, or so it seemed. He had not convinced any of them that their problem was not his emergency.

"Very well. I have little time. I've scheduled another meeting in forty minutes."

O'Higgins acted as messenger boy and led Walden to Sorbatchin's cabin. Walden almost wished the *Hippocrates* had the facilities to lock up the Sov-Lats. Letting them have free run of the ship invited disaster. Their abortive mutiny after coming aboard at Schwann was only a hint of trouble to come.

"Doctor Walden, welcome," the Sov-Lat colonel greeted effusively. "Come, let me propose a toast."

"I don't have time," he said. "And I don't drink."

"With your enemy? Is that what you mean?"

"I don't drink. I've given it up."

"Ah, the recurring ulcer," Sorbatchin said, nodding wisely.

"How do you know about that?" Walden sat down heavily, his mind racing. He wondered if Miko Nakamura was monitoring this talk. He hoped she was. The only way for Sorbatchin to have found out about the ulcer was from records in Leo Burch's keeping. If the Sov-Lat colonel had breached the *Hippocrates'* computer security system, Nakamura would have known instantly.

"Come, let us reason together. Your EPCT major made no attempt to recover the Frinn ship when it floated away."

"You weren't there." Walden looked over his shoulder, but O'Higgins had left them alone. "Ask your puppet. He'll tell you all about liftspace and how unlikely it was we'd be able to bring the Frinn ship back."

"Pedro has been unable to recall much. His mind was blanked by the traumatic experience."

"What was he looking for aboard the ship? A weapons system you could turn against us?"

"Against you?" Sorbatchin laughed. Walden didn't like it. "Hardly. We—you and I—are on the same side, Jerome. We fight the Frinn, even if the NAA released the Infinity Plague which caused them to retaliate against all Earthmen on Delta Cygnus 4."

"I'm ready to believe your version," Walden said. He had run extensive computer scenarios. The most probable result of hostilities on Schwann placed the blame on the North American Alliance researchers.

The Sov-Lats had released anthrax, but it had been in defense when the Frinn began their devastating bombardment of the planet. He also surmised that the Sov-Lats had detected the Infinity Plague and had gone to high security status to defeat it. This was of a lesser probability and hardly mattered.

Both the Infinity Plague and the anthrax had been released. Perhaps some contact had been made between NAA and Sov-Lat scientists.

The Frinn had become infected, had thought the Earthmen had tried to underhandedly destroy them, and had fought back.

Their weapons had been makeshift or constructed on the spot using their extensive robotic equipment.

"One ship left the system early on, possibly carrying the plague," said Sorbatchin. "It is possible the Frinn did not know of the plague then. Their other vessel was destroyed."

"The *Winston* destroyed it," Walden cut in. He didn't know why he felt it necessary to emphasize the NAA's role.

"The third ship built the mass driver in the asteroids and destroyed Delta Cygnus 4."

"It can't be more than a few days ahead of us—and they definitely know of the plague problem carried by the first ship. They don't know we're coming," Walden said.

"A lingering, delayed guerrilla attack will not work," Sorbatchin declared firmly. "We must drive in quickly and decisively and put an end to them."

"You didn't get to hear my briefing," Walden said. "Let me tell you this much. The Frinn are likely to be a decentralized society and any attempt at cutting out their heart will more than likely get our own throats cut first. We won't have a chance to deliver any of our weapons if we're detected and destroyed."

"There are only the *Winston* and *Hippocrates* left," said Sorbatchin. "The *Hippocrates* creates a diversion, the *Winston* delivers the bioweapons." He sat with his powerful hands folded on the desk in front of him. "What is the nature of these weapons you are to use against them?"

"All are fast-acting. We agree the Infinity Plague will work well, but too slowly. We don't dare let them get a hint to Earth's location. We have no defenses against a space-launched attack."

"A pity the defensive shields of the last two centuries were dismantled," Sorbatchin said. "But then, they never worked well and cost so much."

"That's what led to biowarfare. Now, if you'll excuse me, I have to return to my colleagues. We need to make last-minute arrangements for our defense."

"Our offensive, you mean," corrected Sorbatchin. He smiled winningly and slapped Walden on the shoulder. "You are a brave man, a lucky man. It is a pity you work for the wrong side."

"I'm on humanity's side, Colonel. Whose side are you on?"

"Why, Doctor, is it not obvious? I am on my own side. Please hurry. You do not wish to be late for your meeting."

Walden started back toward the wardroom, curious about the exchange with the Sov-Lat colonel. It had been out of character. Why had Sorbatchin not accosted him directly instead of sending O'Higgins to fetch him? The Chilean scientist was no flunky. Walden didn't like the man but had to grudgingly respect his acumen.

He turned to go into the wardroom when he saw Miko Nakamura in the corridor. The woman gestured to him. Walden closed his eyes and tried not to lose his temper. They *all* demanded minutes of his precious time. If he had those minutes rolled together, he could have kept Anita from leaving. They would have had time together. He could have . . .

Nakamura came to his side and patted his shoulder. He recoiled. She had always shown the Oriental's reluctance to touch another. She held up a small furry blotch plucked from his back.

"The colonel oversteps his bounds," she said. Nakamura dropped the fuzzball into a pocket and walked off without further comment. Walden's head threatened to split from the developing headache. Even the simplest of gestures turned into espionage. The Sov-Lat officer had placed a spy device on his shoulder.

Walden entered the wardroom, feeling that he had never left. By ones and twos his team reassembled. They passed their computer block circuits to him. He fed them into the computer and waited for a consensus opinion to be generated.

While the computer worked on the intricate details of bio-warfare, Walden stared at the vidscreen and the clock ticking off the seconds until the *Hippocrates* dropped back into regular space. Frinn space. Enemy space.

The computer beeped. Walden scanned the results and nodded. "I'm transmitting the conclusions to Nakamura and Zacharias," he told the others. "We have enough to launch fourteen genius missiles with seven different vectors. We're going to leave it to the missiles to decide their own trajectories and impact times."

"We can do that," Claudette Wyse said. "Why depend on the missiles?"

"There's no information about the Frinn home world," Walden pointed out. "The *Winston* will gather as much data as possible, then relay it to us. It's up to Nakamura to determine maximum efficiency in deploying our weapons."

"I don't like it. Claudette's right," spoke up Chin. "We can do anything Nakamura can. She's not even in the chain of command. She's only a damned advisor, for God's sake. A civilian!"

"True, but—" Walden saw the countdown for reentry begin. "We shift back in three minutes. Has everyone taken their medication?"

He stripped back the protective seal on a patch of drugs to lessen the physical discomfort. He applied it to the side of his neck. Walden swayed as the potent chemicals diffused through his skin and into his carotid artery.

The senses-twisting transition shook him, as it always did. This time he didn't have Anita or Egad nearby to comfort him with their presence.

"Let's see what's happening," urged Chin, seconds after they had made the shift. "I don't like being left in the dark."

Walden used his priority status as director of research to get a vidscreen display patched through to the wardroom. The screen glowed with the nearness of the destroyer. The *Winston*'s engines kicked in and a long flare showed briefly.

"The destroyer's off to reconnoiter," he said. Tiny yellow-flamed jets showed at the ship's sides; heavily armored scout rockets blasted across the Frinn's solar system seeking life—and where to deliver their bio-death.

Walden swallowed hard. When those rockets reported life, Nakamura would launch the fourteen missiles. He still wasn't sure the Frinn were innocent of anything more than striking back at what they perceived to be aggression against a peaceful exploratory ship.

"We could have gotten the information faster. Those are outdated scout rockets," complained Paul Preston. "I've got CCD cameras able to pinpoint planets up to six light-hours away."

"I've got gravitometers that'd pinpoint a planet just as

quickly," cut in Donelli. Her small, callused hands made unconscious washing motions. Walden wondered if she was as uncomfortable about this as he was.

"They're doing fine," he said. "We need to consider any possible mistakes on our end and let them handle theirs."

"The military will find a way to—" began Chin. He fell silent when Edouard Zacharias and three EPCT marines entered the room, their laserifles held at port arms.

"What do we owe this intrusion to, Major?" asked Walden. He had hoped Anita would accompany the major.

"There are problems, Doctor. Please come with us to the control room. I will explain further there."

"Explain here. These are trusted colleagues. I'll need their help in any circumstance. If the problems are too complicated, you might have to repeat your briefing for them. Telling us all now will save time in the long run."

"They aren't cleared for this information," the officer said stiffly.

"I'm not sure I want to hear it, if they can't," said Walden. He took perverse glee in taunting the major. What did Anita see in the pretentious man?

"You're director of—" Zacharias cut off his angry retort. He took a deep breath and puffed out his medal-filled chest. Only then did he relent. "Very well, Doctor." He gave Walden a coded sequence for the computer access.

Walden punched in the number and adjusted the vidscreen display so that everyone could see it. For several seconds he couldn't understand what it was they witnessed. Then it came to him.

"The scout rockets are reporting back to the *Winston*," he said. "This is the direct information feed from them."

Murmurs started when they realized what they saw, then erupted into loud guffaws among his staff. Walden looked over at Zacharias, whose face clouded with dark, dangerous anger.

"This isn't our fault, Major," the scientist said. "We did our job."

"I am aware of that, Walden."

"What's going on?" came a querulous voice. "I don't understand what the probes are telling you."

Walden took no satisfaction in magnifying the tri-vid photos of the four planets sent back by the rocket probes.

"These," Walden said, "are completely barren worlds. Wherever the Frinn home world is, it isn't in this system. We've been decoyed away from the center of their civilization."

CHAPTER
7

"Every damned world in the system is empty. There's no life anywhere. The pig-faces tricked us!" raged Edouard Zacharias.

Walden stood at the corner of the control room, watching the play of emotion on the faces of Nakamura, Sorbatchin, and Zacharias. The three decided the course of the *Hippocrates* and its mission. With Schwann destroyed, Walden wasn't sure what to do. For the time being, he had no choice but to acquiesce to their decisions.

So far, he hadn't been able to argue with the logic of following the Frinn ship from the Delta Cygnus system. The preservation of his species depended on it. Allow the aliens to locate Earth and they would destroy the planet as they had done to Schwann. But no one had thought the fleeing Frinn ships would use an empty system as an intermediate stopping point.

"Why did the Frinn come here?" Walden asked loud enough for Nakamura to hear him. The woman turned her emotionless black eyes on him. He held up well under her scrutiny.

"I do not understand your question, Doctor."

"Why lift to this particular system?" he said, pressing his point. "They had the coordinates in the navigational computers. They didn't choose this place at random. They came here for some reason that struck them as good."

"They fled after destroying our world," Nakamura said. Interest began to show in her dark eyes, though. Walden sensed she had stumbled across his line of thought and wanted him to pursue it for the benefit of Zacharias and Sorbatchin.

"They thought they'd killed every last human in the Delta Cygnus system," Walden pointed out. "They left the lift sensors to record future ships coming from Earth—and returning. They didn't have any reason to believe we survived."

"We were too damned clever for them," Zacharias said.

"Using the bulk of Schwann to hide us from their probes was masterful," Walden said, giving Nakamura tacit credit for something Zacharias had vocally claimed as his own idea. "They thought we were blasted into atoms. And remember their first ship left *before* they knew the Infinity Plague had been released. They had no reason to come here—unless this is their usual stopping off point."

"But the planets!" protested Vladimir Sorbatchin. The Sov-Lat colonel pointed to the large vidscreen at the far end of the control room. Empty hectares of rocky, airless worlds flashed by as the probes relayed back their photos. "They show no trace of alien presence. No storage tanks, no atmosphere plants . . ."

"On airless worlds?" grumbled Zacharias.

"They have no reason to come here except to throw us off their track," finished the colonel.

"The three ships in the Schwann system were explorers," said Walden, warming to his idea. "They might have feared contagion in their investigation of new systems." He hoped this was so. A quarantine for any length of time would reveal the deadly plague they carried—and which the earlier ship had brought already.

"There is no hint of artificial structure on any of those planets," snapped Zacharias. "Quit outgassing and give us something substantial to work on, Walden."

"He is. I believe he has the germ of an idea," said Nakamura. "Please, Doctor. Continue your thought experiment into the alien psychology."

"They know about the residue left behind in the space-time tensors. They might not want to leave tracks another, more inimical, race could follow." He mentally added "inimical like us."

"They come to this empty system, then lift for their home world?" asked Sorbatchin. "But what is the point? They still leave the mathematical residue we can trace. It is more difficult to find, but the bending of space by the drive lasts for many years. It forms a tiny gravity well that registers as an anomaly. We Sov-Lats can detect it with no trouble."

"So can we," Zacharias said hotly. Letting the Sov-Lat colonel top him rankled Zacharias worse than anything else. Walden almost pitied the man and his sensitive ego.

Was that what Anita saw in him? Vulnerability? Did she pity Zacharias? Or did she really love the man? Walden forced himself back to the matter at hand. Allowing his personal problems to intrude solved nothing—including those problems with Anita Tarleton.

"They come here for whatever reason. This might have been the first system they mapped. They're comfortable. They have pinpoint accuracy on their charts. I think they've got a base here they come to for refitting, for R&R, for quarantine, for command and support."

"Ridiculous. Look at those planets. There's not even a tiny com satellite circling them."

"That's because there isn't any atmosphere. Why drop down into a gravity well if there's no reason?" asked Walden.

"What's your idea?" Zacharias turned away, not wanting to hear. Walden had Sorbatchin's attention, and this kept him talking.

"What did the probes pick up from off the planets?"

"They had seek-and-reply missions on and around the four worlds," replied Nakamura.

"You are saying there is another world we missed?" Sorbatchin shook his head. "I am no astronomer but I know of Bode's Law. We missed nothing in this system."

"What about a space station?"

"Orbiting the star as an artificial world? Where? We look, we see nothing." Sorbatchin's expression told Walden that the idea appealed to him. Something about the Sov-Lat colonel's sudden slyness warned Walden that his idea had found fertile ground—and that Sorbatchin could turn it to his own benefit.

"Space is big. We can wait and send out probes to circle their sun," said Nakamura. She used a laser command wand to transmit the appropriate message to the *Winston*. "A circuit of the star will take many days. Let's prepare for any eventuality."

"There's no space station to be found," grumbled Zacharias. "I'm going to drill my troopers. When we go into combat, it'll be a drop onto a world."

"Still fighting the last battle," observed Walden.

"You would do well to actually fight your last battle rather than continue avoiding it," said Nakamura. Before Walden could retort, she put on a heads-up display helmet and turned her full attention to running the *Hippocrates*.

"Excuse me," Sorbatchin said, slipping from the control room and hurrying away. On impulse, Walden followed. He had learned a little of the spy trade from Nakamura and the Sov-Lat officer. As the colonel had pushed past, Walden had planted a nano-bug of his own devising on the man's sleeve.

Back in his lab Egad sat obediently in front of the computer console. The small vidscreen showed a picture that bounced and bobbed around until the gengineered dog weaved as he watched it.

"Don't stare at it so close," ordered Walden. He sat down beside Egad and put his arm around the animal's whipcord-thin body.

"Dizzy making," the dog observed. "Why watch cat shit coloniel so close?"

"I want to hear what he's going to do. He . . ." Walden fell silent when the officer closed the door to his cabin and went through the procedure of sweeping for spy devices. Walden held his breath. He was no tyro at preparing nano-miniature equipment. As a graduate student he had spent most of his time building molecule manipulators capable of dissecting the smallest organic molecule. One laser-electron beam device he had constructed had been capable of modifying individual atoms in a compound.

Still, spy techniques were different. As Sorbatchin worked, Walden relaxed. He let out his breath and then smiled. Sorbatchin had missed his bug. He put away his detector and opened a drawer in his desk. Walden scowled when Sorbatchin pulled out a curiously shaped device.

It took him several minutes to decide that this hadn't been constructed for human fingers. Whatever it was had been built by the Frinn. The only way Sorbatchin could have obtained it was theft—and he had never left the *Hippocrates*. As the Sov-Lat colonel worked with the device, an idea came to Walden.

Sorbatchin hadn't stolen this from the Frinn ship. He had sent Pedro O'Higgins. Somehow the Chilean biologist had held onto it in spite of his excursion into the gray nothingness of liftspace. He had plucked it from the weapons control room on the Frinn ship and brought it back to Sorbatchin.

Walden rocked back and continued to study Sorbatchin's gadget. The chain of events wasn't quite right. If O'Higgins had brought it back, Leo Burch would have discovered it when the Sov-Lat scientist was taken to the infirmary. Walden heaved a big sigh and shook his head. He kept forgetting. Zacharias had been right in calling Burch a spy. The ship's medical doctor had considerable explaining to do.

Without even realizing it, Walden stroked over the skin inside his left forearm where he had injected the antidote to the poison introduced to him by Burch's cat. Both master and pet were responsible for more than Walden cared to consider at the moment.

A tiny *pop*! of static sounded as Walden turned up the volume on the bug. O'Higgins had joined the GRU colonel.

". . . fix on the pigs' space station," Sorbatchin said. "This device you brought back from their ship must be a direction finder. I can figure no other purpose for it."

"It is well that I risked my life for something that is proving useful," replied O'Higgins.

"This describes a vector," Sorbatchin went on. 'I calculate the spot to be on the far side of the star. If Walden is correct, we have located the Frinn space station. Even more, this is useful to get aboard."

"It sends a recognition signal?"

"*Da*, Pedro, it does. You have done well and will be rewarded when we return to Earth."

The scientist beamed.

"You will receive the Medal of the Revolution. All will

salute you when we ally ourselves with the Frinn against the
NAA.''

"They will believe your story?''

Sorbatchin shrugged, then smiled wickedly. "Why not?
What I tell them is true. The Infinity Plague was released by
the NAA.''

"Only after our scientists learned its secrets.''

"They still released it. They are responsible for the pigs'
deaths, not anyone in the Soviet-Latino Pact. We align ourselves, then use the Frinn to destroy them. So simple. *Da*,
Pedro, you and I are the rising stars. We will be elected to
the Presidium.''

"And then?'' prodded O'Higgins.

"The premiership has been a *troika* for too many years.
You and I can divide it well. You in the Latin countries and
I in the Russias.''

Walden listened to more posturing on Sorbatchin's part,
wondering if the officer meant it or only enticed O'Higgins
to do his dirty work with such sophistry. Sorbatchin knew he
had no chance at being elected to the select Presidium. And
only a major coup would place him in any of the premier's
three chairs.

If Vladimir Sorbatchin spoke to cement the loyalty of his
Chilean scientist, Walden saw that the ploy worked to perfection. O'Higgins beamed at his importance in obtaining a
secret treaty with the Frinn and furthering the cause of Com-
munism in the universe.

Sorbatchin fiddled with the communications device, trying
to figure out how it worked. Walden began to worry about
the quality of his com link. The nano-miniaturized transmitter
he had placed on Sorbatchin was microbe-powered. The small
organism died by degrees; as it decayed, it powered the transmitter. This gave even greater protection against power-sweep
sensors. It also limited the usefulness of the device to the
bacteria's short lifetime.

Walden slapped his hand against the side of the computer
when the probe died. The last glimpse he had was of the
Frinn communicator. He remembered seeing the device attached to O'Higgins' belt when he had returned from the
other side of the liftspace bubble. Walden had been too busy

to examine it then. Now he wished he had been able to when they returned to the *Hippocrates*.

Leo Burch had retrieved it and kept it safe for Sorbatchin. Dr. Leo Burch, would-be assassin and Sov-Lat spy. Walden burned with the feelings of betrayal. He had liked Burch. He had even considered the man a friend.

He turned in his chair to go to Nakamura. He hated dealing with the woman, but she had to know how Sorbatchin tried to turn an illicit discovery into even more trouble.

Miko Nakamura stood in the doorway, eyes fixed on him. Egad stared at her, not making a sound. Walden reached for the gengineered dog but Egad shied away.

"What are you doing to him?"

"He is unharmed. I merely check a supposition. Ultrasonic sound affects him as it does many guard dogs. You must not rely on him to protect you."

"From you?"

"From those on whom you spy so diligently," she countered. "Excuse me, Doctor. I must tend to our Sov-Lat guests."

"You heard—overheard," he amended.

"There is little I do not know that happens aboard the *Hippocrates*. This is my job."

"We can't let them contact the Frinn."

"We must find the space station you postulate before worrying over such matters." Nakamura spun and vanished. Only with her disappearance did Egad let out a howl of outrage and pain.

"Did she hurt you?" Walden dropped beside the dog and rubbed his ears. Egad pulled away.

"Hurt in head. All over hurt. How did she do it? I kill cat shit bitch."

"No!"

"Why not? She make me hurt."

"We need her." Walden didn't like to admit it, but the entire human race might need Miko Nakamura. Dealing with the Frinn was not going to be easy. Either they found the aliens and started shooting or they found the aliens and tried diplomacy. Walden wasn't sure which would prove the more difficult course.

* * *

"We've completely calculated the orbits of the planets," the *Hippocrates'* navigator reported. He looked at Captain Belford, who sat quietly in the corner of the control room. A vacant smile danced on the man's lips. Walden wondered if the former captain of the *Hippocrates* had snapped totally.

"What of the orbital perturbations?" demanded Zacharias. Anita Tarleton stood at his side. She kept her emerald eyes averted from Walden. On impulse he walked around to stand in front of the EPCT major. Anita swung about and stared at Captain Belford. Walden didn't know whether to take this as a victory or a sign that Anita rejected him totally.

"Major, I'm getting to it," the nav officer said irritably. He wasn't used to being interrupted when he spoke and resented the military officer's presence. "The four planets are fair-sized so we got good readings. There's one huge gravitational force being exerted in the system, and it's been acting on the planets for almost two hundred years."

"You can be that precise?" asked Walden. He was astounded at the idea of Frinn presence here for such a long time. The liftdrive was a relatively new discovery for Earth, coming out of quantum chaos theory, advanced use of Mandelbrot and Julia sets, and fractal geometries that spoke of dimensions in fractions rather then integers.

"Yes." The navigation officer wasn't any more pleased answering a biologist's questions than he was an EPCT officer's.

"Why can't we see this reputed gravitational presence?" asked Zacharias. "You're not telling me the Frinn have an *invisible* space station, are you?"

"It's on the far side of the star, Major," replied the navigator. "If my calculations are anywhere near good enough, it ought to be coming out from behind the star's disk soon."

"We'll be able to watch it appear? Will they be able to detect us?" asked Zacharias.

"Major, I'm not a mind reader. Ask her." The nav officer pointed to Nakamura.

"Your confidence is not misplaced, Commander," Nakamura said. "Although I lack telepathic power, I have ordered minimal power usage and blackout shields to reduce reflection. They will not be able to detect us because of star occultation, unless they are extremely lucky."

Walden started to ask about the com device Sorbatchin had retrieved from the Frinn ship. Nakamura shook her head slightly, cautioning him to silence.

"Our recording devices, both on the *Hippocrates* and on the *Winston*, are aimed at the point where their space station will appear." She used the laser command wand to bring up the disk of the star on the vidscreen. The viewing computer blanked out the star's brilliance and left only huge prominences jetting out from the corona. In jerky steps, the magnification increased until only a few radians of the sun filled the vidscreen.

"How long do we wait for this ridiculous space station to show? I say we set course, circle, and come up on them from back-orbit and . . ."

Zacharias' voice trailed off as the Frinn space station slowly swung into view from around the celestial body.

"It's immense!" Anita Tarleton said, speaking her first words since Walden had come onto the bridge.

He had to admit she was right. The space station he had pictured was small enough to orbit a world. The Frinn's station *was* a world.

"So bright," Captain Belford said in a childlike voice. "It shines so much like starlight."

"Starlight," muttered Walden, knowing the name would stick. "We've got to go to Starlight."

CHAPTER
8

Warning lights flashed all over the bridge. Walden resisted the urge to dive for cover under a chair. If the *Hippocrates* was in trouble, simply protecting himself availed him nothing. Any trouble they might find would come in galaxy-sized doses.

"They've spotted us!" cried Zacharias. "They're attacking. Get us into battle condition, dammit," he snapped at Nakamura.

The Japanese woman frowned. Her dark, intent eyes narrowed as she studied the readouts on the *Hippocrates'* control panels. She settled the heads-up command helmet firmly and began working with the command wand. Walden knew she had immense power with both helmet and wand. A wink of the eye could start the ship's engine. A flash of the command wand on a miniature photocell relay might set repair crews into motion internally—or alert the *Winston* to the attack.

"There is no attack," Nakamura said quietly. The collected, serene way she spoke restored order better than anything she could have done. Walden didn't like her personally but had to admire her command skills. She made a better commander than Captain Belford ever had, even with his regal appearance and confident manner.

"Those are approach warnings," Zacharias touched the

com unit at his belt. The marine guard with him looked around the bridge for someone to shoot with their laserifles. Walden hoped their training would hold. He didn't want the *Hippocrates'* controls fused by the potent rifles' blasts.

"They are," confirmed Nakamura. "However, the approach is of the Frinn ship."

"Frinn!" bellowed Zacharias. Walden had no idea what orders the man bellowed into his com unit. He hoped that they wouldn't wreck everything. From the sudden expression of panic on the major's face, he knew his orders weren't being transmitted.

Nakamura idly used her laser wand to restore power to Zacharias' com unit.

"Do not attempt unauthorized communication," she chastised him. "Such transmission interferes with my command ability." Nakamura motioned for the EPCT major to move aside. He did so numbly. Walden saw the slow anger mounting in the man at this easy dismissal. How long before Zacharias exploded would depend on the next few minutes and how real the danger they faced was.

"Observe," Nakamura said. The vidscreen winked away from Starlight and showed a Frinn vessel with a pitted, *dented* hull.

Walden had never seen such a sight. How did a spaceship hull made of composite materials dent? It might spall, it might fracture, it might vaporize or look like a spiderweb of cracks, but dent?

"This is the Frinn vessel that separated from us in liftspace. How it returned to normal space so near us is something best left to the theoreticians." Nakamura looked around the control room. "All hands, record at will. We need copies made and stored separate from the main data banks for review later."

"When we return to Earth," muttered Walden.

"It *followed* us out of liftspace?" asked Anita. "That's not possible. It broke out of our bubble."

"It is possible, Dr. Tarleton," said Nakamura. "It is possible because it happened."

"The com unit Sorbatchin has," spoke up Walden. "Could he have summoned the ship using it?"

"Unlikely but worthy of consideration," Nakamura said.

"What unit? What're you talking about, Walden?" Zacharias belligerently backed Walden against a wall. "Have the Sov-Lats been up to something you haven't told me about?"

"Ask her," Walden said, sliding away from the major without getting tangled in the man's medals. He stared at the vidscreen. Without doubt, this was the vessel that had separated from them in midflight. Even as he studied the ship and its twisted, bent lines, the vidscreen flickered back to show Starlight.

The immense space station orbited past the disk of the star and was fully visible now. Walden had considered it large before. Now he wondered if Earth might not be small in comparison. How many Frinn called Starlight their home? Use of bioweapons on a space station was vastly different from a world of weather and sweeping, open, rainy expanse. The initial plan to contaminate using their fourteen missiles had to be revised—drastically.

"What type of sensors are mounted outside?" he asked. "Can we get even a microbe past them without showing our hand?"

"Analysis of their sensory equipment is in progress," Nakamura said. "From what I see, approach is carefully monitored. There are no fewer than a dozen optical devices used for tracking. What other sensors they employ will require more scrutiny." Nakamura left him to orchestrate the *Winston*'s docking with the derelict Frinn ship.

"Isn't it amazing?" Anita asked him, staring at the vidscreen. Starlight gleamed like a radiant jewel set against the black velvet of space.

"Beautiful," he replied, not sure if he meant the Frinn space station or the woman. "Can we talk later?"

"There's no time, Jerome," she said. Anita still avoided his direct gaze. Instead she turned to look in Zacharias' direction. "He'll get things in order soon. Then we can talk."

"We'll be trying to pry open the station by then," Walden pointed out. "What's wrong with talking now?"

"Jerome, please. This isn't a good time." She turned and faced him. Her eyes overflowed with tears. She made no effort to wipe away the tracks forming on her cheeks. "You've changed. You're not the same anymore, and I can't stand it."

"*I've* changed? Maybe you have, too. We can work—"

Nakamura cut him off. The woman ordered everyone but the *Hippocrates'* flight officers off the bridge.

She pointed to Captain Belford. "Will someone escort the captain to the infirmary where Dr. Burch can tend him?" Without another word, her face vanished once more behind the heads-up display helmet visor. She sat on the edge of the command chair and began playing the controls like a virtuoso working on a synth-organ. Walden wondered where she had gotten so proficient.

He turned to pursue his cause with Anita, but she had slipped out. Walden tried to follow but Zacharias blocked his way. "Don't meddle," the major told him. "I don't like you, I never have, I never will. In the field it's just possible you'll have an accident. Do I make myself clear?"

"Yes," Walden said, glaring at the officer. "You just said in front of witnesses that you'll shoot me in the back, given the chance." He shoved Zacharias out of his way but Anita had vanished.

Walden wandered the corridors aimlessly, not knowing what he should do about Anita, about the Frinn ship, about the bioweapons he and his team had readied. Thoughts of the Infinity Plague kept coming back to haunt him, too. He felt responsible for its release, even though he had known nothing about its development.

"Maybe Anita's right," he said to Egad, who trotted beside him. "I'm taking all this much too personally." On Earth, he had been able to separate his work from the ultimate use of the bioweapons. Since Schwann had been destroyed, it became clearer to him that *he* had to take final responsibility for his discoveries. Leaving the decisions to use or not in the hands of men and women like Sorbatchin, Zacharias, and Nakamura frightened him.

"We go to soldiers?" asked the dog.

"What? We can. Yes, we should." Walden didn't know if Zacharias meant it about murdering him under the guise of combat. The best way of finding out was to talk to a few of the EPCTs serving under him. From the brief foray on Schwann, he knew they didn't think highly of the man's combat ability. He wanted to discover their feelings about Zacharias' temper—and honor.

"Hecht!" he called. The EPCT sergeant turned and smiled when he recognized him.

"Good to see you all hale and hearty, Doc. What brings you down into the belly of the beast?"

"Just wandering. I got a case of the nerves and thought I'd see how you were doing."

"We're fit and ready to shit," the sergeant said, laughing. "What's really gnawing your bone, Doc? You don't pal around with grunts. You drift in the stratosphere with the rest of the mega-IQs."

"You didn't think that when Tanner and I went into the Sov-Lat base," Walden said. He pushed Egad down. He didn't want the dog wandering off, even though he might pick up needed information this way. The dog was more valuable to him studying Hecht's responses.

"Tanner bought it," Hecht said, his face momentarily turning into an expressionless mask. "Getting past him on the Table of Command would have been impossible otherwise. He was a good EPCT." The way the soldier said it sounded like ee-pee-cee-tee.

"Tanner didn't think highly of Major Zacharias. What's your idea about him?"

"About the same. When we get back onto the Frinn ship, it's not going to be pleasant having him underfoot. He gets in the way too much. Meddles. Doesn't let his non-coms do their work."

Walden hid his surprise well. Word that the Frinn vessel had reemerged into normal space was already common knowledge among the soldiers. Even more, they readied themselves to occupy the ship.

"You did know we're going to sneak up on Starlight in the pig ship, didn't you, Doc?"

"No, I didn't." Walden was glad he had come down to speak with Hecht. Although he had been on the bridge when the ship reentered normal space, he hadn't heard any of these plans.

"The major's got this bug up his ass about taking Starlight. He takes it as a personal insult there wasn't a planet to land on and shoot up." Hecht leaned back and hiked his feet up to a plastic crate. "That's his problem. He likes the medals too much."

"He wants a rerun of Operation Pomegranate on Persephone?"

"Seems like it to me, but then what do I know? I'm just an EPCT sergeant trying to do as little as possible before I die."

This simple philosophy had much to recommend it. Walden said so as he left. Hecht's mocking laughter drifted along the corridor as he returned to his lab, Egad silent at his side.

CHAPTER
9

"The whole damned ship's haunted. It's got to be," said an EPCT marine. He hunkered down and clutched his laserifle as if his life depended on it. His gloved finger curled across the firing stud and threatened to send a fiery bolt ripping through a bulkhead at any instant.

Jerome Walden wasn't sure if the man wasn't right. Not only did his life depend on his weapon, the Frinn ship *might* be haunted. He didn't consider himself a superstitious person, not and be a successful scientist. Still, too many details begged for explanation. Little about how the ship had tracked them through the fractal dimensions of liftspace made sense. He might as well believe the impossible: ghosts haunted the Frinn ship.

"Don't give me any of that crap, Mendelssohn," snapped Sgt. Hecht. "We got problems enough without you frosting over on us. We go into the ship, we secure it, we do it. Any questions?"

"No, Sarge. No questions, no problems. We're just stupid do-its," the marine grumbled. Walden saw the expression on his face and knew the chewing out didn't relieve any of the apprehension he felt.

It relieved none of Walden's, either. He shuffled his feet and wondered why he had volunteered for this insane mission. Sorbatchin and Zacharias had concocted the idea of retaking the Frinn ship, then using it as ingress to Starlight. Nakamura had gone along with the plan, neither approving nor vetoing it. Walden thought she saw in it a perfect way of getting rid of her opposition to power.

With both of the military leaders dead, she would be undisputed captain of the *Hippocrates* and commander of the mission.

He shook his head. Anita Tarleton might be right about him changing dramatically. He had grown paranoid. Why should Miko Nakamura maneuver the two officers into such a position? She was leader of the expedition now. What she wanted, truly *wanted*, she got.

"You all right, Doc? You look a mite wasted around the far fringes."

"This isn't what I consider a fun afternoon outing, Sergeant," he told Hecht.

"The ship's empty," Hecht said, more to himself than to Walden. He worked to dispel any vague notion of bad luck attached to the ship and its mysterious behavior. "We're just supposed to get it and waltz on into Starlight. That's why it followed us like your dog."

Hecht bent and patted Egad. The gengineered dog barked and thrust his head higher for the soldier's continued attention. The dog liked Hecht, as he had liked Tanner. Walden still had difficulty explaining concepts like death to the animal. He hoped Egad wouldn't ask again where Sgt. Tanner had gone.

The man—his body—was long since plasma floating through the dusty debris of what had been Schwann. The Frinn had killed him.

Did his spirit haunt the Frinn ship?

"Be careful," he called to a cargo officer and the men using robot loaders. "Don't even think about dropping those canisters."

"What bugs are in them?" asked Luria, the cargo officer. "Anything we ought to wear hazard gear for?"

"Yes," Walden said. "But there's no time to get you checked out. Just don't damage the cylinders or the delivery systems." He studied the vents and valves on one long, slender blue-painted metal bottle. The robot handlers hadn't damaged the microbe-laden flagon of death. Walden looked at the label and saw this bottle contained his gengineered typhoid. Ten seconds' introduction to the Starlight water system and no filtration system would remove the rod-shaped *Eberthella typhosa waldensi* bacteria—except flash distillation.

Walden knew the Frinn would have died of intestinal hemorrhaging long before the idea occurred to them that a genetically tailored bacterium could slip by their purification system.

"Hours," he said aloud. "This works in hours of ingestion."

"Can we breathe it and get zapped?" asked Luria.

"Yes. It'll get into the mucosa and . . ." Walden's words trailed off. He had no reason to explain the process to a cargo officer. "It's deadly to humans and Frinn," he said.

Walden watched them move the containers to the loading bay, where robots finished the chore. The bottles, once inside the small shuttle that would ferry them to the Frinn ship, would have to be delivered by hand.

Walden wasn't a hero. He didn't like the idea of fighting through to Starlight's water system and introducing the typhoid bacteria.

"We can do it," came Sorbatchin's confident tone. "*Da*, we do it now!"

He slapped Zacharias on the back. The EPCT major looked uncomfortable at such camaraderie with a man who had until recently been "the enemy." Walden didn't doubt that Zacharias still thought of the Sov-Lat colonel that way. He knew he did. And he thought of Zacharias as the enemy, too.

Everyone was after him. Everyone wanted something. He closed his eyes and let the paranoia and self-pity wash over him. He tried to tell himself this was only the white waves of fatigue chewing at him. He knew it was more.

"You all right?" came Egad's gravelly voice. He knelt and held the dog's neck, putting his face near the animal's collar transducer. On low power they couldn't be overheard talking—he hoped. With everyone spying constantly on everyone else, he wasn't sure who knew of Egad's intellectual abilities.

Nakamura did, but who else? He didn't want to find out the hard way that he had been used as a pawn in some elaborate game, and that Egad was a piece to be removed from the board.

"I'm fine. We're going to the Frinn ship. I want you to keep alert for anything . . . strange." Walden didn't know how to tell the dog to watch for ghosts. The concept of a supernatural being haunting the Frinn ship was a difficult one to get across to an animal more intent on eating than epistemology.

"I look out for you," Egad assured Walden.

"Good dog," he replied, hugging the animal. Then they had to get into the personnel shuttle going to the Frinn vessel. Walden didn't like sharing the short ride with Zacharias and Sorbatchin, but he had little choice. The sixty men in the shuttle comprised the assault team that would invade Starlight.

The EPCT marines looked the part. Grim, tense, ready to strike out like a coiled steel spring they waited to play their part in the drama.

The two officers drew Walden's attention. Sorbatchin seemed calm and in control. Zacharias' obvious agitation grew by the minute. In this condition he would make errors of judgment. Walden didn't care if Zacharias got himself killed. He didn't want the major taking the rest of the assault team with him.

"Colonel," he said quietly to Sorbatchin. "Who's in charge?"

"What? Such a question, Doctor. Is it not obvious? The EPCT runs this mission well." The sarcasm in Sorbatchin's voice sent a ripple through the marines. One fingered his laserifle as if considering what a single microburst might do inside the shuttle.

"They're loyal," said Walden. "So am I."

"Though reluctantly. I read your kind, Walden." Sorbatchin fastened himself down and sat, arms crossed on his broad chest. "*Da*, I read you like the words on a vidscreen. You are driven by duty, not honor. You come along to be sure your precious germs do not go to waste through misadventure."

"Why are you here, Colonel?"

"I asked to come. They would not allow Dr. O'Higgins or others of my small but select group. I am a soldier. I can aid in the attack." He stared at Zacharias for a moment, then smiled crookedly. "I do not have the medals your major does, but no one has ever questioned my bravery in combat."

The shuttle lurched and jetted toward the Frinn ship. Walden closed his eyes for a moment. He mentally rechecked the bindings on the tanks containing his bioweapons. Nakamura had not wanted him to come along; he had insisted. None of the others in his research team had accompanied this mission. It was just him, Egad, Sorbatchin, and the sixty EPCT marines.

"Good," he said. "I'll stand behind you and let you do the fighting."

"There will be no fighting. Not on the Frinn ship. But on Starlight? *Da*, there our mettle will be tested."

The shuttle reached the Frinn ship in less than an hour. In two they had transferred the bioweapons to the hold. Four of Zacharias' troopers helped Walden prepare the delivery systems for several deadly containers. Rockets with drill warheads would be launched at Starlight from a distance. The laser drills would bore through the space station's exterior, cause sudden pressure loss, then inject bioweapons-laden paste into the evacuated cavity. When the leaks were repaired, the renewed atmosphere would cause the paste to turn to a fine powder. From here it would take only minutes to enter the air system and contaminate an entire section.

Walden had little time to tend to the other diverse delivery systems. Zacharias summoned him to the bridge of the Frinn ship.

"Go?" asked Egad.

"We do," said Walden. "Keep quiet and watch everything. Let me know if you scent anything strange."

"Whole ship bad stink," Egad said. "Frinn not like us."

Walden smiled. The dog thought of himself as human, in spite of his diatribes against bad smells and odd conduct.

He watched as the EPCTs worried his bioweapons and the delivery systems into line. The Frinn ship had no external firing tubes. A few sensor cavities had been converted into crude launch platforms. Walden doubted these would serve them well unless they got within a few light-seconds of Starlight. But such considerations were out of his hands. He had to do what he could and trust to Zacharias for the rest.

As he made his way along the ship's corridors, he was taken by the strangeness of the layout. Nothing blatant struck him; details were subtly wrong wherever he looked. The most peculiar aspect of the vessel were the frequent compartments hardly large enough for an individual that seemed to serve no storage purpose.

"Egad," he asked, "what do you make of them?"

"Frinn smell inside. Fear smell, too. They hide in them," the dog stated flatly.

Walden considered this tidbit. They had seen how the Frinn valued privacy above all else. Each crew member had a separate sleeping room. Many had discrete sanitary and eating facilities. The ship could have carried five times as many humans as it did Frinn.

He made notes to himself as he came to the bridge. This reclusiveness might prove even more of a barrier to overcome than he'd thought. A planet with low population density posed problems in bioweapons delivery. A space station tightly compartmented might be even more difficult to take out quickly.

Walden hated the idea of using atomics against Starlight. The glimpse he'd had showed a beautiful structure, one rivaling anything humanity had constructed in space.

Tears welled in his eyes as he stopped and considered what he'd just decided. He wanted to kill without destroying the material, the property, the outward manifestation of an entire culture. Of the Frinn themselves, he had no feeling.

He had come too far in the bioweapons research, had done too much. He had to find new solutions and not blindly do as people like Zacharias ordered.

"There you are. Come in, Walden," ordered Zacharias. The officer's manner had changed. In total command, he radiated an aura of competence and courage. Walden saw how men could blindly follow a leader like this into the jaws of death.

Walden glanced from Sorbatchin to Zacharias and back. The Sov-Lat colonel sat in a chair, arms crossed and a look of displeasure on his face. Whatever they had decided, the Sov-Lat officer didn't like it. Walden wasn't sure he would, either.

"We're moving what armor we can to the front of the

vessel," Zacharias said. "We need at least six missiles to penetrate and cause confusion, should the need arise."

"What is the attack plan?" Walden paid little attention to Zacharias. Sorbatchin's reaction seemed more important. For all his new air of command, Zacharias would crumble quickly in the face of adversity. Walden thought the Frinn were likely to provide more trouble than any of them planned on.

"We pretend to limp into Starlight," Zacharias said. "We flash lights on and off at random, as if we're signaling. There won't be any other transmission. When we get close enough, we blast into the docking bay."

"From there," continued Walden, "you want missiles to fire into the guts of the space station?"

"Exactly."

"Why not see if we can dock, then release the gengineered typhoid bacteria into their water supply?" he asked. "We stand less chance of incurring loss that way."

"Ah, your trained killer scientist shows a touch of treachery. *Da*," said Sorbatchin. "I like this idea. *Da*! Creep into their tent, then slit their throats before they know it!"

"Silence, Sorbatchin!" snapped Zacharias. "We cannot risk the *Winston* and *Hippocrates* in the manner you advocate."

"What's that?" asked Walden.

"I want to use them as decoys. They pretend to pursue. We rush forward to Starlight. We dock, we disgorge your EPCT. We fight through to the heart of the space station." Sorbatchin looked pleased at the notion of commanding the EPCT.

"It's too risky," Zacharias said. "A station as large as this one has long-range weapons capable of destroying both the *Winston* and the *Hippocrates*. We will do it my way. Our two ships remain on low power, hidden and keeping the bulk of the star between them and Starlight. We come up from back-orbit and overtake the station."

"They'll know we aren't Frinn if we violate their approach patterns," Walden said. "If we can't tell them there's something wrong aboard, what's to keep them from opening fire on us?"

"Nothing," cut in Sorbatchin.

"We brazen it out. Boldness will carry the day. We must

seize the moment. Fortune favors the brave." Zacharias looked less sure of himself than he sounded.

"So said Terence," grumbled Sorbatchin. "I prefer your Samuel Johnson. 'We are all deceived by the same fallacies.' "

"What's that supposed to mean?"

Sorbatchin looked smug. "You mistake Starlight for Persephone. What has worked in one situation may not work again."

Walden said nothing about Sorbatchin defining the wrong fallacy. Humans weren't *always* right. The Frinn had proven themselves worthy adversaries. He didn't doubt that they would again.

Walden watched the two men argue. He drifted away and stared at the control panels. They had been ripped out and partially replaced with instruments more compatible with human hands and vision. He sat down behind the controls and worked through the firing circuits for his missiles. He shook his head. He was no expert in tactics or defense but he saw that they had no chance of plunging the deadly microbe-bearing rockets into Starlight.

Too much time would elapse between launch and arrival, even at close range. And he didn't doubt the Frinn's ability to study the exterior of the ship and see the attached missile ports. If they fired from long enough away, the Frinn could intercept easily. If they crept closer, the Frinn would know the ship had been captured.

Walden touched an intership com. Nakamura appeared instantly on a flat vidscreen.

"Doctor? Is there trouble?"

"The two military geniuses are arguing. I'm worried about Zacharias' plan." Over the woman's shoulder, he saw Anita Tarleton stiffen. Nakamura changed the focus slightly and Anita vanished from sight in a misty blur.

"What troubles you?"

"We need a diversion. Sorbatchin's right. The *Winston*— or the *Hippocrates*—has to keep the Frinn occupied at a greater distance to allow us to slip in."

"That is dangerous to the ship sent to pursue."

"I recommend the *Winston*. It's a fully operational destroyer and might be able to veer away at the last minute."

"Trajectories are not computed in such a dramatic fashion," Nakamura said dryly.

Walden quickly outlined his objections to Zacharias' plan. "Either way, the Frinn will nail us before we can get within delivery range. We need the diversion."

"Get the hell away from there," snapped Zacharias, finally seeing that Walden had activated the com unit and spoke with Nakamura. "Complete silence. That's my standing order."

"Stuff it out the airlock, Zacharias," Walden said. "Here, you talk to him." Walden abandoned his post at the jury-rigged controls and let Nakamura argue with Zacharias.

"You are a curious specimen, Doctor. You object to everything. What do you hold dear? What, besides the successful completion of a project, do you value most?" Sorbatchin enjoyed the dispute among the NAA leaders.

"Getting out of this alive," Walden said.

Sorbatchin laughed. "You are no soldier. We go into battle to die proudly."

"Bullshit," Walden snapped. "You don't die for your cause. You make the other poor bastard die for his."

"Another philosopher of war," Sorbatchin said. "This will be a most interesting encounter with Starlight."

Zacharias savagely toggled off the com unit. Both Walden and Sorbatchin knew that the EPCT major had been overruled by Nakamura. The *Winston* would provide the diversion and they would drive for the nearest docking bay at the alien space station.

Walden left the bridge, uneasy at how the attack strategy progressed. He had the distinct feeling that Zacharias and Sorbatchin fought each other more than they would the Frinn, once they were close enough to engage.

He had a fleeting impression of Nakamura's careful planning in this. If the Frinn ship was destroyed, she got rid of the two officers without blood on her hands. He shook his head at the paranoid notion. What did Nakamura care about removing the two military men? She controlled the *Hippocrates* and *Winston*. Playing on the tensions between Sorbatchin and the EPCT major kept her position secure; no matter what she decided to do, one would ally himself with her.

Walden hurried down to the makeshift missile launchers and worked diligently. He had the eerie feeling of being watched, as if a ghost drifted close enough to jostle his elbow. Egad's presence helped remove such fantasy. But it was no fantasy that the Frinn ship shuddered and vibration filled it when the engines ignited. In an hour, they were beginning their inward trajectory toward the alien sun. In two, they were accelerating to their deadly meeting at Starlight.

CHAPTER
10

"What the hell are you doing here?" Jerome Walden blinked twice to be sure his eyes weren't betraying him—or that the ghost he feared hadn't really appeared.

Pedro O'Higgins smiled hugely, showing strong white teeth. His nut-brown complexion belied any ghost. He enjoyed Walden's startled response. "I am here to aid you, Doctor."

"Does Nakamura know you're here?"

"What does it matter? She is not my superior. Colonel Sorbatchin commands me, not some civilian advisor. You of the NAA have peculiar ideas about chain of command." The Chilean biologist glanced over the settings Walden had used on the missiles. He nodded as he worked his way down the line.

"Do you approve?" Walden asked sarcastically.

"Yes, I do. You are more efficient than others of your decadent society. I applaud your work. If we get close enough, these will destroy the space station."

"They won't scratch the surface," Walden said sourly. "You haven't been paying attention. They're not fools aboard Starlight. Even if Nakamura convinced Zacharias to have the *Winston* chase us in as diversion, we're not going to get to use these."

"Perhaps," the Sov-Lat biologist said. "Perhaps you are wrong. I shall report your excellent work to Sorbatchin. He will be pleased that we are prepared to fight."

"Stuff yourself into a plasma torch for all I care." Walden worked off his ire at being startled. He had almost begun to believe that ghosts stalked the corridors of the ship. That he had been watched only added to his uneasiness at being aboard the Frinn ship.

Walden spun to scold Egad for not warning him of the Chilean's approach. Egad had vanished. Walden cursed under his breath. He knew the gengineered canine had gone to sit with the EPCT soldiers, to listen to their chatter, to gather what tidbits of information he could before the attack. Such data might prove invaluable later.

Now, Walden wanted only to have a companion—and Egad had abandoned him.

The scientist stared at the panels that controlled the missiles just a few meters away. The warheads were laden with seven different forms of bio-death. He had wrought some of them and was no longer proud of his work. Obliterating another intelligent race from the cosmos, even in the name of self-defense, worked at his very soul.

He could do it. Should he?

Walden pushed such questions aside. The quaking bulkheads and deck plates told him it was too late to have any qualms about this. In hours they would spin around the star and overtake Starlight in its orbit. They'd get only one chance to disable the space station.

Walden wasn't sure they'd even get a single shot, but they had to try.

Images of Schwann exploding from its fiery bombardment by the Frinn returned to haunt him more effectively than any fanciful ghost. The aliens had been caught destroying that fated planet. Still, Walden worried about the release of the Infinity Plague. They might never find out the details of who had developed it, who released it, how and why it had been released, where the Frinn came into the complex equation of death.

"Anita might know, and she's not even talking to me," he said. Walden lost himself in double-checking the missiles. The guidance systems were black boxes; he checked only the self-test circuits and the warhead compartments laden with his gengineered death.

"All ready to blast, Doc?" came Sgt. Hecht's voice.

Walden looked up. The EPCT stood in the doorway with Egad beside him, tongue lolling and eyes sharp.

"As ready as I'll ever be. What's our status?"

"Doesn't look good. The engines aren't getting us up to speed. Something got banged up in liftspace. That's the best guess up in the control room."

"Who's doing the guessing?"

"Sorbatchin, from what I hear."

"That's as close to the truth as we're likely to hear," Walden said.

Hecht laughed. He had no respect for Edouard Zacharias, either. "The *Winston* is shadowing us. Their sensors are working better, too. The space gas is that they've picked up a Frinn warship about forty light-minutes away."

"Combat?"

"Maybe," the sergeant said. He idly scratched Egad's ears. The dog's long tongue flopped from side to side as he enjoyed the attention. "I hope we make it to the space station. If we have to fight, I want to be the one doing it. Letting the damned computers do the work isn't right. Makes me feel useless."

Walden nodded. When the *Winston*'s combat computers began working, no human could follow the course of action. Strategists like Nakamura programmed the expert systems with goals. With luck, during the battle they could shift emphasis and change tactics, but the computer mostly ran the military engagement.

"These aren't hooked into the ship's weapons system. Should I tell Zacharias?"

"I asked around," said Hecht. "This ship doesn't have squat in the way of firepower. The MCG cannon is makeshift. They had to rebuild it after every firing. The compact toroid plasma gun must have been on the other ship. This one can't generate enough energy fast enough to charge up an accelerator tube."

"Then this isn't a warship."

"Can't say what it is," admitted Hecht. "I poked around, me and a couple of the other guys, and all we found were robots. The damned ship is packed with them."

"Repair units?"

"They do everything. The pigs must be the laziest damned bunch in the universe. The machines do *everything* for them, including wiping their pig asses."

"That explains why we fought nothing but automated units on Schwann," said Walden. He had long since decided that the Frinn depended far more heavily on automation than did humans. They obviously didn't share the innate suspicion of artificial intelligence machines that plagued humanity.

"I'm not sure, but in the hold is a gizmo that makes main battle tanks. It looks as if they started the equipment and left it to do whatever it wanted."

"They were manufacturing tanks in *this* ship?" Walden found this incredible. He wished there had been more time to study the Frinn craft—and the Frinn.

"Looks like it. Hell, I thought they hauled them all the way from Starlight. Doesn't look like it. Sorbatchin says it's a good way of adapting to different battle conditions. Just build the stuff you need on-site."

Walden looked at the EPCT. "You don't believe that, do you, Sergeant?"

"Not really. I think they ran afoul of the Infinity Plague, then built what they needed to eradicate it."

Walden kept his opinion to himself. The friendly Frinn ventured into human space, established contact, then became contaminated with the chromosome-splitting plague. When they realized that had become infected, they tried to burn out the center of the infection using makeshift weapons.

If this was true, they had acquitted themselves well against two heavily armed NAA destroyers and a full company of Extra-Planetary Combat Team veterans.

"All hands, all hands," blared the speaker system Zacharias had jury-rigged. "We're going into combat. A Frinn cruiser is closing on us. The *Winston* will interdict in fourteen minutes."

"How long before the pigs get to us?" Hecht wondered aloud.

"We make contact with the enemy in eleven minutes," came Zacharias' troubling words.

"Great. This rust bucket has to hold off a warship for a minimum of three minutes until the *Winston* can support us."

Hecht spun and stalked out, bellowing orders as he went. Walden heard the EPCT marines scrambling into combat gear. He looked around and found his own hazard suit. Although it didn't provide the vacuum protection a standard spacesuit did, it gave him needed mobility and dexterity in dealing with the bioweapons.

"Let's get you into a hazard suit, Egad," he told the dog. "Fetch it."

"Don't like suit. Smells."

"Get is and don't argue."

The gengineered dog obediently trotted off and dragged back his hazard suit. Walden took several minutes securing the animal. Then he donned his own gear. What rankled was that Egad was right; it smelled like a rotting corpse inside the suit. No matter what he did to deodorize it, the stench remained.

He hoped his own dead and decaying body wouldn't add to the intolerable smell. Walden adjusted the air flow and it carried enough of the stink away to be bearable. Then he was too busy trying to stand upright to notice.

The ship lurched and seemed to slide sideways. Vibration from the engines increased and the rhythm turned irregular. He scrambled across the room and caught hold of Egad. He soothed the animal and then got out of the compartment and into the corridor.

"What's happening?" he yelled. His throat mike picked up even minor tremors and amplified it. He saw Hecht wince at the loudness in his headphones. Walden calmed and repeated his question in a lower voice. Hecht flashed him a wry smile of thanks.

"We're as much in the black hole as you are, Doc. From the way the ship's behaving, we're using a standard evasion program."

"Sorbatchin," he said, speaking on his command frequency, "report. What is going on?"

"Ah, Walden, you ask the impossible question of me. I cannot say with precision. The Frinn war craft engaged us without warning. Our fame precedes us."

"Can we survive until the *Winston* gets here to back us up?"

"The *Winston* is firing long-range genius missiles, but the similarity in design between this ship and the pig-faces' cruiser makes differentiation difficult.''

''The *Winston* hit us with a barrage?''

''Zacharias is doing what he can to evade.'' Sorbatchin seemed amused at the prospect of being blown from space accidentally by the NAA destroyer.

''Friendly fire,'' grumbled Hecht, listening in. ''Never fails. Those vac-brains at the helm will kill us yet.''

''Has the Frinn ship fired on us at all?'' demanded Walden.

''*Nyet.* No, no fire is evident. All the weaponry is being shown by the *Winston.*'' Sorbatchin's voice trailed off as he turned his attention to other things besides Walden's interrupting questions.

''If we survive our own ship, we might make it to Starlight,'' Walden said.

''An unusual benefit,'' agreed Sorbatchin, distracted. ''Those watching the conflict will think the *Winston* fires at us rather than the other war craft.''

Walden yelled as he was sucked across the corridor and slammed hard against a bulkhead. A tiny kinetic pellet had penetrated the midships and torn a path through both hulls, passing less than a meter from his head. The sudden decompression caused him to slam hard into the wall. In seconds the air pressure had shattered the hull and left a hole larger than his head.

''Get it fixed,'' he ordered Hecht. The EPCT sergeant shook himself and started to obey when a tiny hatch slid open and four robots smaller than a man's hand scuttled out. They followed a geodesic line across the corridor, its walls and ceiling, and found the hole. Within seconds of reaching the gaping hole, they began repairing it.

''They're spiders. The Frinn use damned spiders!''

''No, they're just robots,'' Walden said. The comparison to a spider was accurate, however. Two robots spat out thick strands that covered the hole vertically. The other two worked on horizontal spinning. In less than a minute the hole vanished.

Walden yelped when other robots pushed past his legs. Larger, more powerful devices went to work on the patch, buffing and sanding it until the repair was indistinguishable from the rest of the hull.

"Never seen anything like that," Hecht said. "We could use a few of them critters in the field. Pop a seam or need a battery pack replacement and have them come out and fix us up." The sergeant turned and looked around. "Where'd they get off to? They just upped and vanished into the walls."

Walden saw where the larger robot had gone. An almost invisible door in the deck had opened and swallowed it. The robot would wait patiently until some changing condition triggered it and brought it into action.

"Let's hope the robots in the rest of the ship work as well as this one." Walden checked his exterior pressure gauge and found that the atmosphere had been restored. From the passage of the steel ball to repressurization had taken less than three minutes.

A cold chill ran up and down his spine. If the Frinn used such a complete system on a mobile unit such as an exploratory starship, what systems did they have in place aboard an immense space station the size of Starlight? Even firing the bio-warhead missiles point-blank into the docking bay might have little effect if the repair robots cleaned up quickly.

Walden's paste-into-airborne-dust delivery system wouldn't work, either. The robots would clean up the paste before reintroducing atmosphere. Getting the typhoid into their water system seemed a more reliable system to him now.

"I'm going to the bridge," he told Hecht. "If you want, patch into my circuit and you can listen in."

"Thanks, Doc. I appreciate it. We'll never find out what's blasting, otherwise."

Walden hurried to the bridge and found pandemonium in command. Zacharias shouted orders that sounded contradictory. Sorbatchin sat to one side talking quietly with Pedro O'Higgins. The Sov-Lats looked at Walden as if he were a bug under a microscope when he hesitated, assessing the problems.

He pushed past Zacharias. The EPCT major was too startled to react immediately. Walden shoved his face down toward the vidscreen pickup and spoke directly to Nakamura.

"The ship is loaded with robot repair devices we never

suspected," he said. "We should be able to sustain considerable damage and survive, if they keep working."

"We're in the middle of a skirmish, Walden. Get off my bridge!" Zacharias started to draw his sidearm. He tumbled backward when Egad rushed forward and threw his thin body against the backs of Zacharias' legs.

"The Frinn think we're taking damage from the *Winston*," Walden went on, speaking strictly to Nakamura and ignoring the Sov-Lats. "We might be able to decoy the ship closer and let the *Winston* take it out."

"Do so, Doctor," came the woman's calm voice. "It is regrettable your ship sustained any damage, however slight, from the *Winston*'s inopportune barrage."

"Tell the destroyer to aim better next time." Walden glanced at the readouts on the simplified control panel and saw the *Winston* on an intercept vector with the Frinn ship. The vidscreen display blossomed with thousands of white points; the *Winston* had launched a shotgun-warhead and scattered hundreds of thousands of kinetic weapons into the Frinn's path.

"We took another few pellets," Walden said, seeing pressure readings drop all over the ship on the makeshift control panel. Before Zacharias could force his way to his feet past Egad's helpful nudging, the small robots workers had repaired the holes and returned the ship to working condition.

"I'm in control. Leave immediately or I will shoot you." Major Zacharias had his pistol out and leveled. Walden saw the insane hatred burning in the man's pale, almost colorless eyes and wondered why he hadn't fired already.

"Anita wouldn't like it if you shot me in the back," Walden said, turning back to the vidscreen. A strong hand spun him around. The pistol's muzzle tapped against his hazard suit's visor.

"I'll have you thrown out the airlock. You'll be a victim of the Frinn's aggression," Zacharias said.

"*Da*," piped up Sorbatchin. "We will support your claim, Major. Won't we, Pedro?"

The two Sov-Lats laughed uproariously. Zacharias' face clouded over, his anger barely held in check.

"You've got trajectories to plot and Starlight to take,"

Walden said. "Want to start now?" He backed away from the controls and let the EPCT major back.

"You'll pay for this insubordination, Walden. I swear it."

"None of us may get out of this alive, Major. Don't make promises you don't intend to keep."

Walden glanced back at the vidscreen. "The *Winston* just took out the Frinn ship. We can go in to Starlight unhindered. Better hurry. If they monitored the fight, they'll think we're a wounded survivor of senseless NAA aggression."

"We can sympathize with that," Sorbatchin said innocently. He held his hand up to show he carried no weapons when Zacharias spun on him.

Walden was amazed that the major forced himself back into action without killing someone. The man's training had to be good. He had been pushed beyond the limit and still retained a semblance of good sense. In spite of this, Walden didn't think he had misjudged the man.

Walden stood beside the Sov-Lat, more to listen to their talk than to stay out of Zacharias' way. Egad curled up at his feet and peered up, his brown eye wide. The gengineered dog winked broadly and Walden smiled back. They made a good team.

"We speed up, using the star's gravity well as a slingshot," Sorbatchin said. "This allows approach to Starlight at many times the velocity we would achieve otherwise."

"We still have to slow and match speed," pointed out Walden. "What do we gain?"

"Fast approach and nothing else. Give the enemy less time to study us and decide something is amiss," said the Sov-Lat colonel.

The ship shuddered as the engines came up to full power. Walden looked at the simple, unmarked Frinn controls. Tiny lights winked on and off. He wondered what they meant. They would do so much better using the original controls than the makeshift ones Zacharias insisted on. Still, he understood the major's point. Learning the alien system would require days—months—of work. They might not survive in this star system undetected very long. Best to strike quickly and risk the small EPCT team aboard the ship.

"Sergeant Hecht," Zacharias said into his command circuit. "Prepare for boarding in one hour."

"We're really burning a trail through space," Walden said, knowing the sergeant listened to his circuit, too. "Starlight glows like a small sun ahead of us, even though it is still a long ways off."

"Be quiet, Doctor."

"Sorry. Didn't know I was bothering you. I was just commenting that Starlight rivals the star in brilliance. Have they coated it with reflective material for any particular reason?"

"The space station orbits close to the primary," Zacharias said. "They do not wish to absorb useless radiation."

"They want it to be a beacon," said O'Higgins. "Why else? There are radiation transfer techniques that could turn it jet black. It would vanish in space."

"*Da*, they wish to be seen." Sorbatchin leaned over and worked at the edge of Zacharias' controls. "The size is more than we estimated. From angular measurement, it must be five thousand kilometers in diameter."

Walden whistled in surprise. Starlight was only an artificial space station and yet it held more than five percent of the volume of Earth. Walden closed his eyes and did the calculation quickly. The usable surface area inside Starlight far exceeded the arable land mass of Earth. The Frinn had built themselves an entire world—and more!

"Major, these lights show an incoming message," spoke up Sorbatchin. "They try to signal us."

Zacharias worked to keep the recalcitrant ship on course. "We ignore the signal. We can't decipher it, anyway. We'll pretend to be disabled."

"What was the device you stole from the weapons room, O'Higgins?" Walden asked the question bluntly, staring straight at the Chilean biologist.

"How do you know of it?" demanded Sorbatchin.

"It might be a recognition transponder. There's no telling what it is," said Walden. "We know that the room wasn't really a weapons control center—this isn't a war vessel."

"But—"

Zacharias was cut off when bright points appeared on the rim of Starlight.

"Think of something fast, Major," said Walden, his eyes fixed on the vidscreen. "They've just opened fire on us. Those are missiles—and they'll be here in seconds!"

CHAPTER
11

The ship veered as Edouard Zacharias applied power to one set of steering jets. Even as they crashed about in the control room, Walden knew they weren't going to avoid the missiles. Starlight had sophisticated guidance equipment and had pinpointed them. To dodge now was futile.

Yet they could do little else. The *Winston* came behind them and might be able to pick off the incoming missiles. Walden hoped they could—the chances of it happening were close to zero.

"Stop them!" cried Zacharias into the com unit. "Counter them or we're dead!"

The *Winston* tried. Walden saw tiny pops of light form at the bow of the NAA destroyer as countermeasure missiles launched to intercept those from Starlight. The first shock told him that the Frinn missiles had arrived before they could be stopped.

"We're still alive," Pedro O'Higgins said in surprise. "The missile hit. I felt it. Why aren't we dead?"

Walden made a gesture. Egad tore off to investigate. The direction of the tremor came from the bow of the ship. The gengineered dog could survey the damage and report back faster than any human could reconnoiter.

"I'm picking up static on all bands," Zacharias said, confused.

"The Frinn control boards are alive," said Sorbatchin. "*Da*, they think we are injured. They think we cannot pilot properly."

"After his maneuvering, little wonder," said O'Higgins.

"They send robots to take control and escort us into the space station," finished the Sov-Lat colonel. "We are under their complete control."

"This might work to our advantage," said Zacharias. His hand paused over the com unit. He fought an inner battle. If he tried to contact Miko Nakamura and report, the Frinn might intercept the communication. Yet he wanted to let the woman know that they still lived, that their plan still unfolded according to plan. Almost.

Walden left the control room and caught Egad on his way back. He bent down and opened the visor on the dog's helmet so he could speak directly to the animal.

"What is it, boy? What's happened?"

"Fingers came through wall. Fingers wiggle and sneak into controls in room where cat shit Sov-Lat vanish."

"In what we were calling the weapons control room? The Frinn have gotten robot devices into that room?" The dog bobbed his huge head up and down so hard his whipcord body shook. From the way his long, ratlike tail wagged inside his hazard suit, Walden knew the invasion by the Frinn robots was considerable.

"Are they taking over or just trying to establish a base?"

"Can't tell," Egad said. "Scared, master. I'm scared." The dog drove his head forward and knocked Walden off his feet. He sat heavily and had to cradle the dog's body as Egad crawled into his lap.

Walden sat and thought as he held Egad tightly. The Frinn hadn't attacked, though the flare of rockets made it appear they had. Whatever they had sent entered the ship and worked on the control circuits. He stood and returned to the bridge.

Zacharias fought the controls, cursing volubly when they refused to respond.

"Let them take us in, Zacharias," said Walden. "They've taken over the ship. A remote control device has punctured the hull and entered the main circuits."

"I bypassed the main boards," grumbled Zacharias. "Why won't *my* controls respond?"

"This might not be the main control room," Walden said. "The place where O'Higgins stole their com device is. The Frinn robots unerringly went for it. We've bollixed up our intelligence again and guessed wrong."

"What is this room, eh?" asked Sorbatchin.

Walden shrugged. "I can't say. What I do know is that they think we've been disabled and are pulling us in. If we fight too much, or try to rely on the *Winston* to get us out of this jam, we're going to be blown into ions."

Zacharias gave up on trying to pilot the ship and simply sat and stared. Starlight grew brighter, larger, nearer. Within an hour they saw docking bays awaiting them.

"Walden, prepare your missiles. Fire directly into their docking bay. We can take out the whole damned station with one well-placed shot," said Zacharias.

"It won't work, not in a million years," Walden said. "Starlight is *huge*. And look at how well the repair robots work on this ship—and it's been damaged severely and lost its crew. We should brazen it out as long as we can. To fire now loses us any advantage of surprise."

"The armor plating would withstand the feeble delivery systems available to Walden," said O'Higgins. "See how they cleverly erect armored baffles to keep us from getting a clear shot into the maw of the dry dock?"

Zacharias did. He was a proud and spiteful man, but he was also a soldier. He risked his life only if there was no other way to accomplish a needed mission.

"We need," said the major, "a genius bomb capable of finding its way through their defensive baffles."

"Those aren't for defense," said Sorbatchin. "They are strong, yes, but they are placed more to prevent backwash from rockets leaving the dry dock."

Walden hesitated. He wasn't sure O'Higgins' appraisal was right. The missiles might be able to blast through the plates. A more compelling reason not to try was the one he had given Zacharias. They might sneak into the space station more easily than they could blast their way inside.

And then? Walden wasn't sure he had an idea. Their plan fell apart from second to second.

"My men can fight our way into their control center," Zacharias said.

"Great. Where's that?"

"What do you mean?" the major asked.

"You need to scout the location of their control center," Walden said, suddenly tired of Zacharias and his posturing. "There are millions of hectares inside Starlight. I said it before: this space station is immense. Finding anything by accident isn't likely."

Zacharias fell silent. Walden stared at the vidscreen and watched as the space station's curvature vanished and the side grew like a giant flat wall. A gentle bump announced their arrival in an outer dry dock. Robots swarmed over the hull. Tiny grinding and crunching noises filled the ship as repair work began.

"The missiles," Zacharias said. "Fire them now!"

"There's not much chance we can get them into the heart of the station," Walden said.

"Do it! That's an order!"

Walden looked for support to Sorbatchin, who shrugged, and Pedro O'Higgins, who sat passively. He found neither support nor comfort with the Sov-Lats.

"What's the plan?" Walden asked. Zacharias might be able to pull off something if they did this right.

"My marines go in directly behind the missiles. We fan out once inside. We strike hard, fast. We find their damned control room and take it."

"We'd all better go inside," Walden said. "I don't think the Frinn will allow the ship to survive as a base for our attack."

"We all go," Zacharias said firmly.

Walden knew Hecht and the EPCT waiting below had already heard the decision. By the time Zacharias ordered them to form ranks and prepare for the invasion of Starlight, they were ready. Walden took out a small box with a digital readout and a single button on it.

"Launch at will, Doctor," said Zacharias.

Walden glanced at the vidscreen and the hundreds of robots thronging the space around their ship. He had no idea what had happened to the *Winston*. The NAA destroyer might have veered away and avoided destruction—or it might be rapidly cooling plasma in the orbit behind Starlight.

He didn't want to think about the *Hippocrates* and those still aboard her. Miko Nakamura could take care of herself. But what of Anita?

"Fire, Walden. Fire *now*!"

He lifted the small box and cycled through the digital read-out numbers. The small memory remembered the order. His finger touched the firing button. Fourteen missiles launched in sequence. On the flat vidscreen, Walden saw four crash into baffles. Then the external cameras went black. Either the robots had disconnected them or an explosion had wrecked the hull-mounted cameras. To Walden it didn't matter. He had to follow the EPCTs into Starlight or be left behind.

He gestured to Egad. The Sov-Lats had already left the bridge. Zacharias raced down the hatchways and crashed loudly into the decking far below. The vibrations died suddenly when the atmosphere gushed into space.

"The Frinn have pulled the plug on us," he radioed to Egad. The dog turned mismatched, questioning eyes toward him. He explained. "They thought they could finish us off by evacuating the ship. We were ready with our suits."

"We go into station?" Egad asked.

"We do," said Walden. He arrived at the shuttle launch bay just as the last craft was preparing to leave. Hecht waved to him and held up the launch for the few seconds needed to get aboard.

"You cut it close, Doc," the EPCT sergeant said. "The major ordered us all off on the double. If there hadn't been some trouble with the controls . . ." His words drifted off. They both knew why Zacharias had given the orders he had. He hoped to trap Walden aboard the Frinn ship.

"Thanks," he said. "I owe you one."

"We'll all be owing each other before this day's out," the sergeant said. "Damn, they just nuked the ship."

Walden saw radiation counters mounted in the shuttle wall go wild. No concussion marked the passing of the ship. The nuclear device simply vaporized all debris that might have been large enough to buffet the shuttle.

"Get us in right behind the major," ordered Hecht. He hefted his laserifle and then looked up at Walden. "You need one of these? Bonzo, get the doc here something to warm his hands with.''

The armorer shoved a spare laserifle into Walden's hands. He clumsily checked it out, having had little chance to use such weapons before. He found the stud turning on the red-dot laser sight. All he needed to do was put the dot on his target. The torrent of energy following along the laserifle's real beam would vaporize steel in seconds. Satisfied that he knew enough about its operation, he nodded to Hecht.

''We're almost home,'' the sergeant said. ''The other two shuttles are down and making their way into enemy territory.'' A gentle bump signaled the shuttle's arrival at a spot behind the rocker flare baffles. ''Let's go make bacon out of those pig-faces!''

Walden piled out with the others, Egad beside him. He took a few seconds to look around and get his bearings. His hazard suit didn't have the inertial homing devices worn by the EPCTs. The walls were painted with a confusing array of colors and symbols, none of which made any sense to him.

''Remember our route, Egad,'' he told the dog. Whether the gengineered dog could was a matter of conjecture; the dog depended more heavily on scent than on vision for tracking. Cooped up inside the hazard suit, Egad's most efficient sense was blocked.

''No missile signs,'' the dog told him.

Walden cursed as he followed Hecht's squad past the automated center controlling the landing bays. Not a one of his delivery systems had brought in its deadly load of microbes. He didn't even see the evidence of scratches where the missiles had crashed.

What he did see were thousands of small robots scuttling about, scouring, repairing, making everything perfect. The full impact of any of his missiles would have created more damage than the little mechanisms could have repaired quickly; he had to believe he had failed completely in delivering the lethal cargo.

In a perverse way Walden felt relieved.

''Ambush!'' crackled the warning in his headphones.

He didn't bother to ask who had sent the message. He dived forward, sliding along on his belly. He knew the hazard suit wasn't likely to tear. It had dozens of crossed, laminated layers to keep out even the most virulent virus or bacteria. Walden fought to get his laserifle in front of him and ready for use.

By the time he was ready to fight, the skirmish was over. Molten rain spattered the decks all around him. What had been a Frinn fighting machine lay on its side, its top half blown away by a dozen EPCT laser blasts.

"How many more of them are there?" he asked. It took several seconds before an answer came.

"Don't know that, Doc. This one snuck up on me. Mendelssohn got it before it got me. You and Egad want to get closer and form a unit with me? There's heavy fighting going on inside, about five hundred meters. The major's really stepped into it this time."

Walden scrambled to his feet, conscious of the still smoldering metal droplets on the deck plates. He skirted the destroyed robot and fell in behind Hecht. Egad trotted off to one side, his head moving back and forth like some automated probe. The scientist knew Egad wanted to take off his helmet and use his sense of smell to the fullest.

An involuntary check of the atmosphere and pressure startled him. They were in breathable air. He hadn't remembered going through an airlock.

"Sergeant, we can take off our helmets."

"No!" Hecht's denial was a sharp command. "We stay buttoned up. We don't want them pumping bio or chem into us." The EPCT sergeant hefted his laserifle to port arms and jogged off, assuming Walden would follow.

He hesitated, wanting to give Egad the fullest chance to be useful, yet not wanting to endanger the dog's life. Working on his analyzer fastened to his belt assured Walden that the air was safe and clear of deadly contaminants. The EPCT hadn't brought any biochem weapons; they relied strictly on kinetic and energy firepower. His missiles had failed to penetrate.

"Let me get your helmet off, Egad." He pulled the visor up and fastened the helmet to the dog's back. If needed, the helmet could be refastened in seconds.

"Thank you, master," Egad said, his nose sniffing in all directions. "Pigs nearby."

"Frinn," Walden automatically corrected. He didn't want

Egad falling into the habit of underestimating the aliens just because they looked—and smelled—like Earthly porcines.

"Not many. Much clanking. Robots everywhere."

"They're all dangerous," Walden said. "Let's catch up with Hecht and the rest of the squad." He hadn't gone fifty paces when he realized this wasn't possible. The EPCTs had vanished into the space station's vast interior and hadn't bothered leaving a trail for him to follow.

Walden cursed his bad luck. They didn't need to blaze a trail; they had inertial tracking devices and could find their way back to the docking bays easily. His hazard suit contained more elaborate monitoring equipment than theirs—but it was all technical. They fought, he analyzed.

And he was cut off from them.

"Can you find Hecht?" he asked Egad.

The dog sampled the air and then shook his head. "No trace. No human smell, except yours."

Walden knew he could get back to the docks. What that would accomplish he wasn't sure. If he were the Frinn commander, he would concentrate on demolishing any vehicle giving a chance at retreat. Then he would go after the invaders.

"Let's assume they stayed in the main corridors," he told the dog. Cautiously, laserifle ready, he advanced. The way Hecht and the others had been jogging, they would have far outraced him. Still, Walden didn't feel confident enough in either direction or his own ability to race ahead blindly.

"There," he said, catching motion out of the corner of his eye. "Down this passage."

"Gets smaller," Egad observed. "No human smell."

"Their combat suits are nulled out to keep SAW-dets from detecting them," he said. The surface acoustic wave detectors matched Egad's sensitive nose in detecting random molecules floating in the air. It had been a major technical breakthrough finding material for the EPCT combat suits that could not be SAW tracked.

"No trace of humans," Egad repeated.

Walden rounded a corner. Instinct saved him. He recoiled in fright and pressed the firing stud on the laserifle. The vicious bolt vaporized a robot's questing arm. Walden recovered and fired a second time, this energy blast washing the robot's CPU. The heat fried the artificial brain, even though the laserifle beam failed to penetrate the thick metallic brain case.

"What was it?" whispered Walden.

"Dangerous," came Egad's appraisal. "Smells bad. Burned metal makes my nose twitch."

Walden stepped over the Frinn robot and ran down the corridor. What he had seen had been human, not low-slung metallic robot. Two more sharp corners brought him to a small lounge area filled with destroyed robots. It took him several seconds to realize there had been human casualties during this fray.

Egad sniffed at one fallen EPCT. He had been cut in half, both sides of the cut cauterized.

"Laser beam?" asked Egad.

Walden could only nod. His mouth had turned suddenly dry and his legs shook. He had seen people killed before— not that long ago on Schwann. He doubted he would ever get used to the sight of such violent death. The marine had blundered into the room and a Frinn repair robot had used its laser cutting beam on him.

It took no great intellect to reconstruct this. The robot lay in pieces around the EPCT's body. Someone else had entered and blown apart the Frinn mechanism. The other debris attested to a brief but fierce fight.

"Listen," urged Egad. "Fighting this way." Egad took a position like a pointer. Walden had to smile at the ludicrous sight. Egad's bandy legs, the thin body, the massive head, and the stringy tail weren't those of a pedigreed hunting dog. In spite of this, he knew Egad's senses were as acute—and he was far more intelligent.

Walden turned up the gain on his exterior microphone and immediately heard what Egad had already detected. Hissing laser beams fried metal somewhere down the corridor ahead of him. Walden checked his laserifle and plunged ahead, oblivious to the danger. He knew this wasn't a display of bravery—he just wanted to get away from the ugly death in the lounge area.

He found more death and injury within a hundred meters. Three EPCTs were barricaded in a storage room. They fired

through crates they had stacked in the doorway. Repair robots with welding and cutting torches tried to get to them.
In the corridor lay two dead marines and one who stirred
feebly.

"Egad, wait!" cried Walden. It was too late to stop the
dog. He darted forward. His powerful teeth closed on the
wounded soldier's arm and he began pulling. Walden fired
and blew off a knife attachment on a robotic tentacle. Egad
never stopped pulling until the marine lay behind Walden.

"Who's out there?" came a faint transmission.

"Jerome Walden."

"Yeah, he's the big brain with the dog," came a response.

"The mutt just pulled N'kruma out of the line of fire. Doc,
can you get us out? We're holed up in—"

"I see you," Walden said. "Why's the transmission so
weak? We're not five meters apart."

"The pig-faces are scrambling us. A field must damp com
on all our bands." All the time the man spoke, the EPCTs
kept up a steady barrage at the insistent robots. As quickly
as one was disabled, another took its place—and dozens of
the tiny repair robots flocked to work on the damaged fighting
machine.

Walden frowned. He kept thinking of them as fighting machines, such as the tanks they had encountered on Schwann.
But they weren't. He hadn't seen anything not found in a
well-supplied repair shop. They fought repair robots.

"I'll get them in a cross fire," Walden said. "They'll come
for me. You take 'em out when they do."

The tactic worked well. The instant he opened fire, the
robots shifted their attention to him. The marines in the room
blew the robots apart with their more accurate fire.

"They're not so smart. Wish we had a few of *our* robot
fighters," an EPCT said. "We'd show them how to make
killer machines."

"What's the plan? I got cut off from Sgt. Hecht."

"No time to chatter, Doc. We got to get the Sov-Lat out
of a fix. He tried to help us but was driven back. The pigs'
robots are heavier at the other end of the passageway."

"Sov-Lat?"

"The South American bug chaser. O'Higgins. He fought

like a wildcat. Saved our hides. As much as I hate the idea, we got to go pull him out of the furnace now.''

"What about this one? N'kruma?'' He knelt and checked the man's vital signs readout. "He's still alive, but barely.''

The marine who has assumed the command bent over and touched a small stud. A digital readout glowed under the vital signs. He tapped in a few number combinations.

"That'll hold him for a while. No pain, no consciousness. We'll have to do pickup on him later. Activate his transponder, will you, Doc?''

Walden found the green button on the EPCT's belt and touched it. When the appropriate signal was sent, the fallen man's com unit would reply with his name and condition. Seeing that he could do nothing more for the man without pulling him out of his combat gear, Walden reluctantly left him in the corridor and followed the others.

They found Pedro O'Higgins minutes later barricaded at one end of a huge chamber. The Sov-Lat scientist was the last of a four-man squad. Three bodies had been slashed to ribbons by the Frinn robots. O'Higgins fended them off. From the way his laserifle sputtered and flared, Walden knew he wasn't going to last much longer.

"We'll get you out,'' the EPCT told O'Higgins.

Walden and Egad circled in one direction in the large room and the EPCTs went the other. As fast as O'Higgins damaged an attacking robot, it was repaired by the swarms of smaller repair mechanisms. Walden saw how the Sov-Lat was fighting a losing battle. He might as well have tried filling space with one breath at a time.

Egad snarled and leaped, teeth fastening in a prehensile cable snaking around a corner. Walden stepped away from the wall and fired. The top portion of a robot vaporized. To his surprise, the machine kept fighting Egad.

"Walden, get back!'' came O'Higgins' impassioned cry. "Behind you. They're behind you!''

Walden swung around. His laserifle was batted from his hands by another of the mobile steel tentacles. The wall had come alive with them. They wrapped themselves around his wrists and waist and pulled him toward the bulkhead.

He screamed when he saw the heat drill emerging from the wall level with his chest.

Jerome Walden fought the powerful steel bands encircling his body—and failed. His hazard suit turned a cherry-red from the heat drill and he felt the pain lancing into his torso. The world became black, as death came to claim him.

CHAPTER
12

Blisters popped up on Walden's chest from the heat drill. He sagged in the grip of the steely tentacles. He prepared to die— and then he simply floated on a lazy cloud of muzzy softness.

He lay on his back and stared up at Egad. The dog tried to lick his face but the hazard suit visor got in the way. Walden moved and pain assailed him. His chest had been burned, but not too severely. He fought to sit up and clear his head.

"What happened? Did you save me, boy?" He tried to pat Egad. The dog danced away and retrieved his fallen laserifle.

Walden grabbed it and rolled onto his belly, ready to fight. The wave of red pain washing up from his chest almost pushed him over the brink and into unconsciousness. He grimly hung on and fired in time to cut down a robot threatening O'Higgins.

It took several seconds to realize that O'Higgins wasn't moving. Walden looked around the large vaulted chamber and saw only carnage. The EPCTs who had come with him had vanished.

"Hurt bad," Egad said.

"You are? Where? Tell me, Egad."

"Not me. Him. The cat shit Sov-Lat."

Walden struggled over to Pedro O'Higgins' side. He saw

the trickle of blood inside the sundered suit and knew the man wasn't likely to survive. He popped open the visor and tried to find a pulse in the man's throat. O'Higgins' eyelids fluttered and opened. Blurred brown eyes peered up.

"Saved you," the Sov-Lat biologist said. "Poor trade, my life for yours, but you saved me from drifting forever in lift-space. So empty. Would have gone crazy."

Walden glanced over to Egad. The gengineered dog nodded solemnly. O'Higgins *had* saved him from the robot wall and heat drill and been mortally wounded doing it.

"Thank you," Walden said simply but sincerely. He wanted the precise words to make everything right with O'Higgins. He knew the man was a bloody-handed butcher, but the Chilean had just saved his life. That ought to make a difference, and he wanted O'Higgins to know.

O'Higgins twitched slightly and died without uttering another word. Walden laid him down gently and closed his sightless eyes. To his surprise, the Chilean's sacrifice didn't make much difference in the way Walden thought of him.

Pedro O'Higgins *had* been a savage, vicious, uncaring researcher and deserved his fate.

Walden rocked back and leaned against the barricade that O'Higgins had erected. Would the Sov-Lat scientist think the same of Walden, had he died? Probably.

"Where are the others?" he asked Egad.

"Don't know. Cat shit Sov-Lat saved me, too. Steel string strangled me. He destroyed robot and string fell off."

Walden patted Egad and got to his feet. The robots were deactivated. Even the tiny repair robots had vanished into the walls, possibly frightened, possibly seeking other damaged mechanisms where they could be of greater utility. Not a one of the robots Walden saw could be fixed. All had been turned into molten junk.

Before he checked the fallen EPCTs for signs of life, he perversely returned to the wall where he had almost died. Six mobile tentacles hung limp and useless. O'Higgins' laserifle bolt had destroyed the control mechanism. By exposing himself to the other robots, O'Higgins had died—and saved Walden and Egad.

"What is this gadget?" he asked Egad, knowing the animal wouldn't have any better idea than he did. The tentacles held—what?—and the heat drill bored through it. From the rest of the room, Walden thought this might be a central supply depot, though it lacked the spare parts he associated with even a small repair shop. The deck plates were spotted with droplets of molten metal that had accumulated over long months of use. This robot killer was no more a fighting machine than any of the others he had encountered.

The Frinn defended themselves with repair appliances.

He pulled himself away from the panel and hurried to the side of the nearest fallen EPCT. The man's vital signs read-outs were all nulled out. Walden didn't bother checking to see if there had been a circuit malfunction. From the odd angle between head and body he knew the readings were accurate. The next soldier hadn't fared any better. A laser welder had fused his helmet and his face. The third marine didn't have any arms; his laserifle had exploded in his hands. He had fallen a victim to his own maintenance rather than the enemy's fire.

Stomach rebelling, Walden went to the last of the bodies he saw. To his surprise flickers of life remained.

"Are you able to tell me what happened?" he asked.

From behind the pitted glasteel visor he saw eyes blinking rapidly. A hiss sounded in his ears telling of the interference. Walden adjusted his frequency. Even this close to the radio source, the Frinn efficiently blocked communication.

". . . something with my legs. Took medication nine. No feeling, no feeling." The wounded man's voice vanished like sunlight behind a cloud.

Knowing this, Walden ran a quick check and verified what the man had said. Both legs moved independently of joint or bone. They had been crushed by a Frinn robot. The scientist punched up a report on medication nine, then swore silently to himself when he saw the readout. He knew what the drug did. EPCT slang for it was Love Potion Number Nine. Even as it blotted out pain, the drug produced side effects that might be hurting the man now. Walden vowed to get him out of the confining combat suit and better tend the wounds.

He swallowed hard when he thought that both legs might have to be amputated. A full hospital might be able to save them; even Leo Burch back in the *Hippocrates* could do more. But they might as well be light-years away.

"Egad, is there an empty room nearby? One we can use for a base?"

"Walls have ears," the dog said. "Walls have holes everywhere."

"I don't care about that, as long as they don't have tentacles." He glanced over his shoulder at the bulkhead where the heat drill had scorched his suit and chest. "I just don't want to stay out here any longer."

The gengineered canine trotted off, returning a few minutes later with his report of vacant rooms a dozen meters down an adjoining corridor.

"Good spot, too," the dog said. "Two doors in. No way to get trapped."

Walden hefted the wounded marine in a fireman's carry and staggered out at well over a hundred kilos. Walden was glad he didn't have far to go. He would have had to drag the man the rest of the way if he hadn't stumbled into the room when he did.

"Make a bed for him," Walden commanded. "I've got to retrieve the other one."

Egad started to pull odd bits of cloth and furniture together. Walden returned to the vaulted chamber, slung his laserifle, and cautiously retraced his path. He found N'kruma where he had fallen. Walden wasn't up to carrying the man; he dragged him by his heels back to the small room where Egad finished with the crude bedding.

"Good?" the dog asked.

"You've done a great job, Egad. Want to do more?"

"How?"

"Go fetch any EPCT you can find. You can talk to them, if that's what it takes to get them back here."

"Talk to someone not you or Anita?" Egad was confused. He had spent his life avoiding direct verbal contact with others. He had been created during experiments Walden preferred not to have known, even in classified reports.

"If necessary. We're in serious trouble," he told the dog.

"Pigs all over," agreed Egad. Walden was too tired to correct him. "I fetch everyone back. Even cat shit major?"

"Even Zacharias," Walden said. Zacharias probably knew about Egad's intelligence and ability to speak. Anita must have mentioned it to him. Pillow talk. An unguarded moment. By direct order.

Walden forced himself to forget Anita and relax. He was too tense. If an EPCT squad came up now, he'd probably open fire on them through sheer reflex. He had to keep better control of his emotions if he wanted to survive.

"I'll see what I can do for these two. I'm not a medical doctor but I'm likely to give them better care than anyone else on Starlight."

He waited until Egad ducked through the door. He barricaded it with crates from the corner of the room. The second door was locked. No amount of tugging got it open. Walden settled for a single box in front of it, more as a warning than a deterrent to entry. After placing his laserifle on an upended crate where he could reach it easily, he started into the grisly work of stripping the soldiers of their combat gear and examining their wounds.

He had an immediate problem on his hands: triage. Which of his two patients required the more immediate aid? N'kruma had been under drugs longer and might be more easily saved. Walden went to work on him first using the equipment he had slung on his belt. Although it wasn't meant for such work, it served him well enough in monitoring blood and chemical imbalances. These gave hints to the men's condition and helped Walden through the maze of diagnosis.

From the dilated pupils and the dryness in the man's mouth, Walden diagnosed a concussion. The rents in N'kruma's combat suit showed how he had been slashed and thrown about. Impact against a wall might have jolted him and rattled his brains. Walden studied the list of drugs available and used what he thought would be most efficacious.

Then he burned off the other soldier's legs using his laserifle. To Walden's surprise, the man didn't die immediately from shock. From here he did what he could to treat the cauterized stumps. It wasn't nearly enough but was all Walden could do. He was a biologist-researcher, not a medical doctor.

He leaned back and waited, laserifle across his lap. Sleep crept up on him and dreams of Frinn and O'Higgins and robots turned to nightmares. He came awake with a start, drenched in sweat, when Egad yipped sharply outside the door.

"Come in," he called. "I won't shoot."

The gengineered dog crept in, tail between his short legs. "Sorry, master," he said. "Can't find anyone else to bring. All marines somewhere else."

"Did you hear sounds of battle?"

"Nothing. Entire place silent."

Walden turned up the gain on his com unit and strained to hear even a hint of a human voice through the crackling static. The Frinn blanketed everything too effectively. He tried a few tentative calls to contact someone in Zacharias' squad, then stopped. If the Frinn monitored these channels, they could triangulate and home in on him. He was relatively secure in the storage room and had the two wounded soldiers to protect.

"Let's explore together, Egad." He got to his feet and wobbled. He tried to remember when he had eaten and couldn't. He sampled some of the food pellets from one EPCT helmet and drank his fill from a water canister. His hazard suit lacked such supplies, even if he did carry more weight in instrumentation.

He dropped some of the equipment and slung a spare laserifle over his shoulder. Fighting equipment was more important to him than analyzing tools. He indicated that Egad should take the lead. He followed, finger resting on the firing stud. No matter what they encountered, he was ready for it.

They wandered through long, deserted corridors for over an hour without sighting any living creature—or Frinn robot. Walden began to tire. He even chanced opening his helmet visor and listening for sounds, even though Egad's more sensitive ears had picked up nothing.

"What do you make of it, old boy?"

"Humans gone. Frinn all gone, too," guessed Egad. "Don't know where."

Walden had no idea where the space station's population had gone. Starlight was immense. It should have been able to support a population of hundreds of thousands. If he had discovered a slick travel brochure telling that Starlight's crew totaled a million, Walden would have believed it. Where were they?

He began poking his head into every room they came to. The strange construction used aboard their ships carried over into the Frinn's space station. Tiny rooms provided claustrophobic privacy. Small closets hardly large enough for a solitary Frinn to stand inside were everywhere. He found a dozen along the corridors he explored; each compartment was empty, although a few showed signs of use. The number of sanitary facilities seemed adequate for ten million, and the diminutive food preparation areas were nearly as numerous. But for all the rooms in the space station, he saw no one. Starlight might have been deserted for all the crew he found.

"Any of the rooms recently used, Egad? In the past hour?"

"Empty, deserted. No dust to make my nose twitch."

Walden saw the efficient filtration system used to hold dust in the station to a minimum. Electrostatic precipitators formed only a part of the air screening. From the compartmentalization he saw, Walden wondered if his gengineered typhoid bacillus would have been effective. Each Frinn had individual living quarters. A main tank might supply the water but the purification took place just before the water poured from the taps.

"What kind of culture do they have?" he wondered aloud.

"Untrusting," suggested Egad. "No one wants to be around anyone else."

The scientist had to admit this sounded like a good hypothesis. It certainly fit the evidence they had uncovered.

"I've got to rest," Walden said. "There's a compartment that looks comfortable enough." He stuck his head inside and scanned it. He stopped and stared when he saw the glasteel window sweeping around the perimeter of the room.

He went in, letting Egad worry about ambushes or mechanical traps. The dog didn't warn him so he figured this room was as barren of life as the others in this section of the alien space station. Walden stared out the window into the black velvet vastness of space. Thousands of crystalline points gleamed with manic intensity. The starfield patterns were not much different from this system than from Earth, he decided. A few constellations seemed familiar, but he wasn't enough of an astronomer to tell.

"They aren't agoraphobic," he told Egad. "No one who sought closed-in spaces could tolerate a room like this."

"We hiked to edge of Starlight," said Egad.

"We can see halfway up the sphere, almost to the equator," agreed Walden, craning his neck and looking up Starlight's massive sloping exterior hull. The space station's high reflectivity was caused by millions of crystalline cells that Walden thought might be photovoltaics supplying power to the space station. He wasn't enough of a physicist to understand why they were shiny and not black to absorb the greatest amount of light possible.

He had to admit he wasn't even sure they were photovoltaic cells supplying Starlight's power. The Frinn might consider them nothing more than flashy decoration—or it might be some type of alien billboard advertising a product known instantly to them. He knew too little about the Frinn to make good guesses.

Not for the first time, he wondered what the hell he was doing here. He belonged in a research lab. Glancing at a small compartment in the wall, he wondered if he should enter it to think. Nothing could sneak up behind him. By the same token, he would be easily trapped, and the notion of being pinned inside did not please him. Walden hunkered down, back to the outer wall, and wondered about this and other philosophical problems plaguing him. He had seen too much of what his bioweapons did to ever go back. The man couldn't even reconstruct the rationalization that had allowed him to work on such potent weapons without once considering that they *would* be used. It had been a game to him, and it hadn't involved living, breathing creatures.

Seeing the results of his and others' bioweapons was different from being on the scene when they were used. *He* was responsible now, not someone else.

"You all right?" asked the dog. "You look strange, master. You smell different."

Walden wondered if Egad could smell the changes in his emotions. Apparently his sensitive canine nose could isolate more than his creator had thought.

"I'm fine, old boy. Sometimes I get to thinking."

"You thinking about alien?"

Walden came instantly alert. "What are you talking about? What alien?"

Egad tipped his head in the direction of the passageway. Walden shot to his feet. His fingers clutched the laserifle so tightly his knuckles turned white and his hands shook. He again had to go into battle, personal conflict, with the chance of dying.

Memory of O'Higgins and the others flashed across his mind. The Frinn had done it—their robot killers had. Also entering his thoughts were visions of the missiles he had tried to blast into Starlight's interior. The Frinn were already dying of the Infinity Plague. He had tried to accelerate their awful deaths.

"Let's find ourselves a Frinn," he told Egad. They set off grimly to track down the enemy.

CHAPTER
13

"Robots!"

Jerome Walden flung himself sideways even as his finger tightened on the laserifle's firing stud. His vision was blurred for a moment by the shimmers of heat rising from the destroyed machine. When he got a good look past the demolished robot, he saw the sheen of light off a Frinn's distinctively bald head.

He kicked the smoking machine out of his path and pushed on. Walden wasn't sure if he was the only human still living on Starlight. He had left the two EPCTs medicated and alive, but their conditions were bad and might have grown worse. No one else he had seen was even breathing. The Frinn robots were everywhere, but not humans—and until now, not the Frinn. Curiosity as much as the need to survive drove Walden on.

"Where, Egad? Where did the alien go?"

"Pig-face went down hallway to left. I still hear clicking sounds."

"Clicking? Feet on the decks?"

The gengineered canine shook his head. He didn't know what he heard or, if he did, he had no words or experience to describe it. Walden stared down the long corridor Egad had indicated. Walden clung to the laserifle until his arms shook from strain. He stopped and tried to gather his wits. To go into combat like this meant the Frinn had the advantage.

"No sounds," supplied Egad. "No smell, either. Don't know what happened to the pig-face."

"Frinn," Walden said. "Don't call them pigs again. Promise me."

"Promise," Egad said, "but don't understand why. Other humans call them pig-faces. They smell funny."

"They smell different," Walden said, still correcting the dog. He advanced in a crouch, the laserifle ready for use. He spun and trained the rifle on an empty room.

Walden hesitated. It *seemed* empty but some primitive sense told him to explore further. He entered the room and went around the outside, his back to the wall. He was as curious about the equipment in the room as he was in finding a Frinn.

"Laboratory," he told Egad. "Does it smell like home?" He wanted to determine what experiments might be done here. He recognized the forms of some instruments but failed to determine the nature of the biologic experiments. So much was done with nano-manipulators and molecule splicers that biology had become a quantum science. Walden couldn't remember the last time he had pickled anything in formaldehyde as he had done in college.

He stared at one intricate machine and tried to figure out what it was used for. On impulse, he stuck his eye over what seemed to be an eyepiece and stared at the specimen. Nematodes wiggled in a solution, some moving faster than others. He had to laugh out loud. A computer tracked the velocities of the worms as they escaped from a tiny container and raced to the far, safe, side of the container.

"I've used the same setup to measure the toxic effect of chemicals," he told Egad. "The speed of swimming slows as poisoning progresses. The direction varies according to certain senses-twisting chemical reactions. For all its simplicity this rig does some elegant work."

His opinion of the Frinn went up a notch, as much because he recognized expertise as he did the efforts of a researcher in his own field. Walden examined several of the experiments in progress and saw that someone—a Frinn—had been here recently. The transmission positron microscope element was still hot. He tried to remove the specimen. The stage refused to yield the experiment. Walden finally gave up and prowled the rest of the lab.

"Any trace of the Frinn?" he asked Egad. The gengineered canine shook his head and curled up by the door. With Egad standing guard, Walden felt confident in dawdling. The Frinn wasn't going to leave Starlight.

Walden stopped for a moment and considered that *he* might not be leaving the alien space station, either. If the others had been killed, he was alone. But what had happened to the Frinn aboard Starlight? He hadn't seen traces of more than a handful of living, breathing creatures. Robots, yes, they were everywhere. Only one living Frinn had crossed his path since O'Higgins had been killed. Were they all cowering inside the small compartments spotted throughout Starlight? If so, why didn't they emerge to defend their space station? He had too many questions and no good answers to any of them.

The remainder of the laboratory contained nothing of interest. Walden saw the only running experiment was one of chemical poison detection and identification. He idly wondered if the EPCT had retrieved one of the fourteen missiles he had launched and used its payload-warhead to contaminate some section of Starlight or if this was simply a project with a long history.

It made no difference. He had to find the researcher. Hefting the laserifle, Walden left the lab. "Come on, Egad."

The dog obediently trotted after him. When they came to a crossing corridor, Egad stopped and sniffed. Like a pointer finding prey, he turned. "Pig-Frinn go there."

Walden almost laughed. He had helped correct Egad as he had seen fit. The dog had changed his way of referring to the aliens, but it wasn't what Walden had had in mind.

"Close. Not far away is pig-Frinn." Egad bared his fangs and worked himself into a fighting frenzy.

Walden put a hand on the dog's back and pushed him down. If there was any fighting, he had to do it. For all Egad's ferocity, the animal's body wasn't up to a prolonged scuffle. His legs were too short and Walden had seen a lack of oxygen uptake due to the size of lungs in his greyhoundlike body.

Duplicating his earlier tactic, Walden swung into the room. This one was outfitted as an office. He smiled at the sight of the desk—a secretary had been stationed there—and the ones deeper in the room. Those were executive desks, complete with computer consoles and linkups to databases. One station was turned on. But of the computer user he saw no trace.

He cursed under his breath. He was always a few seconds behind the Frinn. Posting Egad, he slipped into the awkward chair and stared at the computer screen. The controls were odd and the symbols marking the simple set of nine keys undecipherable. At random he pushed one key. The screen display changed, but it meant nothing to him.

For several minutes he played with different combinations of the keys, deciding that each set represented a number or word that coughed up the appropriate data. One key popped up a picture of a long, empty room on the screen.

"Where's this?" he wondered aloud. From behind, Egad jumped up and peered over his shoulder.

"Not far. Back way we came."

"You recognize it?"

"Outside place that smells like home."

Walden assimilated this information. He saw now that the dog was right. Two of the doorways carried symbols he remembered and he had purposefully marked the door leading into the laboratory. He chewed on his lower lip as he thought hard. Why would the Frinn monitor this hallway? Because an alien invader had so recently been there?

"He's gone back to the lab." Walden looked helplessly at the console. He might spend hours finding the controls that brought up different camera views.

He shot from the ill-fitting contour chair and raced back in the direction of the lab. Laserifle ready, he swung around and startled the Frinn working at the lab bench.

"Don't move or I'll cut you in half," he said, the laserifle's red sighting dot squarely centered on the alien's midriff. Walden almost swore in frustration. Ordering an alien not to move in English was absurd.

"You have no need to kill me," the Frinn answered. He spread his hands and bent forward at an awkward angle. His pig snout wiggled and his tiny eyes squinted even more. Walden saw a faint flush cross the bare scalp. The Frinn lifted his arms and held them directly out from his sides.

"Different smells," piped up Egad. "Funny smells. Pig-Frinn surrendering."

"You can scent his submission?"

"Yes. Strong odors now. Glands at work under pig-Frinn's arms. Others on backside confuse me. Pig-Frinn farts for no reason."

Walden sniffed and failed to detect any of the richness of communication Egad relayed to him. All he saw was a porcine creature standing in an ungainly position.

Then it hit him.

"You spoke English!"

"We have studied you for some time," the Frinn said, not moving from his position.

"Still giving up. Still submissive."

"Relax," Walden said uneasily. "You don't have to balance on your toes like that." He became flustered. From his autopsies he knew the Frinn didn't have toes. They had a pliable plate that failed to be a cloven hoof, yet wasn't differentiated into toes.

The Frinn rocked back and lowered his body, keeping his legs bent at an angle Walden thought must be miserable. The Frinn showed no sign of discomfort. He slowly lowered his arms.

"He still gives up. No tricks. Honest pig-Frinn."

"Your pet speaks," the Frinn said, more interested in Egad than in being held prisoner. "We did not know this was possible. None of the four-legged creatures on your colony world spoke in such a clear and intelligent manner."

"Egad's special," Walden said.

The dog thrust out his thin chest and held his head high. He trotted over to the Frinn and sniffed around the alien's feet. Then the dog flopped on the floor just in front of the Frinn. Walden had seen his dog do this before. It signaled trust in the person receiving the honor of his prone presence.

"Egad likes you," he said.

"I have never seen such a beast. Your records were most incomplete on your colony world."

"Schwann?"

The Frinn said something in his own language. He blinked,

his green and gold cat eyes widening. The severely sloping forehead gave the Frinn a look of complete confusion.

"I am sorry. I called the world by its proper name."

"Its Frinn name," said Walden.

"Yes. You call the colony Schwann? I never heard this while on the world."

"You were there?" Walden had a million questions to ask. "Did you leave after the world was destroyed—or were you on the first ship to leave the system?"

"The first. I heard only recently of the disaster that befell the world."

"The Infinity Plague," Walden said anxiously. "Have you isolated it?"

"You refer to the disease that claims so many of us? No, it is a mystery," came the sad answer. "Its progress is sporadic. I fear we have done little to contain it and much to spread it."

"I don't know much about it. How did you contract it? *Where* did you first become exposed?"

"On the world," the Frinn said, curious at the question. "Where else?"

"Which compound? I need to know if you got it from the NAA or the Sov-Lat Pact research station."

"I do not know these names. Do they refer to location?"

Walden found himself explaining political differences to the Frinn, who grew more agitated. "We learned nothing of this," the Frinn said, "while on the planet. Everyone spoke in this language. Does this imply we spoke with the NAA?"

Walden thought about it and shook his head. The Sov-Lats often used English as a compromise language when one group refused to speak Russian and the other Spanish. Among scientists from both factions of the Pact, English might be less of a loss of face than speaking the other's language.

The Frinn squatted down and reached out to tentatively touch Egad. The dog's ears lay back, then he barked. The tone was one Walden had heard often. Egad was welcoming a friend. Still, Walden was reluctant to part with his laserifle. The gengineered dog might have a new friend but Walden wasn't sure he did.

The Frinn had said he was on-planet when the Infinity

Plague broke out. He might have lost friends and family. This brought another question to mind.

"Where is everyone aboard this space station?" asked Walden. "I've hunted for hours and haven't found anyone but you."

The Frinn shrugged, a difficult task with its sloping shoulders. "Do you understand the gesture? It is your shrug," the Frinn said. "I mean to convey the message: I do not understand."

"Is Starlight always this deserted?"

"Starlight? This space station? Yes. We do not need great numbers. We prefer few."

"Privacy," said Walden. He experienced a rush of triumph. From the small clues available he had accurately guessed at a cultural trait of some significance.

"Exactly. We do not like to be around others. This has great benefit. The Infinity Plague, as you call it, has been held back because of minimal contact between ourselves."

"How many has it killed already?"

"More than half the crew of the *Profus*."

"Your ship?" Walden got a quick nod in reply. He heaved a sigh. Carefully putting his laserifle aside, he squatted down and looked at the Frinn over Egad's back. "We've got to work together on this problem. We didn't want to set the plague on you. I'm not even sure it was meant to be a weapon."

"Many of us died." The Frinn's voice remained neutral, but Egad twitched and his nose wrinkled.

"Great sorrow," the dog said. "He smells of loss."

"I lost many of my family," the Frinn said. "How is it your pet is able to know this and you, a civilized creature, do not?"

"Our senses are different. We don't have the capacity for telling one smell from another." Walden frowned. He wasn't telling this well. "Our noses aren't as sensitive."

"Your scent isn't as strong," corrected Egad. "Pig-Frinn has powerful odor."

"Don't . . ." Walden shook off the correction. He needed Egad to translate the alien's moods for him. Without some body language to help him, Walden couldn't read the alien's intentions. Egad could using the scent emanating from the alien.

"Why do you call us pig?" asked the Frinn. "We heard this several times among your kind on . . . on Schwann."

"You look like an Earthly animal we call a pig. It's one of the most intelligent creatures on our planet, second only to humans and dolphins."

"This pig is more intelligent than your pet?"

"Yes," Walden said. In ordinary circumstances this was true. In Egad's case, it wasn't but Walden didn't want to get into a long, involved discussion of why the gengineered dog was different. He had the sensation of time marching by more rapidly now—and the tramping of its temporal feet spelled destruction for them all.

"No one told us of this while on Schwann. We thought we knew your race well. We obviously knew little or nothing of your mores."

"Are you infected with the plague?"

"I do not know," the Frinn said. "I have worked to find out but know little of what to look for. Why do you create such dangerous diseases?"

Walden had no answer for this. Again, it would take long discussion to get the point across. That the Frinn had asked told Walden a great deal about the aliens.

"You don't fight wars, do you? Among yourselves or against other species."

"You are only the third alien race we have found," the Frinn said. "The other two were docile."

"I've got to know for certain. The fighting machines you used on Schwann and here in Starlight—"

The Frinn interrupted him with a question that told Walden everything he needed to know.

"What fighting machines?" the Frinn asked. "We use only repair units to defend ourselves from your curious, singularly unsociable acts toward us."

Walden closed his eyes and took a deep breath. It was as he feared. Earthmen declared war on a peaceful, non-warlike race who responded the best they could when attacked. Zacharias and Sorbatchin had used the most modern bioweapons and attack capabilities of humankind. The Frinn had used nothing more than repair robots to defend themselves.

Jerome Walden was not especially proud to belong to the human race at the moment.

CHAPTER
14

"Do you know if any humans are still alive?" Walden asked.

The Frinn shook his head in a very human gesture. "I do not examine such things closely. I work to study the disease and its spread. Neither is going well."

"We can supply information you're lacking about the Infinity Plague," said Walden. He hardly believed the chain of events that had led him to this point. The Infinity Plague hadn't been intended as a protection against Frinn invasion. It had been released accidentally; a careless worker might have done it. The plague had no obvious effect on humans. That contributed to carelessness.

The Frinn unluckily responded to the plague, either as it had been envisioned or through sheer bad luck.

"You use Starlight as a way station," Walden said. "Have ships gone to your home world that have been in contact with the plague?"

"Of course. We came and left quickly, to get those who had fallen ill during the trip here into more extensive medical facilities. I happened to stay long enough to see the report of the . . . surviving ship from your colony system."

"Will they quarantine the victims on your home world?"

"That is my hope. What the controllers do is something else." The Frinn stared at Walden with his catlike eyes until the scientist began to feel uncomfortable. He had no idea what ideas flowed through the alien brain.

Sensing his discomfort the Frinn turned back to Egad. The alien spoke rapidly, in a low voice that Walden couldn't overhear. The dog shook his head a few times and then barked loudly to punctuate a point. The alien was unimpressed with the responses, if Walden was able to judge the Frinn reaction.

He found that he wasn't.

"The dog values you highly. I trust his judgment in such matters, since I do not know you or your race well."

"You'd believe *him*?" The idea struck Walden as ludicrous, but he kept from laughing. He valued Egad's opinions, too, but Egad was only a dog.

"I have seen what your kind does to create weapons. We knew this world you called Schwann was not your home world, nor did any on it want your home world known. We are a curious people and took measures to locate your birthing planet."

"The sensors scattered throughout the Delta Cygnus system?"

"The passive detectors, yes," the Frinn said. "We will return some day and examine them and learn what you refuse to tell us."

Walden explained quickly how the *Hippocrates* and *Winston* had followed, not wanting to divulge Earth's location.

The Frinn gobbled like a turkey, then settled down and spoke with Egad again. After five minutes of earnest discussion, the Frinn said, "We cannot trust you. I barely know how to respond to your 'pet,' even though he is more honest than any of your race. Have you corrupted him? I think not."

"Thanks," Walden said dryly. He almost pointed out that the Frinn was the prisoner, then stopped. Earthmen had caused the problems and perpetuated them. Enmity had to stop and cooperation begin. If it didn't, the entire Frinn race might be wiped out. Zacharias might not care. He sought combat to enhance his own self-esteem and to win a few more medals to prove the Persephone campaign wasn't a fluke. Medals weren't handed out for meritorious service in diplomacy, especially to EPCT commanders.

"How can I contact the humans who invaded your space station?" asked Walden.

"I am your prisoner. I should not cooperate."

Walden considered all he'd heard, then spoke to his gen-gineered dog. "I want your opinion, Egad. Can the alien be trusted?"

"Pig-Frinn all right," Egad said. "He is not lying. He means what he says."

"I value his opinion, too," said Walden. He handed his laserifle to the alien. The Frinn took the weapon and stared at it for a few seconds. He lowered the muzzle until it covered Walden. The red sighting dot fixed on the man's chest.

"I can kill you."

"Yes." Walden tried not to panic. If he had made a bad decision—if Egad had misjudged the alien—he would die here and now. In a way that thought relieved him. He wouldn't have to cope with the spread of the Infinity Plague on the Frinn home world and the blood of billions of aliens wouldn't be on his hands. He had not developed the Infinity Plague himself, but that was only happenstance. He *might* have been the chief researcher.

Walden didn't want to think of the other projects he had led and the deadly results of each. He was good at his work. Maybe too damned good by far.

"I need only press this firing mechanism?"

"That one." Walden began to relax. The Frinn knew how to operate a laserifle. He saw it in the way the alien held the weapon.

"I have no need to slay you. This one, the one you call Egad, would be my friend. I would be his . . . and yours."

Walden thrust his hand out, then froze. He knew nothing of Frinn customs. This might be an invitation to a duel to the death rather than a sign of friendship. To his relief, the Frinn brushed his hand lightly over the outstretched fingers.

"We do not use this gesture, but I saw it on Schwann," the Frinn said.

"I'm Jerome Walden. You've already met Egad."

He waited for the usual response, but it did not come. The Frinn simply stared at him.

"Isn't it usual to exchange names on your world?"

Walden waited several seconds before the alien answered. "It is an affront to ask for that which is not freely given. We are a very private race."

"I guessed as much from the way Starlight is laid out and the compartment allocations on your starship."

At the mention of the ship, the alien hunkered down even more. "All hands were lost on the vessel?"

"Yes," Walden admitted reluctantly. "We have their bodies in a freezer to preserve them. I had to conduct autopsies on some to determine the Infinity Plague mechanism of infection and transmission."

"You were curious about an alien and wanted to cut one open," said the Frinn.

Egad barked and conversed with the alien. Walden started to order the dog to speak louder, to repeat all the alien said. He held back. He had to take the initiative now and show trust in the alien. He saw how the Frinn still clung to the laserifle.

"Our customs vary," said the Frinn. "You must excuse my behavior. I am not used to dealing with other races. That is a specialty of . . . others."

Walden said nothing. His gray eyes locked with the cat-slit green and gold eyes. The Frinn lowered the laserifle, then handed it back. Walden slung the heavy rifle over his shoulder and squatted beside dog and alien.

"We're got our work cut out for us. I've got two wounded EPCTs to care for. I can't reach the military leaders because of your jamming."

"Jamming?" The alien tried to shrug again. This time he didn't come nearly as close to succeeding, but Walden got the idea.

"You don't know about it? All transmission is damped." He showed the Frinn by trying to communicate with Zacharias. Over his headphones came nothing but static.

"We do not do this. Not intentionally. I am a specialist in biochemistry."

"It's beyond me. I'm a biologist. I saw your experiment. What are you trying to track down with the segmented worms?"

"You know the technique? It is new to us. We could not bring our research specimens to Starlight and required a way of testing for toxicity that would not—" The Frinn cut off his words when Egad leaped to his feet and raced to the doorway. The dog thrust his head outside and ducked back immediately. Hot waves of destruction from a laserifle boiled along the corridor.

"What the—" Walden grabbed for the laserifle, but the Frinn had his hand on it. Walden shucked out of the shoulder strap and left the Frinn holding the weapon when he went to see what went on outside the lab.

"No smell," came Egad's appraisal. "Hot. Boiling hot all over the walls and floor."

Walden tried to tune his com unit better and failed to pick up any chatter between soldiers outside. He swallowed hard. He might be fried by his own side. There didn't seem to be any good way of signaling that he was a human and didn't want to fight.

"Is there any white cloth in the lab?" Walden asked. "We can use it to signal a truce."

The Frinn hunted and found a strip of white plastic. Walden didn't know if it would suffice, but he had to try. He put it on the end of a pair of tongs and dangled it out the door.

He recoiled when the laser blast vaporized it.

"We won't get out this way," he said. "Is there another way out of the lab? If we can't face this guy, we're not going to convince him we're not the enemy."

"You cannot communicate with him?" asked the Frinn. "This static is truly interfering with your unit?"

Walden nodded. He wished he could risk Egad to dash out. The EPCTs knew the dog on sight and wouldn't mistake him for a Frinn. The way the EPCT fired at anything that moved told Walden the man might be injured and frightened—or just following Zacharias' orders. Being out of touch so long put him at a disadvantage. He had no idea what had happened in other parts of Starlight.

"How many are there, Egad?"

"No way to tell. No smell from combat suits. No sounds to tell me, either. Very quiet, very dangerous for me."

"I know, old boy." Walden patted the dog even as he studied the laboratory. He saw no easy way out, except into the corridor where only death awaited him.

"Is this what you seek?" asked the Frinn. He opened a small door recessed in the wall to expose a dark cavity. "It is a direct vacuum link to the landing area."

"This goes to the docking bay?" Walden stuck his head

in and saw nothing but Stygian darkness. Fumbling around revealed a chamber less than a meter in length. "Is there a carrier or tube you use?"

"Cargo is sent directly here. This is an airlock. A simple platform is pulled along by the air pressure differential. Can you use it to escape?"

"Would you try it?" Walden asked the alien. The pig-snouted creature was taken back.

"It never occurred to me to flee. This is my laboratory. I will stay here and defend it."

"The entire space station is yours. No need to make your stand here when another place might do even better." Walden could fit into the small chamber. It would be painful, and Egad would have to follow on his own, but it could be done.

"What other use is there for this?" asked Egad.

"Trash disposal. I place any waste I want evacuated into space or thrown into a plasma torch into this compartment," said the Frinn. "There is nothing to fear. It is not directly linked to the torch. Material from this tube is deposited on a work level for robots to tend to."

Another roar of laserifle fire came in the corridor. This prompted Walden into action.

"We've got to go. We don't dare fight our own side. Nobody wins if we do. Better to get the hell out of here and try contacting them in some other way—some way where we can reach each other visually rather than relying on our com units."

"What will you do once you have arrived below?" asked the Frinn. "Will not your problems be the same?"

"Maybe they will. We'll be on the other side of them, though. That might be good enough to get us in touch with Major Zacharias."

"He is your leader?"

"He thinks he is," Walden said. He climbed into the small compartment. He wasn't claustrophobic; no one used to traveling between the stars through liftspace was. This didn't stop him from closing his eyes for a second and taking a deep, calming breath. He convinced himself the walls were not collapsing around him.

Checking his hazard suit, he gave Egad a thumbs-up gesture.

The door closed and plunged him into complete darkness. Walden sucked in an especially deep breath, trying to forget the sensation of suffocation assailing him. He shrieked in terror when the floor to his world fell away and he descended into a lightless void.

Wind whistling startled him. He shouldn't hear any such noise—unless his suit was leaking his precious air into vacuum. Twisting his head around, he got a readout display to show. He was losing air at an alarming rate from a hole on his chest. Walden tried to clutch his chest where the heat drill had punctured his hazard suit. The narrow walls prevented him from raising his hands past his hips.

He may have screamed. He never knew. Blood trickled from his nose and eyes, and his eyes felt as if they would blast from his head. Then Walden forgot his increasing asphyxia. He crashed hard into a floor. The impact sent a shock wave rolling up from his feet, through his knees and thighs and into his body. A giant hand crushed down on him and threatened to squeeze out the last of his consciousness.

He hung onto the thin thread of his sensibilities long enough to spin slowly and find a single pale yellow light on the wall. He bent toward it and fell heavily onto a floor littered with debris.

He had found Starlight's refuse bins.

Still holding his chest, he checked the air levels and found that he had returned to full pressure. He popped up the visor and sucked in stale, fetid air. To Walden it smelled sweeter than the freshest Earthly spring breeze.

Sitting cross-legged on the floor, he did what should have been done before. He checked the damage to his hazard suit and found the melted areas where the heat drill had blistered and corrupted the tough plastic front. Walden knew how lucky he had been. Another few seconds in the vacuum tube and he would have been dead.

A loud beeping forced him away from lingering over the nearness of his brush with death. The indicator light above the door flashed its pale yellow, signaling another arrival. He opened the door and out jumped Egad. It took only a second to get the dog's helmet free and allow him to speak.

"Fun trip," the gengineered dog said. "But I don't like dark. It scares me."

"It scared me, too," Walden said. He didn't bother going into details. He patted the dog, then asked, "Is the Frinn going to follow us?"

"No suit," the dog said. "He relies on us to save him by biting man who fires at him."

"The Frinn said that?" In spite of the seriousness of the situation, Walden was amused by the dog's interpretation of how to save the alien.

The dog looked confused, as if he couldn't remember exactly what had been said or by whom. Walden scratched the dog's ears and then began looking around the refuse docks for a way out. It took ten minutes for Egad to find the way out. When Walden followed he immediately recognized the landing area where he, Zacharias, and the EPCT squad had entered Starlight.

"All the way back," he said. "I don't know how to get back to where we were. It's a long ways off. I wish I had an inertial tracker like the EPCTs."

"I can find way in a hurry," Egad said.

"You remember the way? Fantastic. Let's go. And keep alert for patrolling EPCTs. We don't want them shooting us before we can identify ourselves."

"Why?" asked Egad. "This is easy way. Pig-Frinn told me about it while you came down shaft."

The dog trotted to a brightly colored wall decoration and pressed his nose against it. Walden reached for the laserifle, only to remember that he had left it with the Frinn in the laboratory. The wall panel changed color and slowly disappeared as if it were nothing but mist evaporating in the morning sun.

Egad jumped inside, turned around three times, and curled up in the back corner. He waited patiently for his master to follow.

Walden stuck his head into the small room. Controls beside the door on the inside told him this must be an elevator. He wondered why he hadn't looked for one earlier. He had been so busy stalking up and down Starlight's corridors that it had never occurred to him to look for anything like this.

"How do you run it?"

Egad replied, "Pig-Frinn did not say. You build machines. You run it. How hard can it be?"

"How hard, indeed," said Walden. He studied the panel until he thought he had an idea what the controls did. He stuck out a tentative finger and pressed the large green button. The door solidified. A low, indirect light came up inside the room. He heaved a sigh of thanks for this. He had no desire to be tumbling down shafts in pitch-darkness again, with or without an adequate air supply.

A few more minutes of fiddling got the elevator cage moving. He had no idea of the coordinates to send the cage. From the jerky motion, the elevator moved sideways as well as up and down in the space station. Trusting that the upper buttons on the panel moved the elevator in that direction, he punched until he thought he had accounted for about the distance into Starlight he had traveled originally from the docking bays.

The door popped open and Walden found himself in the middle of a cross-fire between EPCTs and two Frinn repair robots. The mechanisms thrashed about and used their welding torches as shields to rush the humans' battle line.

"Stop!" Walden yelled. He had no idea if the robots would respond. The marines definitely did not. They concentrated fire on one robot and eventually melted its tracks under it. The welding torch flashed and flared as it cut through a wall. A tiny *pop!* sounded and the robot stopped functioning.

The instant the EPCTs had downed it, they turned their full fire on the other robot. It took only a few seconds of concentrated laser beaming to destroy it, too.

"Can you hear me?" Walden shouted, hoping his com unit could penetrate a few meters.

"That you, Doc?"

"Bonzo?"

"None other. We been looking for you all over this damned place. The sarge said you were running around loose. We found N'kruma and he told us what you did for him."

"What about the other soldier?"

"They zipped him back of the battle lines. If we can get a way off this death trap, they think he can get fixed up just fine on the old *Hippocrates.*"

"Where's Hecht?"

"Who the hell knows? We got split up hours ago. We been roaming in the gloaming trying to mop up. I'll hand it to the major, he's one efficient bastard. He kills anything that moves.''

"This is—" Walden stopped in midsentence. It did no good explaining to a squad leader that this was senseless slaughter and that the Frinn weren't the enemy. If anything, the aliens were the victims of chance and poor containment of what had become the Infinity Plague.

He changed his tack. "Can you find the same corridor where N'kruma was? I had him in a storeroom.''

"Sure, no bad orbits in this outfit.''

"You set your tracker?''

"A couple of us did. I've still got mine set for the landing bay. Say, what is this gadget? An elevator?''

Walden explained quickly what he had found, leaving out the part of Egad learning its existence from a Frinn.

"I'd take you back there, Doc, but there're other halls to check out. The major'll be fit to snit if we miss any of the pigs.''

"Just give me a tracker so I can get there. You need your full force here.''

"Good idea, but you aren't armed. You ought to pick up a laserifle somewhere. Hell, we'll all go with you. Let the major blow a gasket. It'll do him good to fret and sweat for a while.''

Walden tried to dissuade Bonzo, but the EPCT was adamant. They went up four more levels and turned in spirals that made Walden dizzy. If Egad hadn't assured him that they were still on track, he would have thought the soldiers were leading him on a wild goose chase.

"Hey, minimum-wager!'' Bonzo cried when they rounded a corner and saw an EPCT stretched out and using his laserifle. "What they paying you for? To burn photons by the kilo?''

"Bonzo! There's a pig down there. He's got a laserifle or I'd have rushed him by now.''

Walden stepped forward. "That's ridiculous. There's no Frinn here.'' Walden sidestepped Bonzo when the EPCT tried to stop him. He walked quickly down the corridor, his back itching. He knew the soldiers had their sights trained on him. If the Frinn burned him, they would fire directly through the space he had occupied and get the pig.

"Egad, go on ahead. Tell our friend there's nothing to fear—and tell him to hide until I can get rid of the soldiers."

The dog raced on, skidded in the doorway, and vanished inside. By the time Walden got there, the dog sat up, tongue lolling and looking innocent.

He didn't see the Frinn. He waved to Bonzo. The EPCT squad rushed in, laserifles ready for action. Before he could stop them, they fanned out and began a systematic search of the premises. He saw that he would have to do something quickly or they would begin opening doors and firing into corners.

"An empty lab. You do good work, soldier," Walden said sarcastically. He saw the effect on the EPCT who had been firing. The man shook with rage.

"Shit, I *know* there was a pig in here. I saw him!"

Walden turned to Bonzo and said softly, "Combat produces hallucinations, if there's not enough rest."

"Damned linear, Doc," agreed Bonzo. "Come on. Let's find pigs to roast. You coming, Doc?"

"This is a laboratory. I think I'll stay here and poke around. Set your tracker to return here."

"We can't com farther than a few meters. The static is still going like a nova."

"I'll be all right. Check back in a few hours. If I've moved on, I'll leave a note with instructions on where I've gone. Really, Bonzo, I'll be fine. Get back to your duty station."

"The major will slice and dice us if he finds we came up here. You're all right, Doc, no matter what the major says about you." With that the EPCTs left.

Walden waited until the vibration of their footsteps had died out. He asked Egad, "Where is he?"

The dog looked directly at a small compartment door. Walden opened the door. Curled up inside was the Frinn. The alien pointed the laserifle up. When he saw who had discovered his hiding place, he moved the weapon's muzzle away and stood.

"They're gone," Walden said.

"Thank you," the Frinn said. "My name is Uvallae."

It took Walden a moment to realize the import of what the Frinn had said.

"Thank *you*, Uvallae."

Jerome Walden had taken a big step toward the cooperation that would stop the spread of the Infinity Plague.

CHAPTER
15

"There's no way we can get to the control center?" asked Jerome Walden. He frowned as he pored over the readouts Uvallae had called up for him on the space station's computer. The major portion of the schematic was marked as storage or relegated to robot use; only a small section of Starlight had been allocated for living beings. Everywhere he looked in this section trailed red lines indicating EPCTs bent on killing any Frinn they found. Walden might not have liked Zacharias but he had to admit the man had done a fine job of dissecting Starlight. He had unerringly found the principal arteries and cut them.

"He will not reduce power," Uvallae said. "To do so means complete loss of internal atmosphere and gravity."

"How did you arrange the docking bay airlock?" asked Walden. "There weren't any doors that I saw. The blast baffles were in place, but they weren't airtight."

Uvallae shrugged. "I do not know. That is an engineering problem. I work only in biology."

Walden nodded. He understood this problem well. He had run up against physics problems that perplexed him only to be told they were simply solved—by a physicist. There was too much to know and never enough time to learn the skills properly.

126

"Can we use the elevators to reach the control center? We need to know how many of your people are still alive." The words almost choked Walden. Zacharias had been damned efficient. How many Frinn had he slaughtered? Walden changed that to "needlessly slaughtered" since the aliens were not the enemy.

He held back a bitter laugh. From all he had seen, there weren't any enemies and never had been. What the Frinn had done to Schwann must have been in reaction to being infected with the Infinity Plague. And the NAA researchers—or had it been the Sov-Lats?—had never intended it to be a weapon against the aliens. It had just gotten free and unpredictably started the deadly plague.

"You can get through his lines," pointed out Uvallae. "This major will not kill someone of your standing."

Walden laughed at this, too. How could he ever explain that the problems between him and Edouard Zacharias had little to do with logical or even political considerations?

"I don't want to try it. Many of the EPCTs recognize me and wouldn't shoot. Even more know Egad." He looked to where the dog lay sleeping on the floor. The gengineered animal had found this a good time to nap. Walden wished he shared the dog's ability to simply drop off to sleep in the middle of such confusion.

"You are a strange race. You imply this Zacharias would slay you, yet you are on the same side in this issue." Uvallae scratched his severely sloping forehead with both hands in a gesture Walden thought was peculiar.

"There are other considerations," Walden said. "How can we reach the control center—and would we even try?"

"Your Major Zacharias has not taken it. There are indications, even though there is no direct link." Uvallae called up a series of colored lines that looked like spastic worms wiggling across the screen. Walden had no idea what the Frinn saw in them; they did not appear to be writing as much as they were warnings or indicators.

Egad snorted and moved in his sleep. Walden considered sending the dog with a message for the Frinn in the control center, then decided against it. They had no reason to trust Egad. Uvallae and the dog had forged a strange bond of friendship, not Egad and the rest of the Frinn leaders.

"We can convince the controllers to cease resistance, if you can communicate with your Zacharias not to slay them out of hand."

"Turning off the repair robots would go a long way toward convincing the EPCTs that you were friendly," agreed Walden. Somehow he would have to reach Zacharias and tell him to stop fighting. Making it appear that the major had won and the Frinn had surrendered, without either actually occurring, presented Walden with a huge problem in diplomacy.

He smiled crookedly. He was up to it. He had nursed along wounded egos in his research team and induced even better work from his scientists. Zacharias was no different from a biochemist who believed a colleague was stealing his results or a gengineer insisting that his name be listed as primary researcher on an important paper.

First, he had to get the repair robots turned off. With no one to shoot at, the marines might be more amenable to talk. Then he could broach the subject of cooperation with Zacharias.

"We are effectively stopped when we reach level seven," Uvallae said. "Patrols along the intersecting corridors prevent us from reaching the control room."

"Elevators? Can we get past them that way?" Walden wanted the conference with the Frinn leaders behind him as quickly as possible. Too many had died already on Starlight. The real work had to begin soon. The Infinity Plague spread from this space station to the Frinn home world. They had so little time to prevent an entire race from dying through—what did he call it? Negligence? That was the only word he had and it burned in his guts.

He waited for an entire sentient race to be snuffed out because of one careless moment in a bloweapons research facility that ought to have been more careful.

Even worse, it was *his* facility that caused it. Walden wasn't sure if he wouldn't have gloated just a little if the Sov-Lats had been responsible, but the result was the same no matter who had done it. The Frinn died for no reason. He needed time to examine Uvallae and see why he had not succumbed—or if the plague was in initial stages in the Frinn's body.

"They have posted guards to cover the elevators leading

to the upper levels. I am startled at their efficiency. They had not known of the elevators until you told them. Now they successfully prevent our free movement inside the station."

Egad yawned and stretched. One blue eye peered up at Walden. He disliked the idea, but he had to send the dog out on this mission. Zacharias wouldn't listen to Egad. Would the Frinn leaders in their control center?

"Are you up for a little jaunt, Egad?"

"Go to find cat shit Zacharias?" the dog asked. "Can I bite him?"

"No!" Walden calmed himself. The dog was reacting to the situation in the only way he knew how. It was counter-productive to bite Zacharias, as much as the idea appealed to both the dog and his master. "You've got to take a message to the Frinn in their control room. Uvallae will tell you how to get there and give you the message."

"What am I to say in this message?" the Frinn asked. "I have no power with the government agents controlling the space station. In scientific matters they defer to me, but in no other. I am less than a repair robot to them in this matter."

"Too many things have to be done simultaneously," worried Walden. "Let's get to your leaders and take it from there. We'll make them listen. We have to. They have to, if they want help countering the Infinity Plague." The man stopped and considered his own dilemma. If *he* contacted the Frinn, they might take him prisoner—or worse. He was their enemy and Zacharias had shown remarkable skill in deci-mating Starlight's living population.

"How do I go?" asked Egad. "Can't get past those."

"What are they?" Walden asked Uvallae, pointing to the green squiggles on the computer screen. He had no idea how Egad knew their interpretation.

"Robots. My leaders seek to stop your major from reach-ing higher levels by concentrating the repair workers in areas near the control room. Egad is correct. Getting past so many robots is impossible without destroying them."

"There's a way past," Walden said, his brain racing. This wasn't like a building on Earth. A space station had facilities that differed greatly—and had aspects that couldn't be touched on a planetary surface.

Egad barked and got to his bandy legs. The misshapen dog

stuck his head out the door and said, "Soldiers. I hear their footsteps. Go and fetch them?"

"No," said Walden. "We're going to the control room. Fetch a working cutting torch from a damaged robot," he ordered the dog. Egad dashed off, wobbling on his short legs as he ran. To Uvallae, he said, "How do we identify the control room from the outside?"

"Outside?"

"The hull of the space station. We cut through a window at the end of the corridor, get onto the outer surface, and make our way to the control room. We look in the window, you show yourself, and then we figure out how to get inside from there. Unless your design is different than ours would be, there must be an airlock nearby."

"I know of none. As you pointed out, we do not use the same type of locks that you do. Not on a space station," said Uvallae. "But there might be an emergency repair airlock."

"Let's hope so. Do you have a spacesuit?"

"No, but there might be emergency ones stored down a level and near the elevators." The Frinn looked confused. "We have little use for such things aboard this space station. Starlight is . . . safe. The thought of losing atmospheric pressure is awful." Uvallae shook all over and ran his hands over the pebbly skin on his forehead, repeating the gesture Walden had thought so peculiar.

"We can't leave you," Walden said. "That wouldn't be right. Besides, the EPCTs might stumble on you." He looked apprehensively out the doorway and worried that a soldier might poke inside at any instant. Egad had heard someone outside; so had Walden. That meant the marine—or marines—outside had little fear of being overheard or detected as they prowled.

"I can convince the leaders if I can speak with them," Uvallae said. His pig snout wiggled as he sat and thought. Walden's nose wrinkled. He took an involuntary step away from the alien. An overpowering odor rose from the Frinn.

"Let's reconnoiter," said Walden, looking for an excuse to lower his visor and sample the stale air inside his hazard suit. Walden recovered his laserifle and checked it. The weapon had fully charged in his absence. He might need it to reenter Starlight.

He stepped into the hall and was hit in the chest by a purple bolt of laser fire. Stumbling back, more startled than injured, he stared at the center of his chest. The heat drill had damaged his hazard suit; the laserifle fire had left a smoking hole.

"Stop it!" he shouted, wiggling his chin and turning his head to push up the volume on his com unit. "I'm Dr. Walden!"

Only crackling static greeted him. A second bolt of laser energy rippled down the hallway. The energy level was so low the beam sputtered out and left only a shimmery haze behind. The laserifle had run out of power.

Walden took the chance of stepping around and revealing himself to the EPCT. The soldier worked diligently on his laserifle. The snap and flare of a corona discharge around the muzzle told Walden that another attack would carry far much punch and would be a thousand times as deadly.

"Stop!" He waved his arms to attract the soldier's attention, to make him *look* at his target. Walden knew he had failed when the laserifle came up and the red sighting dot pinpointed his chest. A quick spin to the right got him out of the direct beam before the soldier fired.

Walden wasn't even aware of slamming hard into the wall across the corridor, sliding down it, and then bringing his own laserifle up. He fired without knowing he did it. The ravening beam caught the EPCT squarely. Walden yanked his hand off the firing stud the instant he realized what was happening.

He dropped the rifle and rushed to the marine's aid. A quick check of the readouts showed he was too late. Walden opened the helmet and stared at the dead man.

"What the hell is going on?" he asked aloud.

"Know him. He knows you. Why did he try to shoot you?" asked Egad, looking over Walden's shoulder.

"I haven't the slightest idea," Walden said. "He just stood in the open. He hadn't properly tended to his laserifle or he would have fried me with the first shot." He touched the controls on the vital signs readout and froze the information for later retrieval. He wanted to find out why someone he knew had tried to murder him.

Heat of battle was one thing. Such sloppiness wasn't usual in Extra-Planetary Combat Teams.

"Master, look." Egad nudged him until he lifted his gaze from the fallen soldier to the corridor behind. Four EPCTs lay stacked in a neat pile against the wall. Each had been killed with a blast from a laserifle.

"What's going on?" demanded Walden. "If I didn't know better, I'd think he had killed them."

"He must have. All have laserifle burns." Egad sniffed at the burns and looked up, his brown and blue eyes unblinking. "Smells like laserifle."

"Damn."

"Gone crazy, kills friends," said Egad. He continued sniffing around while Walden stewed. He had no reason to doubt the dog's evaluation. But why had a highly trained EPCT done this to his teammates?

He pushed the problem from his mind and examined the bodies. Stripping them of their combat gear, he pieced together two complete units. He fit into one well. The other would have to do for Uvallae, even if the Frinn's body wasn't designed for a human spacesuit.

"Let's get out of here," Walden said. His gorge rose every time he looked at the dead men. Focusing on what he had to do helped—but not much.

"I cannot wear this," said Uvallae, holding the combat gear at arm's length.

"We're not at war. You won't be shot as a spy," Walden said, misinterpreting what the alien meant. "Either of us is as likely to be shot by our own side as the other."

"The smell is intense. I can barely stand being near you."

Walden started to retort that the Frinn's body odor was extreme, too, then stopped. "We don't have much choice, do we?" he answered instead. "Can you stand it for a little while?"

"Strong smell," agreed Egad. "Why not use coverup?"

"A good idea. Do you have any chemicals in your lab that will mask the human scent? Or kill your own sense of smell?"

"Not that!" Uvallae's outrage at destroying, even temporarily, his own sense of smell was real. "I am sorry. It is like asking you to blind yourself."

"I understand. Do what you can. We can try to find those emergency suits . . ."

"I will force myself to use this," Uvallae said with great

dignity. He worked at his chemical cabinet for several minutes, pouring various concoctions into the suit and then rinsing it out. Walden knew this wouldn't work. The suit's inside had been made of a spongy material that trapped perspiration, acted as heat exchanger, and added to body protection from external trauma. The complex circuitry wouldn't easily be defeated, either.

Uvallae climbed into the suit, doubling up in ways Walden found startling. He hated himself for thinking of the alien as a true piglike creature. Uvallae had no direct ancestor with Earthly pigs. He had no direct link with Earth.

"I can survive for a time," Uvallae said, shaking himself into the combat gear. "I will be unable to carry anything heavy, however. I am unable to get my leg muscles under my body properly."

Walden saw the difficulty Uvallae had in walking. He patted him on the shoulder. "We'll get by. This won't take too long. One way or the other." Walden knew his initial enthusiasm for this scheme had been misplaced. Dressed as EPCT marines, they might be shot at instantly by the Frinn defending Starlight. With EPCTs killing their own men, they might be lasered by either side.

They hurried to the room with the expansive windows. Egad dragged along a cutting torch he had taken from the damaged Frinn repair robot. Walden turned on the torch, made sure his and the others' suits were airtight, then applied the torch beam to the glasteel. The clear material turned milky, then began to flow under the hungry tongue of the cutting laser. Cracks began radiating out from the center; they spread as air pressure popped the core out.

Walden slammed hard against the window as the air rushed from the room. Emergency doors closed behind them to limit air loss. Dozens of tiny robots scampered from the walls to repair the leak in the hull. Walden found himself working to cut a hole faster than the robots could repair it.

"Ambitious buggers, aren't they?" he muttered.

"I do not understand. Is this an idiomatic expression?" asked Uvallae. When Walden didn't answer, the Frinn turned to Egad. The two conversed for some time while Walden struggled with enlarging the hole in the window.

"Never mind that," he said. "Get outside. The combat

suits have both magnetic and adhesion soles. What's the outer hull made of?" Walden helped Uvallae through. Egad jumped up and hung suspended, half in and half out. Walden booted the dog through. The animal's hazard suit lacked the sophisticated traction gear. Simple ropes fastening him to both the Frinn and his master would have to suffice.

"I do not know," Uvallae said. "This is another matter outside my field of expertise."

Walden tumbled through and clung to the edge of the glasteel window for a moment. He got his feet under him, found that the adhesion setting worked better than magnetic, and pulled his hand free in time to keep it from being sealed up in the window by the scurrying repair robots.

He tested his footing and found it adequate for walking slowly. After securing Egad to his belt with a short rope, Walden tried the com unit. He hadn't fitted it properly to Uvallae, but the unit worked well enough for their purposes.

"The interference is just as bad out here," he said.

"I can barely hear you," came back Uvallae's response. Walden walked closer and banged helmets together. "We go in that direction," the Frinn shouted. The contact allowed sound conduction between the helmets.

"Walk slowly," Walden cautioned. "Plant your foot securely before lifting the other. There's no rush. We have all the time we need."

"I understand," came Uvallae's reply.

Egad kept tugging at the rope. He wasn't used to a leash and didn't appreciate this. Walden tried to contact the dog but the interference drowned out any chance of talking with him. The dog's suit wasn't designed for external work and his feet kept slipping off Starlight's slick surface.

Only when Egad got to the field of circular glass cells did the going get easier for him. Walden moved to press his helmet against Uvallae's.

"What are these?" he asked. "They're what made us give the name Starlight to your space station."

"Homing beacons. Our ships lock onto cells radiating at different frequencies. We can guide as many as a thousand ships at a time using this system."

Walden saw the complex of circuitry underneath. The Frinn ships must use a negative feedback recognition system, he decided. The incoming vessel sent out a beam, it went through the cells and radiated back a guidance beam. The full duplex system allowed constant contact between station and approaching vessel.

They walked across the field of cells until Walden's leg started to cramp. The movement of picking his feet up squarely and then making certain he was securely fastened to the surface tired him more quickly than he had anticipated. He motioned for Uvallae to stop.

"Rest," he panted. "I need to rest. Getting hot. Sweaty. Hard to catch my breath." He looked back where they had been and ahead where they were headed. Something nagged at him, something he had overlooked. He was so tired—too tired to think straight.

Egad bounced around, tugging at the rope and making a nuisance of himself. All Walden wanted to do was sit and stare at the brilliant stars above. He thought they had chosen well their spot to leave Starlight's interior. This side of the space station faced away from the primary. They didn't have to worry about hard radiation from the nearby star. Even better, his view of the firmament wasn't ruined by the star's brilliance.

"Move. Keep moving," the dog urged. Again came the annoying tug. Walden almost cut the dog free. Only Uvallae's hand on his wrist prevented it.

The alien bumped helmets. "We must do as our friend suggests. Let us hurry to find our way to the top of the space station."

"Top? What top? There's no up or down in space. There's nothing but pretty stars. Look at them. Aren't they the prettiest sight you've ever seen? But the space isn't really black. More a purple. Maybe that's the helmet visor. Different from mine. Had to abandon my hazard suit. It had holes in it."

"We must go."

"In a minute. Let me rest. So tired." All Walden wanted to do was talk, to rest, to enjoy the lovely airless sky.

A suspicion nagged at him. Airless. He had a suit. Why airless? He didn't hear any hissing of escaping gas. He had a fine EPCT combat suit on. They didn't leak. They wouldn't dare leak.

Uvallae jerked hard on his arm and got him moving. Egad bounded up and crashed his helmet against Walden's.

"No air, master. You're not breathing. Readouts show no air."

"I've got all the air I need," Walden said. He moved at a dizzying pace. He raced along. He just couldn't figure why the dog and the Frinn kept ahead of him so easily.

"Tired," he said. "Let me rest again. Sticky stuff on my boot soles is holding me back."

"No, Walden," said Uvallae. "There is no oxygen circulation in your suit. Something has been damaged."

"I tested it before I left." He hesitated. He *had* checked it. He remembered. Or had he? Everything had been so rushed. What had he missed? Something, he knew, but what? He wobbled but Uvallae held him erect. There wasn't far to fall. Starlight's shiny exterior was only an arm's length away.

But the stars! To fall to infinity!

Walden tried to take that route. To the stars. To the wondrous stars above.

CHAPTER
16

"Go 'way. Wanna be alone." Jerome Walden tried to fight off the legions of annoying demons. He fought and kicked and tried to scream. The words jumbled in his dried throat. Eyes barely focusing, he looked up and saw Egad. He tried to pat his dog but something went wrong. His hand slapped hard against the gengineered dog's head, driving him back.

"No, come here," he mumbled. He had a curious sensation of floating above his body, away from, separate from the pain and confusion he experienced so strongly.

"Master still not right," came the dog's appraisal.

"I'm all right. What's wrong with *you*?" Walden tried to sit up and found he lacked the strength. Part of him worried about this. The other part, the part floating somewhere beyond his reach, thought it was funny. He heard laughter and finally recognized it as his own.

"Do all humans react to death this way?" came a strange, gravelly voice. The pitch was lower than normal. What was normal? Walden tried to put everything together and failed.

"No air. Not dead. Just a bad suit. He is getting careless," said Egad.

The dog's words snapped him back. He sucked in deep breaths and rode out the giddiness this produced. His vision cleared and he found himself reunited. No longer were there

137

two of him. Both parts functioned now—and both hurt like hell.

"The suit," he croaked out. "There wasn't any air flow. I was living off oxygen trapped in the HEM. The heat exchange membrane released it slowly enough so I didn't feel any discomfort until we'd been outside and exercising hard."

"Never did like exercise," Egad grumbled. "This proves badness for you."

"Where are we?" Walden looked around, expecting to see Starlight's control room. The walls were lined with storage cabinets and the floors had a curious cross-hatching pattern on them.

"We entered the first room available. I am unsure about this room's function. The floors indicate drainage was required. I have not had a chance to explore." Uvallae walked around, arms extended to shoulder height. Walden guessed that the alien either was sniffing at the room or leaving his own scent marker.

"That's all right. We've got to get to Starlight's control room. We've got to talk to your people so I can get to Zacharias and stop him and—"

The words cut off suddenly. He had been oxygen-starved longer than he had thought. He had convinced Uvallae and Egad to walk on Starlight's hull all the way to the control room. If the control center was perched at the nominal "top" of the space station, that was a hike of more than two thousand kilometers.

Walden tried to stand, only to find Egad working against him. The heavy dog bumped behind his knees and forced him to sit down heavily. He started to scold the animal.

"Stay," Egad said firmly.

"You are weak," added Uvallae.

"We can't wait around," Walden said, not wanting to agree with them. He knew he could make it. He had to. If a truce wasn't declared soon, Zacharias would wipe out the Frinn. Walden had seen enough to know their peaceful nature couldn't contend with the EPCT major's drive to conquer and win some measure of self-respect in the process. They fought skill and combat-proven weapons with repair robots.

"We do not wish to risk your life," explained Uvallae. "You seem incapable of making rational decisions."

"I'm fine." Walden's mind raced. Outside was still a good way to reach the control room. They could jet around the space station. It might take far longer than he had originally, and mistakenly, thought but it was better than walking. "Let's get back outside and get to it. We've got to do it differently, though. We can . . ."

"Can't," said Egad. "No way to cut through glasteel. Window all fixed by cat shit robots."

Walden glanced up at the clear window looking at the infinity he had wanted to sail into. No hint of crack or break existed. He didn't see the scuttling spidery robots, either. They had already done their work and returned to their niches in the walls.

"The laserifle. We can use it—" He broke off and looked around in panic. The weapon had vanished.

"The rifle burned out when we used it to cut back through into the space station when your distress became apparent," said Uvallae. "It was discarded as useless."

Walden looked to Egad for confirmation. The dog bobbed his shaggy head up and down.

"We don't need it," he said forcefully, more to convince himself than the others. "We can find another way out and still get back in. The emergency airlock you mentioned. It's close to the control room. We can use it."

"Will you risk your life again?" asked Uvallae. "Your suit does not work. I have no way of causing the repair robots to work on it. Can you hold your breath so long?"

Walden knew he couldn't. If the air system had failed on an EPCT combat suit, serious repair work was needed to fix it. The suits had been designed to take incredible punishment and allow their wearers to survive.

He stripped off the damaged combat gear and left it on the floor. If it wouldn't protect him and furnish oxygen when he needed it, he saw no reason to lug its weight around.

"Can you still use your com unit?" asked Uvallae.

"I detached it, but I don't know what good it is. Are you sure the interference isn't your doing—your commander's doing?"

"There is no reason to jam our own frequencies," Uvallae said. "We are as hindered as you by this."

Walden doubted that. The Frinn were on known territory.

They could dispatch their robots and have a good idea what would happen. The EPCT had to blunder along, fighting as they went.

"I'm going to be fine," he told his two friends. "This isn't false bravado speaking. We *have* to get a truce soon or nobody's going to leave Starlight alive."

"That is so," mused Uvallae. The Frinn made his odd gesture of rubbing his forehead with both hands. "You can eradicate my kind; once set into motion the repair robots will continue to hunt your soldiers until they are dead. There is no way to disable all our repair machines before you run out of men."

Walden remembered how he had gotten the suits to make the foray along Starlight's outer hull. Why had the EPCT killed his comrades-in-arms? It made no sense, yet it happened. Events moved too swiftly for him to understand. He had to establish the cease-fire before anything else. That he knew. That he could do.

He hoped.

"The control center. We've come a ways up in Starlight. We might be behind your lines, ahead of Zacharias. Let's try to get to the control center by elevator." Only by such single-mindedness could Walden prevail. Everything jumbled in his head. Zacharias. Anita. The Infinity Plague. The combat inside Starlight. Even the interference over the com units struck him as odd. He had to believe Uvallae when the Frinn said they weren't responsible. Then who was?

Uvallae stepped from the storage room and studied the corridor beyond. For several seconds he shifted weight from foot to foot. He finally gestured for Walden to join him. The scientist forced himself to walk with a steady gait. His bout with hypoxia had left him weaker than he cared to admit.

"There is a com unit in the wall," said Uvallae. "We can reach the controllers through it."

"It's hard-wired?"

Uvallae stared at him without comprehension.

"The unit uses foptics? Fiber optic cables?"

"I do not know. It just . . . is." Uvallae went to the device and pressed his snout against the acceptor plate. Walden stepped away when the alien exuded a powerful stench that almost choked him. Egad pushed past Walden, nose working overtime. The gengineered canine sniffed and finally got the pheromone message straight in his mind. He dropped beside his master, head on his tiny paws and eyes watching as Uvallae called his superiors.

The Frinn began grunting and cackling, more like a chicken than a pig. When he flapped his arms, the smell almost overwhelmed Walden. There was no denying the intensity of Uvallae's emotion. Curious, Walden edged closer, breathing in shallow pants to avoid being knocked out by the alien's body odor.

He nodded when he got a clearer look at the com unit. He wouldn't call it a vidscreen with visuals as much as he would a surface acoustic wave detector similar to the SAW-dets used by the EPCTs. Whoever received Uvallae's message knew without question the identity of the speaker and how agitated he was.

An idle thought crossed Walden's mind. Was there ever a case of mistaken identity among the Frinn? Did their scent patterns form a unique identifying characteristic, as well as a clue to the emotional state?

"The controller is upset at my friendship with an enemy creature," Uvallae said. "I have tried to pacify him. I have failed. He promises the direst consequences for me when I present myself for his judgment and punishment."

"He's acting as judge, jury, and executioner," muttered Walden. He had feared this might happen. During war, even the least competent assumed positions of command. Small men rose to great heights, until their ineptitude caught up with them. He shouldn't expect any less in Frinn circles.

"Let me talk to him. I can—"

"He will not deal with an enemy," Uvallae said. "In addition, there is no easy way for you to use this com unit. It communicates in ways other than pictures."

"I know," said Walden. "It relays odor as well as picture." Uvallae's bony ridges rose in surprise that Walden had figured out the device so easily. "Can't he take me on just visual?"

"How can any not so trained trust an alien capable of masking his emotions so completely?"

Egad barked and pushed past Walden. "Let me talk to

your master. Too many die. Some deserve it. Some aren't fit to be dog food, but many good men die.''

Walden grunted as he lifted Egad to the plate. The dog's nose pressed into the SAW-detector plate. He yelped once and sniffed hard to receive the message from the other end. Even Walden's insensitive nose wrinkled at the odors emanating from the com unit. Egad belched and farted and barked, interspersing this with words in both English and Frinn.

Walden was amazed at the dog's command of the alien language, odors notwithstanding.

Egad jerked around, twisting so fast in his arms that the man dropped him.

''Run,'' the dog urged. ''He sends robots to kill us.''

Before the words were sounded from the dog's transducer, Walden heard the rattling of repair robots. It took several seconds for him to locate the source of the noise. By then he was trapped between closed doors and a corridor-filling robot brandishing a variable frequency cutting laser.

Walden wished he still had the laserifle—but he didn't. It had burned out getting him back inside Starlight. All he had to fight the machine were his wits and luck.

He didn't feel very lucky. He shot across the corridor and smashed hard into a door, trying to get it open. If he could get out of the robot's path, he might be able to fight it from behind. The door refused to budge. He swung around, looking for either Uvallae or Egad. Both had vanished into the bowels of the space station.

Fire across his arm forced him back. The repair robot wasn't fast, but it approached with an inexorable speed that hinted at an absolute quantity in the universe. It would not be denied its victim.

''Egad! Where are you? Uvallae!'' Walden back-pedaled from the robot, wondering where his friends had gone. They had simply vanished. He danced in front of the robot like a fencer without a sword. The robot came on, cutting laser held in an immobile arm.

Walden tried to use this seeming flaw in design to duck down and get past the robot. He failed. Small tendrils of steel cable flicked out from the sides and gripped at him. He barely escaped their clutchès. The repair unit grappled with whatever it was designed to cut apart, the tentacles moving the object of its attention in and out of the stationary cutting beam.

Behind him was a cul-de-sac. The doors to either side refused to budge. He had let himself be cut off. And where had Egad gone? He shouted again.

This time a muffled bark answered him. He glanced up at the overhead. Part of a ceiling panel had been pulled away. The dog's ungainly head thrust through it. He barked again, this time in greater agitation. Walden wondered why the dog didn't speak. Then he found himself completely boxed in by three walls and the robot with its deadly laser torch.

"Here. Up here!" came Uvallae's soft words. "Do not alert it. You must help yourself as much as possible. Trust me!"

Walden had no choice. The Frinn reached down only a few centimeters. Walden gathered his wits, got his legs under him, and launched himself upward like a rocket blasting into space. His pants legs caught fire as the robot rushed forward, its laser burning at the space where his body had been only a few milliseconds before.

He dangled, the Frinn hanging onto his wrists, until he kicked hard enough to swing his body up and over the edge of the ceiling panel. He lay flat, panting harshly.

"Why didn't you help me?" he demanded.

"Quiet!"

The Frinn's warning came too late. Walden looked below and saw added danger. The robot's shining dome parted. Clamps opened as they rose on an extensible arm. The three-fingered prongs snapped and gripped at his feet. Using only his elbows, he worked his way forward. Hot geysers sprouted all around him.

"The laser. It has a laser in its top! Get away. Hurry, and be quiet. It tracks by sight since it works on our shuttle rockets and other vehicles."

Egad barked, urging him on. Walden didn't need the dog's goading. He had ample reason to scuttle along as fast as he could. More hot spots flared around him. When he came to a narrow crossing tunnel, he saw the Frinn and the dog down a branching tunnel. Wiggling around air baffles, he crawled next to Egad.

The dog barked and nipped at Walden's sleeve. He saw

the reason for Egad's silence. The transducer had come loose from his throat, preventing the computer from analyzing the throat muscle contractions and turning them into words.

"There is no time," Uvallae said. "The robot will stalk us. It knows we are above it. We must get away."

"We will, we will," Walden said, working on his dog's collar. He finally got the transducer back into place. Egad swallowed, belched, and bobbed his head eagerly.

"Thanks," was all the gengineered canine said.

"We can go now," Walden said. New burn holes appeared behind him. The robot had alertly followed when they switched air ducts. Looking ahead, Walden saw their luck had run out. The branching ducts turned too small for either Uvallae or him. Egad might save himself, but the fit would be tight.

"Here," he said suddenly. He kicked at a grating and followed it into a room. Egad tumbled after him. What seemed an eternity later, Uvallae dropped into the room. Outside in the corridor they heard the repair robot rattling along.

"Can he track us in here?" whispered Walden.

Uvallae shook his head. The Frinn's pebbly skin took on an unhealthy sheen. He sank to the floor and put his back against a wall. He scoured his sloping forehead with both hands in what Walden had come to interpret as a sign of frustration or even rage.

"We are *trapped*. We cannot reach the control room. Even if we do, *that* is the reception we can expect. They have forsaken me!"

"We can get away from that laser-wielding hunk of junk," Walden said. He found another door leading from the room into a larger area that had once been a lounge. Chairs strewn around had been overturned and two low tables had been broken. Laserifle burns on the walls told of a quick but vicious fight. Walden closed his eyes for a moment when he saw a flash-heat dried spot of blood. He wasn't even sure if it was Frinn or human—but it had been blood before it had been boiled to a dark black spot on the floor.

"Find cat shit major?" asked Egad. The dog had tracked his own thoughts perfectly. He patted Egad, then pulled the dog close and hugged him.

"We've got to get to Zacharias. If the Frinn won't let

Uvallae talk with them, this is our only way of getting a cease-fire.''

"Master squeeze too hard."

"You're more loyal than a human ever could be, Egad. I love you for it."

"Hear footsteps in corridor. Human footsteps. Might be EPCTs. I don't think it is."

"Who else might it be?" he asked.

"Cat shit Sov-Lat. Don't like him, either. Why won't you let me bite him?"

"Sorbatchin?" Walden rushed to the door and levered it open a few centimeters. At first he saw nothing. Then the big, raw-boned, blond Sov-Lat colonel strode past. He had two laserifles slung over his shoulders and carried a third one.

Walden started to call out to him. He wanted to reach Zacharias and thought the Sov-Lat could help him. Something made him stop. Sorbatchin spun in the hall and looked around, his cold blue eyes looking like chips of polar ice. His manner made Walden hold his tongue. Sorbatchin made a precise military about-face and vanished into the room across the corridor.

Trying to make as little noise as possible, Walden slipped from the room and went to the entrance. Sorbatchin hadn't closed the door. From inside he heard the all-too-familiar hissing and crackling of the interference that had blotted out communication inside Starlight. Sorbatchin hummed to himself as he worked—and the static vanished.

Walden edged around to get a better view of what went on inside the room. The Sov-Lat officer worked over a small device hardly larger than his hand. He placed it on a table and took out an even smaller com unit.

"Come in, Patriot. Can you read me, Patriot?"

"What?" asked Egad.

"He's calling someone—and I don't think it's inside Starlight. Be quiet and listen. Your ears are better than mine."

"Patriot, we have achieved goal. Casualties minor. O'Higgins lost. Two others wounded. What is happening aboard *Hippocrates*?"

The answer was too low for Walden to make out, but Sorbatchin seemed pleased.

"Scrambling once more. You have done well, Patriot. You

will be rewarded when we make definitive contact with the pigs.''

Sorbatchin cut off the com unit and stuffed it inside his voluminous uniform blouse. He worked at the other device for several seconds. Walden heard the popping and hissing from his own headphones and knew that Sorbatchin was responsible for the jamming.

Colonel Vladimir Sorbatchin caused the jamming—and he had spoken with someone on the *Hippocrates* using a code name. Walden had worried that Nakamura was paranoid and seeing spies around every corner. He knew now that the woman was right. Doris Yerrow hadn't been the only spy. Another one was on the ship.

Walden knew his earlier poisoning hadn't been an accident. Patriot had tried to kill him.

He grabbed Egad's collar and pulled the dog back into the lounge across the hall. He got the door almost shut when Sorbatchin dashed into the corridor, laserifle leveled and ready for use. He had heard something and was ready to fry any moving target.

Walden turned cold inside when Sorbatchin moved toward the lounge. Without a weapon, Walden knew he had no chance against the Sov-Lat colonel. Even with a rifle, he lacked experience or the killer instinct the man had already shown.

A rattle and a clank saved him. The repair robot with the cutting laser mounted on its front hove into view. Sorbatchin spun and fired in a well-coordinated move. The robot returned fire, but Sorbatchin's aim had been exact. The repair robot continued to wheel and crashed directly into the far corridor wall. Its laser torch cut through the bulkhead and it would have rumbled on except that Sorbatchin's second blast destroyed its guidance computer. The robot let out a tiny wheeze that was almost human, then died.

Sorbatchin kicked the robot, then hurried off, switching laserifles as he went to allow the one he'd just fired time to recharge. The Sov-Lat officer was a flesh-and-blood killing machine and more than a match for any metallic repair robot. Even so, Walden was happy to have the robot put in an appearance when it did.

''Hear other feet,'' Egad said. ''EPCTs near.''

"That can wait," Walden said anxiously. "Tell me everything you overheard. Could you tell who Sorbatchin contacted aboard the *Hippocrates*?"

"Damned cat noise."

"What?" Walden was irritated at Egad's insistence on calling everything he disliked cat shit or cat noise.

"Voice muffled electronically, but I heard a damned cat. Cannot recognize human but there was a cat meowing."

Walden looked up in time to see Uvallae making his way across the room. Whatever private hell the Frinn had gone through upon realizing his superiors had abandoned him and had even branded him a traitor, he had recovered from it.

"We must stop this warfare," Uvallae said. "You are correct in this assertion. I have been weak. I apologize for my lack of confidence in you and myself."

"Egad heard our troops nearby. If I can think of a way of attracting their attention without getting my head lasered off, we can find Zacharias and—"

The door into the lounge turned cherry-red, then exploded in a rain of molten metal. Colonel Sorbatchin kicked through the smoldering fragments and leveled his laserifle at them. Walden saw the tiny red sighting dot flare against his chest and knew death was only milliseconds away.

CHAPTER
17

Walden tried to brush the red sighting spot off his chest, even though he knew this was futile. He waited for the laser beam that would rip through his body.

The dot jerked from his chest and the laserifle tore away the overhead, sending a cascade of debris falling on him. Walden stared at his body, touched the spot where the sight had been and found no hole, then looked up. He went weak in the legs at such a near miss with death. He finally forced himself to look at Sorbatchin to see why the Sov-Lat colonel had relented at the last possible instant.

The answer didn't please him. Sorbatchin would have killed him if Sgt. Hecht hadn't smashed his laserifle under the colonel's, knocking it off target.

The anger clouding Sorbatchin's face wasn't a pretty sight. He said something to Hecht, who only smiled back and shrugged. The colonel spun and vanished.

"You still orbiting, Doc?"

"I'm all right," said Walden. He wanted to say more but his mouth was dry. He took a step backward and dropped onto a chair. It didn't matter that the furniture had been designed for Frinn physiology. Support was what he sought until the shakes left him.

"Sorbatchin's got it in his head that anything moving is

enemy. Can't prove it but I think he fried one of Bonzo's squad." Hecht looked thoughtful and added, "It's going to be a damned pity if the colonel has an accident."

"He wanted to kill me," said Walden.

"You're lucky I happened by, Doc." Hecht took in the room for the first time. When he saw Uvallae, he moved with lightning speed to bring up his laserifle and fire. This time Egad came to the rescue. The dog bowled over the EPCT sergeant, amid flailing arms, kicking legs, and loud curses.

"Dammit, dog, get off me. That's the enemy! That's a pig-face!"

"Pig-Frinn," Egad corrected, standing over Hecht.

"Sergeant, it's all right." Walden looked at Uvallae and shrugged, a helpless look on his face. He tried to convince the alien that what he said now was essential to their mission of forging a cease-fire. "He's in my custody."

"You took a pig-face prisoner? Hell, Doc, we been having a hard time even seeing them. They send their robots after us rather than fighting us face-to-face."

"I'm sure they think we're as ugly as they think we are," said Walden. "I've got to talk to Zacharias right away. It's important. I can stop the fighting."

"He wants to talk to you, too. He sent me to ferry you to base HQ, but he couldn't care less about the fighting. We got 'em penned up where they belong. There's no way they can win now. The major's got it into his head that this might not even be a real combat unit we're facing." Hecht scratched himself mechanically. Walden wondered what the sergeant accomplished through the thick combat suit but said nothing. "Don't know if Zacharias hasn't hit on something, for a change. All I've seen are repair robots."

"That's what I've got to talk to him about," said Walden, feeling better. He tested his legs and found he could stand without shaking. Sorbatchin had a way of always surprising him. He had never considered outright murder to be part of the Sov-Lat's makeup. He seemed the type to resort to more subtle plans.

Like Miko Nakamura.

"You sure he's not going to turn on us?" Hecht stared at Uvallae, then slung his laserifle. "I can take him, if he gets too fired up. Move it out, p—" Hecht stopped in mid-word and looked at Egad, who growled loudly. "Move it out, Frinn," the sergeant amended.

"Move what out?" asked Uvallae.

"Just another idiom, Uvallae," said Walden. Hecht's eyes widened in shock at hearing such perfect English spoken by the alien.

"Smart pig-Frinn," said Egad. "Smarter than cat shit major."

"No argument on that, Egad," said Hecht. "He talks better, too." Hecht's mouth fell open when he realized the dog spoke, too. He looked at Walden, then shook his head in wonder. Hecht motioned for them to precede him. Walden stepped into the corridor, gingerly avoiding the still-smoking door Sorbatchin had lasered. He expected a bolt of energy to fry him as the Sov-Lat shot from ambush, but the colonel had vanished.

Walden wasn't sure if this worried him more than another attempt on his life. Had Sorbatchin seen him spying when he contacted the *Hippocrates* and "Patriot"? He would have to live looking over his shoulder and worrying about Sorbatchin's intentions.

"The major's down a level," said Hecht. "We've been gliding smoother than a shadow through vacuum, but he's in a snit fit over something."

Walden started to tell the sergeant about the Frinn and how Uvallae had aided him so many times. He decided against it. When Zacharias was convinced, then the orders would go down the line. He had no illusion about Hecht or any other EPCT disobeying a direct order from their superior. They were too well trained to think for themselves.

Walden saw where the EPCTs had blown a hole through the floor. Hecht pointed and said, "Down. You first, Doc. Then the dog, then the prisoner." Hecht stared hard at Egad, waiting for the dog to argue. Egad only barked.

Walden didn't bother correcting him. Let Hecht think what he wanted. Zacharias held the key. He kept repeating this over and over to convince himself. He was going to do battle—albeit verbal—that was every bit as important as any the EPCT had engaged in since landing on Starlight.

"Glad the sergeant found you," Zacharias said, looking up from a map display on his small combat computer. Grids flashed and tiny dots crawled throughout the maze. It took Walden a few seconds to realize the EPCT had somehow explored the lower reaches of Starlight and had mapped it completely. Only the upper levels had gone unsurveyed.

"I need to talk with *you*, Major," said Walden.

Zacharias held up his hand and cut off the flow of words already bubbling up to Walden's lips.

"This is more important." Zacharias saw Uvallae enter the room. His hand went to his sidearm. When he saw Hecht had made no move with his laserifle he relaxed. "You caught one? He's the first prisoner we've taken."

"He's not a prisoner," Walden said. His mind raced. He had to choose his words carefully or Zacharias might order Uvallae vivisected to develop specific bioweapons. "He's a diplomat—an ambassador come to negotiate a cease-fire."

"We don't need to talk with them," said Zacharias. "We're almost finished with Starlight. It'll be ours completely in another day. Their robots are—"

"Their robots," interrupted Walden, "are *not* war machines. The robots are repair tools. You've been fighting appliances, not expert system robokillers."

Hecht coughed and then stood silently, a smile creeping across his lips. Walden guessed that the sergeant had told his superior this at the onset of hostilities and had been ignored.

"Things are spinning faster," muttered Zacharias. "We have too many items to cover before dealing with this." Louder, he said to Hecht, "Sergeant, see to our . . . ambassador. We'll speak with him in a few minutes."

Walden motioned for Uvallae to accompany Hecht. Egad trotted after them, much to Uvallae's relief. Walden found himself regretting the gengineered dog's absence, but it was for the best if it kept the Frinn happy in trying times.

"I've found out something else," Walden said before Zacharias swung into his own harangue. "Sorbatchin is generating the interference blocking our com."

Zacharias sat down heavily. He rubbed his temples, then opened his pale eyes and vented a gusty sigh. "That son of a bitch should have been tossed out the *Hippocrates'* airlock. He's caused nothing but trouble since we boarded Starlight."

"I overheard him contacting the spy still aboard the *Hippocrates*," Walden went on. "He didn't call him by name—

only used the code name 'Patriot,' but I know the spy's identify.''

"Later,'' Zacharias said, startling Walden. On the *Hippocrates*, the major had been obsessed with finding spies. To
push it aside meant he had more important matters to deal
with. Walden wasn't sure he wanted to know what they were.

"Colonel Sorbatchin has found a laboratory in this area.''
Zacharias swung the computer vidscreen around so the scientist could see it. "We have reason to believe it is the Frinn's
research center and contains certain bioweapons capable of
wiping out all life on Starlight. *All* life,'' he emphasized.
"Including ours.''

"A doomsday weapon?''

"It might not have been developed for that, but Sorbatchin
is not above using it in that fashion.''

"What's happened?''

"Our men have died in peculiar ways,'' Zacharias said.
The strain had turned his swarthy complexion pale. Walden
saw the evidence of sleeplessness in the major's eyes. Even
his usually steady hands shook slightly. Walden perversely
wanted Anita Tarleton to see her lover in this distraught state.
It might change her mind about the medal-wearing, pompous
EPCT.

"How?'' Walden had other matters to discuss. Zacharias'
paranoia had always run unchecked. He didn't consider the
Frinn laboratory any threat. He had talked briefly with Uvallae about their research and had confidence that the Frinn
only tried to stop the Infinity Plague, not generate their own
version to kill humans.

"Two marines have gone insane and killed others in their
unit.''

This brought Walden up straight in the chair where he awk-
wardly perched. "I came across a soldier who had killed four
of his squad. I thought it was strain of combat.''

"No. None of my men can crack under combat conditions.
They've been trained in such a way they will die before
breaking.'' Zacharias smiled wanly. "You're skeptical. In
this you can trust me, Doctor. They *can't* go berserk and turn
on their own troops.''

Walden didn't ask what had been done to them. The NAA
had psych warfare officers who were every bit as good at their

jobs as he was at his. If he guaranteed the efficacy of a bio-weapon, that meant it worked exactly as he predicted.

"You think they've picked up some microbe from the Frinn labs?" Walden shook his head. "That's not likely. They haven't had time to do such detailed workups on our physiology. Even if they had, look at the labs. They aren't geared for bioweapons work. In some respects, they are at a very primitive level compared to what we can do."

"You're not putting it all together. Sorbatchin has found something. The Sov-Lat *must* be responsible. Your arguments are good and I accept them—I thought of them myself."

"Sorbatchin is a military man. He's no scientist." Walden couldn't help remembering how Pedro O'Higgins had lost his life. The Chilean didn't have to die to save Walden—and he had. A debt had been repaid. Of all the men and women with Sorbatchin, only O'Higgins had the skill to produce a plague vector in such a short time.

"Others with him . . ." Zacharias started.

"O'Higgins is dead." Walden quickly explained what had happened.

"Sorbatchin has stumbled onto something we can use without scientific translation, then. I don't believe he had it with him when we rescued him on Schwann. Nakamura or I would have noticed."

Walden wasn't sure they knew what to look for, but he bowed to their skill in espionage. In a way, his and the EPCT major's concerns came together in the same subject: Vladimir Sorbatchin.

"He's jamming your communications, he's relaying data back to the spy aboard the *Hippocrates*, and he might be responsible for killing off some of your men." Walden tried to put everything together, but the pieces wouldn't form a clear picture. "How does he gain by killing EPCTs aboard Starlight?"

"He wants to negotiate with them," said Zacharias.

Walden remained quiet. He hadn't been the only one eavesdropping on Sorbatchin and O'Higgins while they plotted to subvert the Frinn and form an alliance against the NAA.

"By presenting himself as the leader of the force, he can do anything he wanted."

This made no sense to Walden and he said so. "Sorbatchin ought to be stopped. Just order your men to shoot him down."

"Nakamura doesn't want it. We discussed the matter before we left the *Hippocrates*."

Walden shrugged this off. If the major couldn't take the initiative for himself, that was his difficulty. "She's out of com with us and we're here. What's your problem?"

"I cannot go into all we discussed, Walden. It's too complex for—"

"For a mere scientist?" Walden said angrily. "You're not doing a great job here, Zacharias. You've lost a lot of men, you're letting a Sov-Lat colonel wander around unchecked, and now you tell me there's a bug loose driving your men crazy. Does that sum it up?"

"Will you help me find the lab and counter it, Doctor?"

"Take Sorbatchin out of the equation, then I'll help."

The EPCT major made a sour face, touched a stud on his com unit and said, "Get Hecht in here on the double."

The sergeant slipped in and stood silently at the door. Egad dropped beside the man, tongue lolling. His mismatched eyes fixed on Walden, silently telling him that all was well with Uvallae and that Hecht could keep quiet about Egad's verbal ability. Walden felt more in control now. Uvallae was safe; Sorbatchin was on his way out as a threat. All that needed doing was forging a cease-fire and getting down to the real work of stopping the Infinity Plague before it wiped out the Frinn.

He laughed without humor. *All that was needed*, he thought. It might as well have been a life's work ahead of him.

"I want our Sov-Lat colleague shown how we conduct rear echelon maneuvers. Do I make myself clear, Sergeant?"

Hecht smiled crookedly. "I'll show him around, Major. He might not want to inspect the troops right away. How much grease can I use with him?"

"As much as necessary."

"The body will go out their whizzer airlock," Hecht assured his superior.

"No! I mean, not unless it's necessary." Zacharias glared at Walden, as if accusing him of this problem. "Do it right away. We have to step lively or Starlight will get away from us.''

"On it, Major." Hecht did an about-face and vanished. Walden felt better. Of the soldiers, he trusted Hecht to do a good job. He regarded Sorbatchin removed as a threat. Walden considered talking quietly to Egad and having the dog convey the desire to have the Sov-Lat colonel tossed into space without a suit, then stopped. Carelessly playing such a valuable card as Egad's intelligent spying capacity was poor gamesmanship. Hecht knew of the gengineered dog's verbal ability. That was enough for now.

"There's something more, Major."

"The laboratory, then we can discuss other matters." Zacharias' cold eyes fixed on Walden and convinced him that further concessions weren't forthcoming. Find the laboratory, destroy or contain whatever suited Zacharias, *then* bring up the issue of a cease-fire. That had to be the order if anything was to get done and save lives, both Frinn and human.

"I'll need Uvallae's help. He's a scientist and can get us around the lab levels faster than blundering on them ourselves."

"Can he be trusted? He is a pig-face."

"He's also a diplomat come to help forge a cease-fire," said Walden, working in his own claims.

"A scientist diplomat?" scoffed Zacharias. "Ridiculous."

"Agreed. It's as silly as a soldier diplomat, isn't it?" Walden brushed past Zacharias. He summoned Egad. The dog trotted along obediently, the weight of his slim body pressing against Walden's leg to guide him toward Uvallae.

"Walden," came the Frinn's aggrieved voice. "Why do they hold me like this? You said I was an ambassador. Are there not certain prerogatives that go with such a station?"

"The major's in charge right now. We've got to find a lab that might have loosed a bioweapon on our troops. Zacharias is sure it's a Frinn weapon."

"No!"

"I told him that. If there is one, Colonel Sorbatchin is responsible for its release."

"He used our lab to generate this bioweapon?" Uvallae looked appalled at the idea.

"We don't know. I saw some evidence of the disorder

among the EPCTs, but I'm not sure they contracted it aboard Starlight." Walden turned the problem over and over in his head and decided it couldn't be anything released on the space station. The EPCTs had never opened their suits; contamination through their impervious combat gear was almost unthinkable.

"We do not pursue such research. I told you this."

"Right. Let's go scout around and see what we can find. Truth will always outweigh speculation."

Four EPCTs moved behind them as they started toward lower levels. Uvallae wandered around, checking signs and following a path that left Walden confused. He was glad the soldiers had their trackers on—and that Egad wasn't easily put off by such turnings and twistings.

"Here is the main laboratory. Any research done will be recorded in the master data bank." Uvallae seated himself in front of the flat two-dimensional screen and began working on the keys. He rubbed his forehead twice with both hands, then returned to work at the console. After ten minutes, he glanced back over his shoulder.

"I do not understand. My data has been corrupted. I cannot tell what work has been done here in the past ten days."

"Sorbatchin?"

"No human could access the machines and obtain the proper codes to do this. The controllers must have done it. I cannot understand why. This work is of no military use."

"They might be keeping us from learning your real capabilities." said Walden. He had worked around military long enough to know how they thought. Keeping information hidden was as much a part of their credo as defeating an enemy.

"You do not use me for this selfish end, do you, Walden?" asked Uvallae. The Frinn's green and gold eyes flashed and the cat-slits narrowed in suspicion.

"No," he said simply. All the denials in the universe wouldn't mean anything if Uvallae didn't want to believe them.

"Very well. I can believe the Infinity Plague is an accident of immense proportion. I will help you now in return for your help later."

"We'll get through this," said Walden. "We've got to

find out why you didn't come down with the plague. The other Frinn responded to infection in about two months."

"Many aboard the ships returning to our home world were similarly unaffected," said Uvallae. "But not all." He looked somber. "Perhaps it is slower working in me."

"If it is, we have to find out why. We can retard its progress and gain more time to stop it."

"You are more advanced in such matters. That is apparent," said Uvallae. "We are lucky you are willing to aid us."

The guilt Walden felt for belonging to the same species—and probably the NAA research team responsible for the Infinity Plague—almost overwhelmed him. What he did wasn't altruism as much as it was an attempt to expunge the culpability.

"We go on the assumption that your controllers removed the data you sought on experimentation. I'd also go on the assumption that Sorbatchin hasn't had anything to do with introducing a new bioweapon found in your labs."

"Has this one introduced any plague at all?" asked Uvallae.

"There's no reason for him to. Zacharias is looking for an excuse, and the Sov-Lat officer was convenient. Sorbatchin's not to be trusted. Don't get me wrong on that, but I don't think he's responsible for the outbreaks among the EPCTs."

Walden started to present another working hypothesis for Uvallae when Zacharias burst into the laboratory. "Have you learned what he did? Do you have a handle on it?"

"Major," Walden said slowly, thinking hard and trying to formulate his thoughts as he went. "Uvallae says the Frinn leaders have interdicted the computer data. If one of their own scientists can't access it, how could Sorbatchin?"

"I don't know," snapped Zacharias. "How?"

"He could not," spoke up Uvallae.

"What are you saying?" Zacharias began pacing, his hands locked behind his back and his sidearm slapping his hip as he turned at the end of each circuit.

"Neither Sorbatchin nor the Frinn have introduced a bioweapon. Whatever is working on your troopers came from the *Hippocrates*."

"The spy aboard the ship caused this?"

"Possible," said Walden. "It might even be probable. If I'm right, all the damage has been done that can be. We can work to repair other fronts by destroying Sorbatchin's jamming unit."

"We can speak with my controllers," said Uvallae.

"Sorbatchin first," cut in Walden. He knew Zacharias and his linear thinking. "Find him, find out what he knows. He might have instructed the spy aboard the *Hippocrates* in what to release—and we need to find out what he thought he'd gain by doing it."

"Very well," Zacharias said glumly. "If you're correct about Sorbatchin and the jamming device, we can at least regain contact with the *Hippocrates*. That will be a great help in other matters."

Walden didn't ask if Zacharias sought orders from a supposedly civilian advisor. Miko Nakamura was the true commander of this mission, whether anyone liked it or not.

"Major," came Hecht's crackling, interference-riddled com. "We're cut off from the Sov-Lat."

"What's going on?" A panicked look crossed Zacharias' face, making Walden wonder how much in charge the officer was.

"Robots. We got robots up to the ass. Sorbatchin is trapped in a room. Should we fight through to rescue him?"

"We'll join forces in five minutes. Maintain position until then," snapped Zacharias. The EPCT major raced from the room.

Egad's head rose from where he had rested it on crossed paws. Uvallae stared at Walden. Everyone looked to him for orders. He heaved a deep sigh and said, "We're not getting anywhere staying here. Let's see what Sorbatchin has to say for himself."

Jerome Walden didn't add, And maybe get ourselves killed doing it. Both Egad and Uvallae knew the chance existed. He silently thanked both for joining him as he trailed after Zacharias. It didn't seem quite as lonely.

CHAPTER
18

"Cat shit major upset," said Egad. "Why does he want to save cat shit Sov-Lat colonel?"

"I don't know," Walden said, resting his hand on the dog's head. He began to worry about infection from the mysterious disease that Zacharias was sure either the Frinn or Sorbatchin had introduced to Starlight. If humans caught it, even with combat gear on, Egad might be a prime candidate for contamination because of the long periods he had run around the space station without his helmet.

Walden wondered about himself. He hadn't worn his helmet much of the time, either. The air was good, the pressure and composition right. Why bother?

He forced such speculation away. Dying from a laserifle bolt was of more immediate concern.

"Nakamura doesn't want him disturbed. It has to be her doing that Zacharias is so frightened to even speak with the colonel."

"Don't like her. She doesn't have any smell. The pig-Frinn know how to talk right," the dog said. "Don't like their smells sometimes, but they talk right."

Walden checked his com unit and heard the roar in it when he tried to reach Zacharias. For a few meters com was fine.

Beyond that, it fell apart quickly. Whatever Sorbatchin was using to jam their equipment, it worked well.

"What is happening?" asked Uvallae. Two EPCTs stood immediately behind the Frinn, laserifles ready to use. They distrusted their "enemy." Walden didn't blame them. They had seen their friends killed by the Frinn robots. Uvallae was the first prisoner to be taken aboard Starlight. All Walden had to do was convince them and their leader the Frinn weren't the enemy.

"The robots have trapped Sorbatchin. We've got to reach him if we want to find out what he has done."

"You truly think one of your own released a plague that destroys you?"

Walden shrugged. They had more questions than answers. Sorbatchin, Zacharias, and Nakamura would have to stop distrusting one another and start cooperating if they wanted to get anywhere. Walden knew this wasn't likely to happen unless something catastrophic happened. Even then, he wondered.

"Robots, Doc!" came Hecht's loud call in his headphones. Walden recoiled. The EPCT sergeant couldn't be too far away for the warning to come so strongly.

Seconds later Hecht and three other marines came around the corner in the corridor ahead of him. Even as he watched, one EPCT toppled forward, the front of his combat suit a smoking ruin. The two tried to pull him back. Walden heard Hecht's sharp command to leave the dead man. Walden's eyebrows shot up. The EPCT prided themselves on retrieving their dead for burial, if possible.

"What's the trouble ahead?" he asked Hecht.

The sergeant leveled his laserifle and pushed him and Uvallae back down the corridor. "We got ambushed. At least seven of the machines caught us in a cross fire. We didn't have the firepower to stop them. I'm calling up light artillery."

"You can't use it inside a space station," protested Walden. "You'll breach the walls if a round goes off next to an exterior hull section."

"I'll blow 'em all into space," vowed Hecht. "They killed Bonzo. He was a damned fool, but he was my friend."

Hecht kept pushing them faster and faster. Uvallae turned

and broke into a trot. Walden had to lengthen his stride to keep up. Egad ran easily beside him. The dog looked up, his expression clear. He had important news and wanted to speak.

Walden didn't see how they could take the time to find a private spot. In the confusion he took a chance. "Tell me, Egad. Make it fast," he ordered the dog.

"Robots all around us. They circle us!"

"Hecht, we're heading into an ambush," Walden said. "We've got to re-form and get with Zacharias. If we don't, they'll keep sniping at us and remove us one by one."

The sergeant's face was contorted as he shouted into his microphone. Walden couldn't hear; the EPCT tried to reach Zacharias on a command frequency closed to him.

The suddenness of Hecht's voice in his ears hit Walden as a wave of pain.

"We got big trouble. The major's surrounded, too. We've got to get him out before we can even think of finding Sorbatchin." Hecht turned and made a hand signal. Two soldiers came up, pulling thick tubes from their packs. "Use 'em. *Now!*"

Walden crashed against a bulkhead as rockets flared from the launcher muzzles. Two huge holes appeared in the floor. The composite material began to burn. In seconds the rocket-diameter-sized holes grew to ones larger than a man in combat gear. Walden didn't hear a command, but the EPCTs began jumping down the holes blasted in the deck. He, Uvallae, and Egad were soon the only ones left.

"Company," warned Egad.

The Frinn robots clanked and rattled around the corner. Walden winced when he saw they rolled over the fallen body and left behind blood tracks as they advanced. A laser beam touched the wall beside his head. If Uvallae hadn't tackled him and taken them down into a heap on the floor, the swinging cutting beam would have sliced off his head in one easy motion.

The robots now used long-range weapons.

"Down," he told Egad. The gengineered dog looked into the hole skeptically. Walden swept his arm along the floor, caught Egad's backside and shoved the animal through. He heard a mournful howl as the dog fell and an even more anguished yelp when he hit. Walden followed quickly, snaking through and dropping. He struck the next level sooner than anticipated. The shock momentarily paralyzed. Again Uvallae came to his aid and saved him.

The robots had halted at the holes and trained their laser weapons downward.

"Stay low," warned Walden. The EPCT had re-formed. A half-dozen laserifles began firing up through the hole. Molten pieces of robots began raining down.

"Doc, you live a charmed life. You and that mutt of yours should have been fried up there. Sorry about leaving you like that but things are worse here."

Even as Hecht spoke, rockets launched from the tiny tubes in the hands of the two EPCTs. Walls vanished and composite materials burned with greasy smoke filling the corridor. Laboratories were revealed through the crude path until the smoke billowed up and obscured them. Uvallae began coughing. Walden started a few seconds after. Only Egad escaped the smoke, being lower to the floor where the heavier oxygen formed a layer.

Walden and Uvallae dropped to hands and knees and scuttled along until they got away from the worst of the smoke.

Walden tapped his com unit. "Hecht, you there? Where are you? We were separated."

"Not for long, Doc. This way." A hand grabbed his ankle and pulled. Uvallae followed him into a small storage room. Six EPCTs crowded into it, laserifles pointed upward. "We need to get with Zacharias' bunch." Hecht stared at Uvallae, not sure if he wanted to burn the Frinn or let the pig-face trail along.

Walden read the sergeant's thoughts accurately. "He stays with us. He wants an end to this, too."

"Have him call off the damned robots," Hecht snapped.

"He can't. Sorbatchin is jamming all the frequencies he needs to reach his controllers. We have to talk to them if we want to turn off the robots."

Walden looked past Hecht. A marine stirred strangely, shrugging his shoulders and bumping hard against the men on either side of him. His movements became more violent. Walden saw the laserifle lowering and knew they were in for trouble.

Egad sensed the danger and launched himself at the EPCT.

Walden grabbed the barrel of the laserifle and grimly forced it back toward the overhead, even as it began to quiver with power as the marine fired it in a continual blast. Their efforts availed them little. The man had the strength of five. He tossed them aside and bellowed incoherently.

Even when Hecht drew his sidearm and fired point blank into the soldier's chest, the berserker struggled. His laserifle drilled a hole in the ceiling. His thrashing knocked men aside as if they were small children. A third and fourth shot from Hecht's pistol still didn't quiet the raging man.

"Let 'im out," grunted Hecht. He turned to the side and used a judo maneuver to send the marine reeling into the smoke-filled corridor. "Now burn 'im. Fire, damn you all. Fire!"

Three of the EPCTs nearest Walden responded. Their laserifle bolts cut the man in half.

"Mutiny will not be tolerated," Hecht said in a low, fierce voice. "Nobody gets out of here alive if he panics. Is that understood? We're in this as a unit. We're in this _together_."

Walden barely listened to Hecht's speech. Whatever had set off the EPCT, it wasn't panic. The expression on the man's face had been one of rage rather than fear.

"Sergeant, was he one who had been on Schwann with us?"

"Him?" Hecht sniffed indignantly. "He might have been. It's hard to remember."

"Check it when you can."

"Sure, Doc, when I can," Hecht's tone told Walden this would be when they returned alive to the _Hippocrates_—another way of saying when hell froze over.

"He acted like the other," said Uvallae. "Can it be the Infinity Plague affects your kind, also?"

Walden had to consider it a possibility. He hadn't found any way for the plague to infect a human—it only unraveled the extra chromosomes the Frinn possessed. It took two months to manifest itself among the aliens. What if it took longer in humans?

A cold chill raced up and down his spine. It hadn't been _that_ much longer than two months since they had unearthed the plague on Schwann. The combat on the planet's surface had been quick, bloody, and definitely ended when the Frinn destroyed the world. Between the destruction and lining up for the lift to Starlight had taken only a month. Two months transit and another week in this system.

Walden knew they guessed at two months' gestation period in the Frinn before the plague worked on their autonomic systems. It might have been three or four months.

It had been this long since the *Hippocrates'* complement had been exposed.

They might be carrying the seeds of a deadly plague inside them all. For the first time, Walden was glad Nakamura had prevailed and that they had chased after the Frinn ship. Returning to Earth would have spread the Infinity Plague among the billions infesting the planet. He felt sick over the prospect of destroying the entire Frinn species. To have the human race added to the death rota would have been more than Walden could have coped with.

"I'm locked on the major. We go and rejoin forces. Then we push through and get Sorbatchin. I've put the route into your charting systems. Ready?" Hecht checked his laserifle before going to the door.

"Wait." Walden grabbed the sergeant's arm. "What about Uvallae and me? We don't have your computer system. We don't even have suits."

"Doc, I feel for you. I do, but I got orders. You and the pig-face got to make it on your own." Hecht pulled free and stepped into the corridor. His rifle erupted flaming death instantly. With a purple ionization trail marking his passage through the smoke, he started away from where the marine had been cut in half.

"Egad, fetch the laserifle." The last of the EPCTs left the room before Egad returned with the fallen man's weapon. Walden hefted it, not knowing what good it would do him. The weight comforted him, though, and anything that made him feel better was a worthy addition.

"I can see them," the dog said from the lower vantage point. "Follow me."

Walden and Uvallae coughed and choked on the acrid smoke in the corridor. Keeping close to the dog helped. The electric crackle and roar of the EPCTs' laserifles also kept them on track. When they got free of the smoke caused by the burning walls, Walden almost collapsed. He hadn't realized how much the smoke drained him of energy.

"There. Your Sorbatchin is hiding in a physics laboratory," Uvallae said. "He is nowhere near the biology section."

"That wouldn't matter to Zacharias. When he gets an idea stuck in his head, it becomes permanent."

The EPCTs had formed in a small lounge area at the end of the long hallway. Sorbatchin kept the Frinn robots at bay, but Walden knew he wouldn't last much longer. The flare from his laserifle lacked the intensity of a full-charge bolt. He might have carried three of the rifles; he was down to his last joule now.

"Cat shit major wants you," said Egad. "See how he jumps around and looks stupid?"

"Come on," said Walden. "We need to get this over as fast as we can. The situation is turning more serious by the second." He worried as much for the people left aboard the *Hippocrates* as he did those trapped on Starlight. If Uvallae was right and the Infinity Plague had come up from Schwann, the entire human party was at risk.

Even if their problems stemmed from something Sorbatchin had released, they had to resolve matters quickly. They had invaded Starlight in strength. Walden worried that the eleven EPCTs gathered around Zacharias were all that remained.

"Hecht, have one of your rocket men take them out. Do it without damaging the Sov-Lat."

Rockets trailed down the corridor and blew apart robots until the metallic parts littered the corridor in knee-deep piles. As deadly as the rocket barrage was, it barely stopped the waves of machines struggling to get into the fray.

"There's too many of them, Major," observed Hecht. "We can't get to Sorbatchin without cutting through the walls."

"You cannot do that quickly enough," said Uvallae. "The walls are specially lined for radiation experiments. Lead, steel, other types of baffles were installed. This is not my field, and I cannot tell you the details."

"He's not lying, Major," said Walden. "He wants to stop this as much as we do."

"Cut the power to the damned robots," grumbled Zacharias.

"Each is independently powered," said Uvallae. "The central controller can turn them off. No one else can without approaching them. I am sure they have been reprogrammed to prohibit this."

"Nobody gets within five meters of them," agreed Hecht. "We tried to sneak up on them. Their sensors are too good. Can't even find *where* the sensors are."

"The shining domes hold much of their circuitry," said Uvallae, "but the main controlling unit is hidden deep within. They are cargo and repair robots. It would not do to have them disabled by simple loading and reconstruction accidents."

"They survive too damned well when we hit them with our laserifles," complained Zacharias. "Is there any easy way to disable them?"

Uvallae shook his head and then rubbed his forehead with both hands to show his frustration.

"Can you lure them from Sorbatchin?" suggested Walden. "Give him a chance to escape and . . ."

"He won't budge. Whatever he's got in that lab is his, he says. The fool is going to die with his discovery."

"Can you contact him?"

Zacharias shook his head. "That static is the most intense here of anywhere we've been in Starlight. You're probably right about the colonel causing it. He won't even turn it off to save his own life. The damned fool!"

"Let's let him be, Major," said Hecht. "We don't need to kill the static. We've done all right up till now."

"All right?" bellowed Zacharias, infuriated at his sergeant. "Look around you. This is it. These are the only ones who have survived. We've taken eighty percent casualties!"

A blast of heat came down the corridor that singed Walden's clothing. He spun and fired blindly, not caring what he hit. The laserifle beam tore apart a robot carrying a tiny but deadly laser welder. When he saw the dozens of other small robots, each with a welding device, he went crazy. He fired until the floor turned to a liquid puddle. His weapon lacked the power to burn completely through the deck.

The ten laserifles joining his blew a large cavity in the

deck. The small robots fell into it and vanished. Walden heard them scampering about under his feet, trapped between levels in the space station. He knew it wouldn't be long before they tried to give him a hot foot. They would turn their miniature welders upward and try to kill him.

"Code red, code yellow, code zero," barked Zacharias. As one, the EPCTs rushed down the hall, weapons firing in deadly cadence. The robots trying to reach Sorbatchin turned to meet the new threat. The air superheated as lasers on both sides fired.

Walden, Egad, and Uvallae hung back, knowing they stood no chance in that inferno. The biologist kept looking at the deck, waiting for the small robots to come after him. He knew it was paranoid thinking. He just couldn't stop himself.

"Chewing noises," commented Egad. "Robots?"

"Let's move," Walden said uneasily. He had no idea where it would be safer than in the lounge area. Zacharias and the EPCTs fought a half-dozen meters away, but following them would be suicidal. He barely stood the intense heat boiling back from the scene of combat.

Without a combat suit, he would be fried in seconds.

"There," said Uvallae. "A lab. The flooring will be heavier. It is a radiation lab."

Walden discharged the laserifle just as tiny craters began appearing in the floor. The robots had worked their way back upward with machinelike determination.

"We get cut off from cat shit major," protested Egad. The dog danced around, barking and snapping at the robots poking their way through the floor. He didn't seem to notice that his helmet visor was still locked down in place.

"Here, Egad, come here," ordered Walden. He couldn't fire at the emerging robots without hitting the dog.

Egad reluctantly broke off his futile attacks and joined Uvallae inside the lab. He dropped into a corner and put his head on his crossed paws, not liking any of this. Walden fired twice and vaporized a robot poking its welder through the floor. The other machines he let work. After a quick glance down the hall at the battle scene, he ducked into the lab and closed the door.

"We don't want to get cut off from them," he told Uvallae, "but getting killed before they've got Sorbatchin isn't too bright, either."

"These walls will protect us," Uvallae said. He studied the foptic communicator sitting on the desk, but the controller refused to accept any com from him. The Frinn's expression didn't seem to vary, but Walden sensed a deep disappointment and even resignation.

"We'll get to them," Walden assured him. "Starlight isn't doomed. We aren't, either."

Silence fell. Walden began pacing, clutching at his laserifle and wishing they were back aboard the *Hippocrates*. He needed to study the bodies of the EPCTs who had gone crazy and turned on their fellows. If the Infinity Plague somehow acted on them, the entire expedition was in danger.

His thoughts turned to Anita Tarleton. What were her orders? Had Dr. Greene told her to work on the Infinity Plague once she arrived on Schwann? Walden had not bothered to pursue the point while they had been in liftspace going to Delta Cygnus 4. Now he had to know. She might know more about it than anyone, if it had been her assignment. Anita might hold the difference between extinction for the Frinn— and humanity—and survival.

"Silent. There's no sound outside," said Egad. The dog poked at the door, trying to nose it open. With his helmet in place, he couldn't do it.

Walden strained to hear. He couldn't find any hint of the battle that had been raging. Pulling the door open a fraction of a centimeter, he peered out. Bodies littered the corridor— too many bodies for the EPCT to claim a victory.

He pushed through and saw Hecht and Zacharias going from corpse to corpse, recording the condition for their reports. Hecht looked up and shook his head.

Zacharias saw Walden and left his sergeant to the grisly work. Favoring a burned left leg, the major came up. "We got to Sorbatchin. He's going to live, but he's been injured."

"What about the robots?" Walden looked at the deck. Even here he saw no indication of activity.

"We drove them off," Zacharias said. "It cost me all but five of my men. God, the Starlight campaign is a disaster! Ninety percent casualty rate!"

Walden thought the major was going to break down and

cry. The man's body shook with emotion and his fists clenched and relaxed, only to tighten into gristly balls once more.

"Did you find the jamming device? If we contact the space station's controller, we might stop further attacks."

"We burned it," Zacharias said bitterly. "How he smuggled it aboard the *Hippocrates* is beyond me. He didn't build anything that sophisticated aboard the ship. He didn't have the time or skill."

"Can he talk? I need to ask about the—"

Walden didn't finish the sentence. A shock wave echoed down the corridor and caught them in a powerful, invisible fist that smashed and crushed.

Walden found himself pinned under Zacharias. It took several seconds for him to realize the blast had come from the lab where Sorbatchin had been. He didn't know if the Sov-Lat colonel had been caught in it or not. He couldn't even tell what had happened to Hecht and the others.

"Get off me, Zacharias," he said with ill grace. "You're too heavy for me to support."

He shoved hard and the major rolled to one side. Walden went cold when he saw Edouard Zacharias' face through his combat suit's helmet. Starlight had just claimed another casualty.

CHAPTER
19

"Get Hecht. Get him here right now!" Walden struggled to open the front of Zacharias' suit. The fastenings had been damaged by the blast. Walden finally gave up. There wasn't any way he could get inside. Thinking about it, he decided he didn't want to. The man's guts must have been turned to jelly from the force of the blast wave that had ripped along the corridor.

"He is hurt a lot," came Egad's report. "Want me to drag him away from here?"

"Any robots in the area?" Walden clung to his laserifle as if this would save him. He knew better. The company of EPCTs had fought throughout Starlight and had been reduced to only three or four. He had no hope of surviving if those well-trained combat veterans hadn't been able to.

"There are none," came Uvallae's calm evaluation. "There is no static on the communications channel, either."

Walden snorted in contempt. It did little good getting rid of the interference now there wasn't anyone to link with—except the *Hippocrates*. This thought buoyed him and kept him going as he went from marine to dead marine, checking their vital signs readouts and verifying their condition.

He had anticipated finding one or two still alive. Walden swallowed hard when he realized that all were very, very dead. The Frinn robots had efficiently killed, just as they had been programmed originally to efficiently repair.

"What about the colonel?" came a voice loud and clear in his headphones. Walden had to readjust his gain to keep from going deaf. He looked around and saw an EPCT propped against a wall, his helmet blown off.

"Hecht! What caused all this?"

"Bomb. Blew at the end of the tunnel. Venturi effect caused a real hurricane along here. The major didn't make it, did he?"

"He . . . died saving me." Walden said, aware that this half truth would end up in Edouard Zacharias' record. Zacharias had died and had saved Walden, but the act had been entirely unintentional. Walden knew the major might earn another medal for this, if they ever returned to a place where such trivial considerations mattered.

"Always had a flair for being a martyr," grumbled Hecht. "Prefer having officers more interested in getting *me* back home in one piece." Hecht coughed.

Walden studied the man's readout and saw he had suffered compression trauma. He might be spitting up blood, but his lungs were intact. A quick check of his mouth showed where Hecht had bitten his cheek. Most of the blood he spat out came from this insignificant injury. A last check of the vital signs readout showed that the circuits hadn't been damaged and gave accurate reports.

"You'll live. You were lucky. What about Sorbatchin? You said he was in bad shape."

"Can't say. He wasn't wearing his suit for me to get at the readouts. He was knocked out and looked gray. You know how a body looks after it's been dead for a week? He had that look to him."

Walden called over his shoulder, "Egad, round up everyone still ambulant. Get them together. Whoever—whatever—set the bomb is likely to do it again since it worked so well." He looked up at Uvallae and asked, "Can you reach the controllers now?"

"I believe they will speak to me. There is nothing else to do." Uvallae rubbed his sloping forehead until the pebbly skin turned a rusty red. His agitation was so great Walden hoped the Frinn wouldn't do anything rash.

"Let's see about Sorbatchin," Walden said to Hecht. The pair cautiously approached the door to the lab where the Sov-Lat colonel had made his stand against the Frinn robots. Walden peered in, then moved more quickly. Sorbatchin sprawled across a deck, his bloodied fingers leaving a red trail on the plastic surface.

"That's the damn jammer he was using," said Hecht, pointing to a charred spot on the floor. "I flamed it myself."

Walden pressed his fingertips into the Sov-Lat's neck. The pulse was strong, vital. "At least someone came through this alive," said Walden. He rolled Sorbatchin over and lifted an eyelid to check for pupil dilation. The pupil responded quickly to the increased light level.

"He's tough, damn him. As much as I hated Zacharias, I'd trade this son of a bitch for the major any day and twice on Sundays." Hecht prowled the lab, poking into piles of equipment and opening drawers. When he finished he returned to stand beside Walden and the still-unconscious Sorbatchin.

"I'm going to give him a little stimulus," said Walden, looking through the drugs he had pillaged from the dead EPCTs' supplies. "I don't know what most of these are for. I'm giving him one cc slow release of pentagan. If he's in pain, this will loosen him up. If he's not, he'll be able to walk through walls and never feel a thing."

Walden applied the drug patch behind Sorbatchin's right ear. In less than a minute he stirred, moaned, and sat up, hands grasping. Hecht grabbed the powerful man's wrists and held him easily.

"You stay in orbit, Colonel. One bit of eccentricity and I land you—hard."

"Your jamming device is destroyed," Walden said. Sorbatchin's eyes hardened and focused on him. "I know who your contact is aboard the *Hippocrates*, too. I know who 'Patriot' is. Did he supply your jamming device?"

"He did. He inherited Yerrow's stash of such devices. What is it to you, Doctor?"

"Nothing. It means nothing unless we get off Starlight. Most of the EPCTs are dead, including Zacharias." This provoked an even greater response from Sorbatchin. "We're dead in space if we can't get to the Frinn controllers and have them turn off the robots. Are you going to help us or are you going to continue your own espionage games?''

"Does it matter?"

"Only to you, Colonel," said Walden. "Sgt. Hecht wants to kill you very badly. I'm the only one standing between you and his laserifle."

As if to emphasize his desire, Hecht twisted slightly. Sorbatchin's gray face turned even paler. Walden wished he had vital signs monitor on the Sov-Lat officer. It would help to know how much pain he could endure before blacking out. This would indicate the truthfulness of any answer he might give concerning cooperation.

"Time is precious, Colonel," said Walden. "We can't take forever getting you to help us." He looked up and nodded to Hecht. Sorbatchin's response was immediate.

"Wait! I bow to your crude tortures," the man said. "I am injured. I cannot take more pain."

"He's not hardly hurting yet," Hecht observed. "I'd wager a month's salary he's running at nominal. The drug's just now kicking into light speed in him."

"I am injured," insisted Sorbatchin, "but as a Sov-Lat officer, I can continue in spite of my intense distress."

"The jamming device is destroyed?" asked Walden.

"There was no—''Sorbatchin screamed when Hecht applied pressure on his arm. Sorbatchin's flinty blue eyes fixed on the EPCT sergeant. "The device is destroyed," he said, relenting. Hecht released the man's arm and went to the doorway, peering out.

"We've got to move soon," the sergeant called back. "The pig-faces' robots are closing in on us again. This time it looks as if they mean to exterminate us completely."

"One more thing, Colonel. Did you introduce any type of bioweapon into Starlight? Aimed against either the EPCT or the Frinn?" Walden watched the Sov-Lat's reaction closely.

"I introduced no such weapon. Nor did O'Higgins, unless he did it on his own. I doubt he would do anything without seeking my approval."

"You believe this space gas?" asked Hecht.

Walden said, "Yes." He hurried to where Hecht covered the corridor with his laserifle. A half-dozen Frinn robots were forming a wedge, preparing to roll forward. Gears ground harshly and the hiss of lasers charging filled the air.

"Egad, let's go." Walden slipped from the laboratory and slid along the wall, trying not to draw attention to himself. He kept thinking of the machines as being human. Their sensors were more sensitive than any human's eyes or ears—and they were never distracted. Walden hit the slippery deck just ahead of six slashing laser beams intent on cutting him in half.

Hecht and the other EPCTs returned fire, giving Walden and Egad time to wiggle along to the far end of the corridor. Walden had sought sanctuary where he could regain his senses. He wasn't used to being fired at constantly. Instead, he found a nest of small worker robots repairing the larger ones. Their mission had been delayed by the large number of wasted machines littering the decks. Walden pulled his rifle around and began blasting at the smaller repair robots. He sent them hurrying for cover. The longer it took for them to repair the heavier machines, the more likely it was for the humans to escape this death trap.

"We're with you, Doc," came Hecht's sharp, clear voice. "You need to get into a combat suit."

"No time. I've got a com unit. Give me your frequencies." Walden shook his head as the headphones buzzed.

"All done," said Hecht. "Combat programming's a time saver, isn't it?"

"It is," Walden said, head still reeling. The computer dump of information into his com unit gave him full range of useful frequencies. All he needed to do was use the chin switch to change from one band to another and he would be privy to all EPCT com.

"We got to get higher, or so says your pig-face."

"Frinn pig-face," correct Egad. "He is ambassador to your species."

Hecht laughed harshly, not noticing it was the dog who had spoken. "Call him whatever you want. What's our mission?"

It took Walden a second to realize the sergeant looked to him for orders. With Major Zacharias and the other officers dead, he was the closest to the chain of command remaining, even if he wasn't an EPCT.

"We've got to reach the space station's control center. Once there, we try to convince the Frinn to turn off their robots. We can work together to stop the Infinity Plague. We—"

"Doc, I don't care asteroids for the reasons. Tell me what to do and I'll do it. You worry about why, I'll worry about how." Hecht spun and fired from the hip at the approaching wedge of robots. The air filled with slashing lasers, driving them deeper into the station. Hecht and another EPCT took a few seconds to blow a huge hole in the deck to slow the robots' advance.

"Where's Uvallae?" Walden asked. The Frinn silently stood beside him. "How do we get to the upper levels? The robots are becoming more aggressive."

"They are learning how to cope with you," Uvallae said.

"Expert system killers," mumbled Hecht. "We got to move *now*. They just cut off our rear guard."

Walden saw an arm on the deck. He didn't know where the rest of the EPCT belonging to it had fallen. Fighting not to think too much about it, he held down his gorge.

"How many of us are left?"

Hecht did a quick tally. "You, the dog, the Frinn, me, and three others. Seven, all told."

"Can we use an elevator to reach the upper levels?" Walden asked Uvallae. The Frinn shook his head, then rubbed his forehead. "Are there stairs?"

"There. Emergency lifts. They are difficult to use. We must be careful."

"We'll be whatever it takes," said Hecht. "If we stay here, all we'll be is dead." The wedge of robots progressed toward them slowly, somehow skipping over the hole Hecht had burned in the floor. A new hole wasn't likely to stop them any more than the last, but Hecht tried. Oily smoke from the vaporized composite material cloaked the advancing death from sight, but Walden knew the robots' sensors peered through the haze easily.

"The emergency lift. Get us into it, Uvallae. Hurry!"

The Frinn led the way through the corridors, winding around until Walden was totally confused. He glanced at Egad. The gengineered dog barked once to let his master know he remembered where they went and that the alien did

not lead them astray. Uvallae stopped and pressed his hands
against a bright green panel. It slid back to reveal a large
bucket attached to a simple chain.

"It is dangerous unless you keep your hands inside the lift
understructure."

"In," Walden said, heaving Egad up and over the bucket's
lip. The dog sat, head cocked to one side and waiting for the
others to join him. Walden went next, then Uvallae and one
EPCT.

"Go on, Doc. I'll follow the others."

Walden saw Sorbatchin standing to one side. The expression on his face was indecipherable. He vaulted from the
bucket, grabbed the Sov-Lat's collar, and dragged him into
the bucket.

"I protest!"

"Hecht is bringing up the rear. We're honored guests in
front, Colonel. Any objections?" Walden left it unsaid that
Hecht would cut down anyone trying to run.

Walden motioned to Uvallae to start the emergency lift.
He was driven to his knees by the sudden acceleration. The
chain flashed by just centimeters from his face. Walden lost
track of how long they were in the emergency lift, but he
knew it had to be at least an hour, possibly longer. His legs
began to tremble from the strain and he wanted to scream at
the noise and closeness in the tunnel. The sudden stop sent
him flying upward to crash into the overhead.

"You all right?" asked the single EPCT with them. "You
don't take ac-changes too good, Doc."

"I never cared for acceleration in the first place, much less
rapid changes," groaned Walden. He was the last to leave
the bucket. He expected to see it drop back for a return trip
to pick up Hecht and the remaining marines. Instead, it folded
into the wall and made way for the next bucket. Hecht and
only one EPCT climbed out a minute later.

"It's getting hot in here, Doc," the sergeant said. "I don't
know what they used on us down there, but you're lucky you
missed it."

"Nukes?" demanded Sorbatchin.

"They wouldn't use anything that powerful inside a space
station," said the sergeant. "Can't say that it was, but it

melted damned near everything in front of it. They even took out a dozen of their own robots to reach us.''

"For them, that is a good exchange,'' commented Sorbatchin. "They outnumber us heavily. Every twelve-for-one trade diminishes us more than it does them.''

"Thanks for the tactics lesson, Colonel. I'll try to remember to not let them trade for me,'' Hecht said sarcastically.

Walden stepped between the two men. "Uvallae says we can reach the control center by going down this corridor and up a ramp. There will be a concentration of robots at the base of the ramp. Then we're inside and able to negotiate.''

Walden raced along the corridor, then slowed when he noticed a crunching under his boots. He looked down. Everywhere he stepped he broke one or two of the small repair robots. They poured from their storage niches in the walls and filled the deck like a plague of metallic cockroaches.

"What's going on?'' demanded Hecht. "They aren't attacking. They just get in the way.'' He stomped hard and broke five of the tiny robots, sending bits of metal and computer innards flying.

"They mean to slow us until they can form an ambush ahead,'' said Sorbatchin.

Walden looked to Uvallae for confirmation. The Frinn shook his head. He had no idea what the robots did. Their actions struck him as irrational and contrary to their primary programmed mission to repair other equipment.

"Ignore them,'' ordered Walden. "Egad, scout ahead. Don't do anything foolish.'' He watched the hound race ahead, wishing he could go with him. Egad was impetuous—for all his gengineered intelligence he was still a dog with a dog's instincts and drives.

"May I attempt to communicate once more with those in the control center?'' asked Uvallae. He indicated a foptic com unit on the wall. Walden motioned for him to try. Hecht faced the rear with the other two EPCTs, guarding against a surprise attack. Sorbatchin stood beside him; he didn't want the colonel near him but had no choice. The corridor was too constricted to allow much room for privacy.

"They will not negotiate,'' Sorbatchin said. "I tried to communicate the Soviet-Latino Pact's desire for peace and they spurned me. They are savages who can learn only through total defeat."

"Starlight has been ravaged, Colonel. How many Frinn did Zacharias kill?"

"Several. Their robot killers destroyed more of your marine force," the Sov-Lat officer said. "They are in control. They have no need to bargain for peace. They will kill us all unless we return to the docking bay and flee."

"If you're right, that won't do us any good. Surprise is gone. They could train Starlight's weapons on our ship and blow us out of space before we got a kilometer away."

"The *Winston* and the *Hippocrates* can lay down protective fire for us," the colonel insisted. "A well-coordinated attack will distract the aliens."

Walden cursed himself for forgetting that the interference blanket had been lifted. He could reach Nakamura and arrange any support the ship and its complement could provide. They had reached this far in Starlight without Nakamura's aid. He decided to push on. Even with the woman's cleverness and any possible firepower the NAA ships might offer, Walden saw little opportunity to get back to the docks unscathed. Better to plead their case before the Frinn leaders.

Egad came running back and skidded to a halt. The dog was obviously upset over what he had seen. Walden turned his back on Sorbatchin and flipped open Egad's visor. Reaching inside the dog's hazard suit, he turned down the volume on his computerized transducer so that the dog would speak in a whisper.

"What is it, old boy? What did you see?"

"Robots!" the dog cried. "Everywhere the cat shit machines run. Snap here, bite there. They are dangerous. Packs like dogs of them and they attack!"

"Calm down, there, there," Walden soothed. He turned Egad's volume back up after cautioning him to remain silent. A single glance in Sorbatchin's direction reminded the dog of the danger here as well as ahead.

"Sergeant, there are packs of robots guarding the ramp leading to the control center. We can't fight our way through, can we?"

"Not this orbit, Doc. Not in a dozen orbits. We're about drained. Three—four—fighters doing any real good." Hecht reluctantly included Sorbatchin in his estimate of their fighting inventory. Walden felt mildly annoyed at being left out. He had done his share along the way, even if he wasn't an EPCT.

"Uvallae?"

The Frinn stood beside the SAW communications unit. The expression on his swinish face eluded Walden. He thought Uvallae was perplexed, though he couldn't tell. He looked to Egad. A whisper rose from the dog's throat, "Bewildered."

"What's wrong, Uvallae?" Walden asked loud enough to mask Egad's comment, in case any of the others overheard it.

"The controllers are . . . not."

"They aren't what?" demanded Hecht. "We've got no time left for games. Come to a decision, give us the least energy orbit and let's blast fast."

"The controllers have lost control," Uvallae explained. "Never before has this happened. They programmed the repair robots to repel invaders. Something went wrong."

"What do you mean?" Walden looked nervously back down the corridor. He felt vibration through the deck. Something heavy came up on them from behind.

Hecht started forward. The others went with him rather than face whatever caused such rumbling along the wide corridor. Sorbatchin and Walden hurried to match Uvallae's pace. Both wanted a fuller explanation of the situation aboard Starlight.

"They ordered the robots to destroy all invaders," Uvallae said nervously. "Somehow, the systems are evolving and becoming more expert—and they have interpreted the controllers as being a part of the invasion."

"The robots cannot turn on their makers," scoffed Sorbatchin. "There are safeguards."

"There were," admitted Uvallae. "Not now. When you blasted your way into the docking area, the controllers worked to remove those safeguards. Protecting the space station was paramount to caution. Now they pay the price for their rush."

"Hold up, Doc," came Hecht's command. "We got problems again. The metallic sons of bitches are everywhere. Look at 'em, will you?" The EPCT sergeant's laserifle roared as he melted thousands of the small, scurrying repair robots.

"The ramp leading to the control center," Uvallae said in almost reverential tones. "It is up there that we will find allies among my people."

A Frinn emerged from the vaultlike steel door at the top and gestured. Uvallae started to respond when the air filled with dozens of flashing laser bolts. The heavy garlic odor of ozone from the massive discharge choked Walden.

When the after images had left his eyes, he saw only a smoking pile of charred cloth and bone at the top of the ramp. The Frinn's own robots had killed him.

"We might have worse problems than we thought," he said. All around them, the defending robots' sensors flashed and winked—and homed in on the insignificant human strike force.

CHAPTER
20

"Fire! Fire on them all!" shrieked Uvallae. The Frinn exploded into a frenzy of activity. He jerked the laserifle from Walden's hand and began firing wildly into the metallic mountain of advancing robots. The mechanisms responded instantly, firing their own laser weapons at the small knot of humans.

Walden and Egad worked together to knock Uvallae to the side. Their luck held. They crashed into a door and knocked it open. They tumbled into the room, the laser bolts searing the air above them. How the EPCTs and Sorbatchin fared, Walden didn't know. He was too busy trying to wrest the laserifle from Uvallae's thick fingers.

"Let go, dammit," he raged at the alien. "You're making it worse. You got them aimed in our direction."

"They were killing my leaders," sobbed Uvallae. The Frinn raked at his sloped forehead and clawed at it until thin trickles of blood oozed from the gouges. "We will never defeat them. We can never survive. The Infinity Plague. The robots. *Our* robots!"

"We got this far," said Walden. "We'll stop them. There has to be some way of turning them off or reprogramming them."

"Do you think my people are so stupid that they have not tried everything you mention?"

"No," said Walden. He swung around and pumped several actinic bolts through the doorway at smaller robotic units coming after them. The tide of machinery would overwhelm their position in a few seconds. He tapped the side of his com unit and said, "Hecht, get out of here. We're inside the room to your right."

"I'm coming for you, Doc. You got a wall of robots piling up outside. It doesn't look good for you."

"No, get back and—" Walden never finished. The explosion knocked him flat. Air gusting from his lungs, all he could do was sit and stare, trying to suck in enough oxygen to stay alive.

"Blast bad," moaned Egad. The dog had been thrown across the room by the concussion grenade Hecht used against the robots. "Hurt all over."

Walden soothed the dog, then tended to Uvallae. The Frinn had been knocked out by the blast. Only then did Walden check himself. He found some bleeding from the ears and nose. He had bitten his tongue and had a splitting headache. Other than these minor injuries he was in remarkably good condition.

"My luck is still holding," he told Egad as he patted the dog's head. Egad shook him off and went to the corner of the room to lie down. He began licking himself, only to curse when he found he did a poor job through the holes in his hazard suit.

"Hecht, get us out of here. You damned near deafened us and mashed us flat."

"We got more problems, Doc. You think those pigs at the top of the ramp want us camping on their doorstep?"

"Why?"

"There aren't any happy campers left down here. By count, we're facing a thousand robots—and each of them is waving around enough laser power to fry us sagans of times over."

Walden shook Uvallae, knowing this might further injure the alien but needing him awake, if not alert. Only he could communicate with the controllers inside their protected chambers. Uvallae moaned and tried to speak. Nothing coherent came out.

"I help," said Egad. The dog dashed past and dodged through the robots between the humans and the top of the ramp. Once at the top Egad began yelping loudly. Some Frinn noises came, followed by more frenzied barking.

"Help me get him up," Walden said when Sorbatchin poked his head into the room. The Sov-Lat colonel obeyed without questioning the orders. Together they supported Uvallae and got him up the ramp. Hecht's concussion grenade had cleared the path—for a few more minutes. At the top of the ramp Walden looked back down the corridor and almost dropped the alien in his surprise.

Hecht hadn't exaggerated when he said they faced billions and billions of watts of laser death. The three EPCTs backed up, their rifles firing steady streams of energy into the robotic horde. As they fired, their weapons weakened visibly until one EPCT got only tiny sparks from the muzzle of his laserifle.

"Egad, are they going to let us inside?" Walden lowered Uvallae and pulled out his own weapon to add to the three marines.

Sorbatchin looked at the scientist as if he had gone insane. The Sov-Lat officer jumped when the steel door began cycling open. Egad yipped and barked and danced around as it swung wide enough for a man to slip inside.

Two Frinn came out and grabbed Uvallae. They carried him inside. Walden waited, watching Egad for a clue to what they were supposed to do. The dog barked and tossed his head, showing that the Frinn had given them sanctuary.

"In," he told Sorbatchin. "And I cut your tongue out if you try to subvert them until we join you."

"You are a strange fellow, Dr. Walden," the colonel said. "You have worked a miracle, though. I salute you." With that, Sorbatchin ducked through the heavy door and vanished.

"Watch him, Egad," Walden called. Then he rushed back down the ramp to join the three soldiers. He handed his weapon to the man whose firearm had completely discharged. The EPCT took it and used it far better than Walden ever could have.

"You're all right, Doc," said Hecht. "Now orbit your asteroid up and inside. We can hold them at bay long enough for that. But not too much more!"

Walden joined Sorbatchin and Egad inside the Frinn's control center. The room looked nothing like he had envisioned it. To control the vastness that was Starlight he had imagined huge control panels and dozens of controllers using laser wands to command the legion of robots bent on repair and service.

A single panel with a half-dozen winking lights constituted the entire central control unit. From all he could determine, the room was about one-third of the way up the core of the space station, as measured from the lading docks. He had assumed wrongly that their control center would be perched on the "top" of Starlight, antipodal to the docking bays.

Uvallae sat up in a chair. Another Frinn tended him, a small buzzing computer device in his hand.

"He heals me, Walden," said Uvallae. "I will be whole again in a few minutes."

Hecht and the other two EPCTs backed into the room. Hecht tossed his laserifle to the side and drew his pistol, its beam feeble in comparison to the more powerful rifle. Only when the Frinn closed the massive door did the three marines relax. One collapsed to the floor. The other began a steady string of curses and wouldn't stop. Hecht looked pale and shaken.

"You came close on that one, Doc. You don't win any medals, either. Try to do one or the other—play it safe or get something to pin on your chest."

Hecht laughed and shook his head. He looked around the control center and shrugged, as if saying, Is this it?

Walden waited until Uvallae stood and stretched. He asked the Frinn, "How many controllers are here? What can they do about the robots rampaging outside?"

"There are the fourteen," spoke the Frinn who had tended Uvallae. "We are the controllers of this station you call Starlight."

"How—"

"We listen everywhere on Starlight," the Frinn explained. "We do not have leaders in the way you humans do. I am a controller and, as such, as much in command as any of us."

"Can you stop them?"

"Uvallae explained our predicament. We unleashed them to repel your invasion force. They have exceeded the bounds of their programming—we have done our job too well. You are defeated." The Frinn hung his head. "So are we. They have taken control of our space station."

"All they do is kill," said Hecht. "That can be used against them, can't it?"

"What do you mean, Sergeant?" asked Sorbatchin.

"They can be turned against each other easier than they can be reprogrammed to love our hot little bodies. There's not much repairing being done by the little buggers. If the bigger ones are decommissioned, their offensive will fall apart."

"Can you give them that additional command?" Walden asked the Frinn controller.

"We never considered it. You are the enemy."

"We don't want to be," Walden said earnestly. "We're facing mutual problems. The robots are only a part of that problem. The Infinity Plague affects us, too."

Sorbatchin stared at him curiously but said nothing. Hecht pushed past the Sov-Lat officer and asked, "You mean we're likely to die from that damned plague, just like the pig-faces?"

"Frinn," Walden corrected. "And that's right, Sergeant. Do you remember the EPCTs who went crazy?"

"How can I forget them? I had to laser one." His voice turned colder, more distant. "He was a good friend, too, and he tried to fry me."

"That's the Infinity Plague working on us. It's just taken longer for us to show symptoms than it did among the Frinn."

"Wonderful," the soldier said. "Robots and plague. This entire damned mission has been totally plucked and fucked from the start. I knew I should never have shipped under Zacharias."

"Work on the reprogramming," Walden said, unconsciously taking command. "I want to contact Nakamura and see what she can do from outside. Are there any weapons trained on our two ships?" he asked the controller.

"Weapons? We have none on Starlight, except for the guidance lasers we use to pilot vessels in to our docking area."

"What about warships in the system?"

"There are several on patrol. When the *Prolum* returned from what you call Schwann—"

Walden realized for the first time how pervasive throughout Starlight the Frinn observation had been.

"—we put several ships on patrol to protect ourselves, should you choose to pursue and complete your unprovoked attack. This course was hotly debated since the world was totally destroyed. We prevailed on the side of caution and posted the sentry vessels. It is well that we did, though they failed to detect your entry into our system."

"It was all an accident. Hasn't Uvallae explained this?"

"We find this explanation too fantastical for belief."

"You *do* believe we have to work together if any of us are ever going to leave Starlight alive?"

"We are your prisoners. Do with us as you see fit." The resignation radiating from the Frinn almost overwhelmed Walden.

"You are not prisoners. We are allies. We have to work together." His own frustration ran high trying to make the alien understand. "Tell him, Uvallae. You know."

"I have been your prisoner, Walden. That is all I know."

"No!" Walden started to protest when he saw an immense vidscreen display behind the Frinn light up. It showed the robots beginning work on the exterior sheath on the steel door. Hundreds of lasers turned their intense coherent light onto a single spot. Even Ultimate Strength Steel would yield under such concentration of energy. The Frinn vault door was no exception. It turned a cherry-red and began to sparkle and pop as the metal vaporized.

To Egad he said, "Talk with them. Convincing them we're allies, not enemies. And get them to work on reprogramming. We won't last long if the robots cut through that door."

A quick look around the control center showed no other place to run. The door was their sole protection. As a defensive it left much to be desired, he saw.

"*Hippocrates*, come in," he said, switching his com unit to a hailing frequency used by the ship. "I need to speak with Nakamura right away."

A faint hiss from solar static filled his ears, then the woman's voice came through, quiet, firm, tranquil. "You have waited long enough to contact me, Dr. Walden. What is your current situation aboard the space station?''

He detailed it quickly, finishing with, ''Land the rest of the EPCTs. We need a diversion behind the robots.''

''The marines are already dispatched. Two shuttles will reach Starlight's docking bays within four hours.''

Walden cursed under his breath. He wasn't sure they could survive another four hours.

''You allude to the identify of another Sov-Lat spy aboard the *Hippocrates*,'' came Nakamura's implacably calm voice. ''Are you referring to Dr. Burch?''

''I . . . yes,'' Walden said, feeling deflated. Nakamura knew who Sorbatchin's other spy was. ''How did you find out?''

''Captain Belford and Major Zacharias both suspected him. I concentrated on your scientist, Doris Yerrow, since she had revealed herself to me earlier on Earth.''

''The cat gave him away when Sorbatchin contacted him,'' Walden said. ''There's something about the cat that's not right.''

''Dr. Yerrow's cat has a remarkable interior,'' said Nakamura, laughing softly. ''The animal is filled with spy devices of every imaginable description.''

''That explains its lethargy. It's too weighted down to move.''

''It is hardly alive. I have taken steps to remove the creature's burden. It also has a curious defensive system, exuding a neuro-poison if touched for any length of time by any not trained in its ways. Petting the animal introduced the poison to your system.''

''What about Leo? He's a good doctor. We can use him.''

''He is accompanying the EPCT contingent en route to Starlight. He is no longer a threat to the NAA since his duplicity has been revealed. Use him as you see fit. Is there anything else you require of me, Dr. Walden?''

''Prayer. We need it if we're going to keep the robots out of the control room until help arrives.''

''I have confidence in you. We shall discuss this matter at greater length when you return to the *Hippocrates*. Good day.''

The connection terminated abruptly, leaving Walden with

the feeling there ought to have been more said and resolved. What, he couldn't say. He wanted Miko Nakamura to tell him what to do, how to make everything come out right.

"They aren't having much luck," said Sorbatchin, looking at the Frinn's work on the control panel. "The robots resist any change in their mission program."

Walden found himself staring at the vidscreen. The robots burned out their lasers and moved aside, letting others with charged cutting torches in. The door never cooled. Molten puddles formed at the foot of the door, then began running down the ramp. It looked as if some artificial volcano erupted and spewed forth long lava trails of liquid steel.

Walden forced himself to calmness. Nakamura never appeared rattled or out of control. She was the one to emulate, not the hot-blooded fire that had characterized Edouard Zacharias. He glanced over at Egad. The dog spoke with several intense-looking Frinn congregated at the far corner of the control room. He hoped the gengineered dog convinced them of his sincerity in wanting to cooperate against both the plague and the robotic menace.

Keeping his emotions in check, he tried to think through all the possibilities open to him. A slow smile crossed his face when he hit upon a scheme that might just work.

To the Frinn working so diligently at the control panel, he said, "All the robots are originally repair appliances, aren't they?"

"All," the Frinn confirmed.

"Can you return all but the largest ones to their original task? The command to repair is stronger than to fight," he guessed. "Define any unit as requiring repair that is unable to function properly."

"Fool! We only hasten our own death," Sorbatchin said angrily. "They repair themselves and provide even more firepower against the door."

"They can't get too many more robots up there," said Walden. "I want to take out as many replacements as possible for the ones working on the steel door."

The Frinn spent almost ten minutes working on the slight reprogramming. He turned and stared at the vidscreen. "I have done what I can."

"Good, good." Walden had worked through the plan in

his head while the Frinn labored. He knew it gave them a slim chance, but this was better than trying nothing. "They're repairing each other. Now try turning the few left against each other."

"One responded," the Frinn said.

"Have the repair units tear it apart for examination."

Sorbatchin whistled tunelessly through his teeth. "This will not work, Walden. It is too difficult to remove them one by one from the force arrayed against us."

It grew warmer in the control room. Walden wasn't sure if it came from his concentration on the Frinn and his work or if the robots' cutting torches warmed the thick steel to the point it heated the room. Either way he felt the pressure of time on his shoulders. They had just about used up any grace period they had earned by ducking into the vaultlike room.

"Change the repair parameters to one hundred percent efficiency," ordered Walden. "Have any robot failing to meet these specifications torn apart for complete repair and reconstruction. Do not try to reprogram any of the bigger machines still working on the door. Let the repair units go after them."

"What if none are working below maximum efficiency?" asked Sorbatchin.

"Just wait, Colonel," Walden said. "I've never seen a robot work at complete efficiency for long. Humans always oversee their actions because programming cannot take into account every contingency. Even zero-defect robots that can learn and adjust never function at one hundred percent."

"Those are human-built devices," pointed out the Sov-Lat officer. "These are Frinn machines. They use them for everything. Each is an expert system. They will not fail."

Walden began to think the colonel was right. A few of the Frinn robots slowed and ran afoul of their own repair companions. Most of the machines cutting through the thick door continued to work unhindered by their metallic friends.

"Another one fell below one hundred percent," said the Frinn. "That leaves only fourteen robots cutting through the door. None of those out of order have been returned to service yet."

Walden stared into the vidscreen display. He couldn't take his eyes off it. The fourteen machines became thirteen, then twelve, and finally eleven. Changing the repair parameters to impossible precision kept the machines out of service—but the ones still working showed no sign of flagging.

"They're too damned good. The Frinn build their robots too damned good for my liking," he grumbled.

"We can use them, Doc," said Hecht. "Think of a legion of robokillers on *our* side. Nothing could stop them. We could drop them as shock troops and follow with an EPCT landing."

Walden said nothing. He had worked in bioweapons research too long not to know the arguments for developing any given weapon or tactic. It was always "nothing could stop it."

"Look," said Uvallae. "There are only four robots still cutting at the door."

That's what the vidscreen showed. What worried Walden more were the tiny holes appearing on the steel door's inner panel. The robots' persistence paid off; they had almost cut through. Four remained out of the thousands that had started, but it would only take one to finish the job and kill them.

And, as Sorbatchin had pointed out, some of the robots would be repaired and returned to service soon.

"How many laserifles are still working?" he asked Hecht.

"We got two that might light a cigarette," the sergeant admitted. "We'll club them when they come through, if that's what it'll take to stop them."

Walden saw that the shuttle with the EPCT support was still an hour from docking.

The metal lining on the door warmed, heated, then blazed white-hot and turned into a sieve. The Frinn's robots had finally cut through and would come after their victims in minutes.

CHAPTER
21

"Another robot is operating at less than perfection," Uvallae said softly. "There are only two robots working at the door."

Jerome Walden couldn't take his eyes off the white-hot patches spreading across the steel. He motioned to Hecht. "Get your laserifles trained on the door. Get the robots out of action as fast as you can. It's our only chance."

"Why use the rifles?" asked Hecht. He pulled out a concussion grenade. "I've got a couple left. Might as well use them now. Get everyone under cover. These suckers make a hell of a noise when they go off."

The inner panel fell free from the door. Sgt. Hecht twisted the grenade timer and heaved it. In the same motion, he dived and slid on his belly until he came to rest under the Frinn's simple control panel. The blast deafened Walden.

He shook his head and wiggled free of the chair he had ducked behind. The metal door cooled visibly. No laser torches sliced through the metal to seek out their tender flesh.

"The grenade damaged the robots," came Uvallae's triumphant shout. "The others are repairing them."

"Get control back as fast as you can. Shut down whatever you can," ordered Walden. "I don't want repaired robots coming after us again. I don't want any robot after me."

He sank down and threw his arms around Egad's neck.

The dog wetly lapped at his face. Walden was too happy to even pull back. It was good to be alive.

"We expected to fight our way onto Starlight," said Leo Burch. The medical doctor sauntered behind the heavily armed EPCT marines. "You're more efficient than I'd've thought."

Walden gauged the distance, rocked back, and delivered a blow to the point of the doctor's chin. The impact rippled all the way up his arm and into his shoulder. Walden grunted as sharp pain told him he might have broken fingers with the punch. The sight of Burch sprawled on the deck was enough to make him forget it.

"You son of a bitch," Walden said. "You sold us out. You were in league with Sorbatchin."

"I've already been over this with Nakamura," Burch said, sitting up. He wiped blood from his mouth. His cut lip bled profusely. "It's nothing I'm proud of. It just happened."

"Doris Yerrow," Walden started, swallowing hard. The real scientist had been replaced—probably murdered. "She died so a Sov-Lat spy could take her place."

"I didn't know anything about that until close to the end. Nakamura maneuvered her into getting lasered."

"You took her cat," accused Walden.

Burch shrugged. "I found out about the spy equipment inside the cat by accident. It proved useful while I had it. You know I don't especially like cats."

"I thought you were my friend."

"It was an accident, you getting poisoned like that. You should have avoided the cat. It was something Doris had set up. When you petted the cat, you infected yourself. Some defensive mechanism. You've got to believe me, Jerome. I didn't know anything about it. I was innocent of that. I *like* you."

Walden restrained himself from hitting Burch again when the doctor stood. His anger has been drained off. He'd always liked Leo Burch. He just couldn't understand what had driven the man to spy for the Soviet-Latinos.

"You need to do complete autopsies on the EPCTs," Walden said. "There is a good chance we're starting to come down with the Infinity Plague."

Burch's bushy eyebrows shot up. "Nakamura didn't mention that."

"Maybe she didn't want you spilling it to Sorbatchin." Walden said. He damned himself for such a cheap shot at the doctor. The Sov-Lat colonel already knew as much about the possible Infinity Plague infection as Walden did. "I've tagged the marines who went crazy. Start with them—and be damned careful. The plague might spread in any number of ways we haven't even guessed at."

"How exact you've become in your diagnoses," muttered Burch. "I'll check the crazies out. I need to get the bodies back to the *Hippocrates* for a complete workup. I need Albert—and it'd be nice if you were there helping, too."

"I'll be there," said Walden. He spun and stalked off. He had work to do here. The sight of Leo Burch still caused him to boil inside. Walden needed time to cool off and come to grips with the man's betrayal.

"The place is worse than we thought, Doc," said Hecht, falling into step beside him. "The first reports show damned near eighty percent Frinn casualties. What Zacharias and the Infinity Plague didn't polish off, their own robots did. The entire space station is still running, though. They do wonders with computer equipment."

"I prefer letting the machines do menial tasks," said Walden, distracted. "What's Nakamura's word on who controls Starlight?"

"The Frinn still do," Hecht said, startled. "I never got orders that we're taking it over. I wouldn't know where to start. This place is *huge*."

"Carry on, Sergeant," Walden said. He went to a small room and sat down in the uncomfortable Frinn chair. He twitched his chin and got Nakamura's command frequency.

"Yes, Doctor?" came the woman's soft voice.

"We need to get started immediately on researching the Infinity Plague. The surviving Frinn are infected; they must be. Uvallae was on Schwann. Their worst cases have already lifted for their home world—which heightens the problem. They're carrying the seeds of their own destruction. I don't believe their bio-containment facilities are anywhere near as good as they have to be."

"If our own soldiers contracted the disease on Schwann,

you are right. It has been thought for some time that the EPCT combat suit was impervious to any vector.''

Walden licked his lips, his mind racing to formulate his request so that he would get it. ''I need help with this,'' he said. ''I need someone who is a specialist in the Infinity Plague.''

''So it seems.''

''I need Anita's help.''

''Why do you believe Dr. Tarleton is such a specialist?''

Walden explained how Anita's project was classified and how he was prohibited from knowing the details. ''I am in charge of the research mission. Dr. Greene didn't see fit to let me know. What other project could they have worked on?''

''Why hasn't Dr. Tarleton volunteered this information?''

''We haven't been talking much lately. She might not even know of the Infinity Plague cases among our troops.''

''She has been informed,'' said Nakamura. ''She refused to volunteer any information to me, but this is acceptable. I have no need to know. You, as project director, ought to be aware of her expertise and orders from Earth.''

''I want to return as soon as I can to the *Hippocrates*,'' Walden said. ''Put me in isolation. Use the quarantine wards. I need the equipment to carry on the research into stopping it—into finding what it does to humans.''

''Very well. Return on the shuttle. Bring those aboard Starlight who can aid you most. I see that this is a major undertaking and requires full cooperation among all your staff. Those who remain aboard Starlight must accept it as isolation.''

Nakamura's voice faded in his ears as the woman cut the connection. Walden heaved a deep sigh. He had persuaded the military advisor of his need, of the stark importance of finding how the plague propagated and how to stop it.

''Egad!'' he called. ''Fetch Uvallae and any of the other Frinn who want to go to the *Hippocrates*. We're going home.''

The gengineered dog barked and raced off. In less than an hour Walden was on his way back to the hospital ship. In five he, Uvallae, and three other Frinn scientists, and Egad were safely quarantined in the sealed ward in the belly of the *Hippocrates*.

At least, Jerome Walden hoped it was safe.

"Find somewhere to sleep," Walden said. Knowing the Frinn obsession with privacy, he showed the three aliens who had accompanied Uvallae private rooms they could use. Uvallae he gave a larger room with an adjoining office.

"It is small," murmured Uvallae, "but will suffice. I need access to my computer files. I have worked some on the Infinity Plague but have gotten nowhere."

"They'll be furnished. You can access my data banks, too. I've got the results of autopsies on all the . . . on your starship crew." Walden swallowed hard. He had worked long hours on those analyses. Had the Infinity Plague invaded his system? Did it already work to drive him insane, as it had the EPCT marines aboard Starlight?

"You are helpful." Uvallae cocked his head to one side and his pig snout wiggled. "Did you do this to aid us or to prevent spread of the disease in your own kind?"

"We've got to find a stopgap treatment. Otherwise, your home world will be wiped out in the span of months. The Infinity Plague works fast in your species."

Uvallae nodded and turned to the computer console. He worked a few minutes at it, getting the feel of the new equipment. Walden left the alien to his work. There wasn't too much difference between the operation of Frinn and human computers. What dissimilarity there was could be easily overcome by the Frinn's expertise.

He settled down onto a bed at the far end of the ward and arranged his own equipment in a semicircle. Best to let the Frinn have their privacy. Walden knew how little any of them would have in the isolation ward. Everywhere he looked he saw the rice-grain-sized camera lenses that constantly monitored everything. A tiny icon winked at the corner of his computer screen.

"Yes?" he asked.

"Jerome?" The screen flashed once and Anita Tarleton appeared. He knew from the dark clouds of anger twisting her face that she was not pleased with him.

"I'm sorry about Zacharias," he said.

"I read the report. You killed him, you filthy son of a bitch. I ought to let you die for that."

"He died protecting me," Walden said, putting a hint of verisimilitude into his tone. Zacharias hadn't even known the danger existed. It had been pure chance that his body had blocked Walden from the concussion that had killed the major and left the scientist unscathed.

"I know a little about the Infinity Plague," she said sullenly. "I can't believe your report on it affecting humans. Every report that came back from Schwann said it was a lost cause."

"You were sent to Schwann to work on it?"

"Yes, but not under the name Infinity Plague. I have no idea where that name came from. Some Sov-Lat stole it and wanted to make it sound worse than it was."

"We have to find a way of stopping its action in the Frinn. You've read my report on that, too."

"This Uvallae and the others were exposed but have survived. It's not as bad as you make it out to be."

"Anita!" he exclaimed, shocked at her callousness. "We're dooming billions of innocent Frinn to death."

"They destroyed Schwann. They're not *that* innocent, Jerome. What's happened to you?"

"Humans and Frinn are not enemies, Anita. We have no reason to kill each other. The contracted the Infinity Plague and thought we had released it on purpose. They only wanted to purify the planet—and get even."

"They did that," she said. "Let them die."

"And me? You want me to die from your plague, too? Do you hate me that much?"

Indecision crossed her face. "No, I don't hate you. There's not much I can tell you about the plague you don't already know. I . . . I'll free my classified computer files. That might help you find something."

"I need *your* help, Anita. You're as close to an expert on this that we have on the *Hippocrates*."

"Very well," she said, her tone frosty. "I have a few ideas how to proceed. What induces the insanity is a mystery to me, but the chromosomal unraveling in the aliens might be retarded." She launched into a long discussion of how the Infinity Plague had been intended as a gene-splicing technique and then progressed into a self-perpetuating plague that changed form as it spread.

Walden heaved a sigh of relief that the plague had never achieved its goal. Destroying the Frinn autonomic system was bad enough. To have the plague alter itself before infecting another victim would have truly been tracking down an infinity of death.

Walden transferred Anita's files to his own and began computer searching for similarities, differences, anything that might give him a clue to blocking the progress of the plague. As he worked, he wondered if he did it for the Frinn, who had been innocent victims of NAA and Sov-Lat bioweapons research technology, or if he did it for some other reason.

Guilt? He filled with it until he wanted to explode. None of the weapons he had worked on were supposed to be used. They gave the knife edge balance of anxiety to diplomatic relations between the two political power blocs.

Walden fell asleep over his computer console, something he was destined to do many more times before he found the blocking agent for the Frinn.

"This isn't a cure," Walden told Uvallae. He punched up the three-dimensional depiction of the complex molecule on the vidscreen. Another touch of a key set the molecule to rotating, showing its every secret to the Frinn scientist. "At best, it duplicates your natural immunity to the chromosomal splitting."

"The side effects are severe," said Uvallae, working on his own console. "Still, this is a small price to pay for protection against certain death."

"The manufacturing process for the molecule is relatively simple, too. Inexpensive. You can provide huge dosages at low cost and get it to every Frinn on your home world."

Uvallae said nothing.

Nakamura's face appeared on Walden's computer. She had been listening to the byplay. "We need to know where your world is. There were no coordinates in Starlight's computer. Even worse, we have been unable to locate the residue of liftspace drives because Starlight is so close to the primary. The star's strong gravitational field badly distorts the tensors we need most in our analysis. They have been efficient in preventing us from learning of their home world.''

Walden couldn't tell if Nakamura approved or not. She had been thwarted—but the Frinn had been clever. With the military advisor, this counted for a great deal in determining who earned her respect.

"We protect ourselves," said Uvallae. "You have shown great resolve and determination in your pursuit of this preventive measure. Still, it is difficult to know the proper course to follow.''

Walden sought the right words to assure the alien that they wanted nothing more than to help. The words didn't come. He knew differently. For three and a half weeks he, Burch, and the others on his research team had worked tirelessly to formulate this immunizing formula. Sorbatchin and Nakamura had discussed other matters—all military and all revolving around conquering the Frinn.

Walden didn't know if they realized his own organically powered spy devices were planted throughout the ship. Nakamura and Sorbatchin were foes but they shared a language. They sought to expand their respective power bases, and the Frinn presented an opportunity unparalleled in human history.

An entire world—possibly many worlds—lay ripe for the taking if the Infinity Plague worked its deadly magic on the alien population. Even as Walden toiled to prevent the plague, the two plotted to subjugate. All the while, they never lost sight of their mutual antagonism. Walden didn't understand it. He didn't care to. Somehow, he had to work with them and deliver the antidote to some of the Frinn trouble.

For a real cure, more extensive work was required. And he hadn't even scratched the surface of the Infinity Plague's action against humans. The only consolation was the lack of new cases since Starlight's invasion.

"Uvallae," he said, "the plague is already rampant on your world. How long ago did your ship leave Starlight for home?''

"Months," answered the Frinn.

"Your reclusiveness as a race might impede the plague's transmission. I don't know. What I do know is that we have the way to keep the plague from spreading more than it has. Your world is doomed without this. We've got to try it out on you and the others, but I'm confident it will work as I outlined.'' He tapped the computer screen where the tiny molecule still revolved in synchronization with the larger projected image on the ward's vidscreen.

''I have studied your work, Walden,'' said the alien. ''You have performed miracles, even with Tarleton's basic information to aid you.'' Uvallae closed his eyes and rubbed his forehead. His snout wiggled and his entire body shook in agitation. ''I have discussed this matter with the others. You are sincere in your desire to help us. Egad has convinced us further of your wholehearted support for our planetary independence.''

''I don't speak for everyone aboard the *Hippocrates*,'' Walden said.

''We know. We have reached a difficult decision in the face of such contradictory feelings among your kind.''

''You will give me the coordinates of your world?'' asked Miko Nakamura.

''Yes,'' said Uvallae.

Walden didn't know whether to shout with joy or fear for Uvallae and his race.

He touched the Frinn's arm and said softly, ''We'll keep the plague from obliterating your people. I promise it.''

Egad barked once and moved between them. Walden had no idea what the gengineered dog added to his heartfelt statement, but it put Uvallae at ease. He wished he was as pleased with the decision.

Uvallae gave Nakamura the needed coordinates.

The *Hippocrates*' engines stirred as it positioned itself to enter liftspace and race toward the blighted planet. Jerome Walden knew he wanted to help. He just hoped he wasn't saving the Frinn for Vladimir Sorbatchin and Miko Nakamura.

THE FINEST THE UNIVERSE HAS TO OFFER

__THE OMEGA CAGE Steve Perry and Michael Reaves
0-441-62382-4/$3.50
The Omega Cage—a hi-tech prison for the special enemies of the
brutal Confed. No one had ever escaped, but Dain Maro is about to
attempt the impossible.

__THE WARLOCK'S COMPANION Christopher Stasheff
0-441-87341-3/$3.95
Fess, the beloved cyborg steed of Rod Gallowglass, has a host of
revealing stories he's never shared. Now the Gallowglass children are
about to hear the truth...from the horse's mouth.

__THE STAINLESS STEEL RAT Harry Harrison
0-441-77924-7/$3.50
The Stainless Steel Rat was the slickest criminal in the Universe until
the police finally caught up with him. Then there was only one thing
they could do—they made him a cop.

__DREAM PARK Larry Niven and Steven Barnes
0-441-16730-6/$4.95
Dream Park—the ultimate fantasy world where absolutely everything
you ever dreamed of is real—including murder.

For Visa and MasterCard orders call: 1-800-631-8571

FOR MAIL ORDERS: CHECK BOOK(S). FILL
OUT COUPON. SEND TO:

BERKLEY PUBLISHING GROUP
390 Murray Hill Pkwy., Dept. B
East Rutherford, NJ 07073

NAME_____

ADDRESS_____

CITY_____

STATE_____ ZIP_____

PLEASE ALLOW 6 WEEKS FOR DELIVERY.
PRICES ARE SUBJECT TO CHANGE WITHOUT NOTICE.

POSTAGE AND HANDLING:
$1.00 for one book, 25¢ for each ad-
ditional. Do not exceed $3.50.

BOOK TOTAL	$ ____
POSTAGE & HANDLING	$ ____
APPLICABLE SALES TAX (CA, NJ, NY, PA)	$ ____
TOTAL AMOUNT DUE	$ ____

PAYABLE IN US FUNDS.
(No cash orders accepted.)

281

Frank Herbert

The All-time Bestselling
DUNE
MASTERWORKS

__DUNE	0-441-17266-0/$4.95
__DUNE MESSIAH	0-441-17269-5/$4.95
__CHILDREN OF DUNE	0-441-10402-9/$4.95
__GOD EMPEROR OF DUNE	0-441-29467-7/$4.95
__HERETICS OF DUNE	0-441-32800-8/$4.95
__CHAPTERHOUSE DUNE	0-441-10267-0/$4.95

For Visa and MasterCard orders call: 1-800-631-8571

FOR MAIL ORDERS: CHECK BOOK(S). FILL
OUT COUPON. SEND TO:

BERKLEY PUBLISHING GROUP
390 Murray Hill Pkwy., Dept. B
East Rutherford, NJ 07073

NAME_____

ADDRESS_____

CITY_____

STATE_____ZIP_____

PLEASE ALLOW 6 WEEKS FOR DELIVERY.
PRICES ARE SUBJECT TO CHANGE WITHOUT NOTICE.

POSTAGE AND HANDLING:
$1.00 for one book, 25¢ for each ad-
ditional. Do not exceed $3.50.

BOOK TOTAL	$ ____
POSTAGE & HANDLING	$ ____
APPLICABLE SALES TAX	$ ____
(CA, NJ, NY, PA)	
TOTAL AMOUNT DUE	$ ____

PAYABLE IN US FUNDS.
(No cash orders accepted.)

253